Additional Praise for *The Barbarian Parade*

"A great story to tell, one that is by turns sensuous, carnal, tender, and often brutal. With its original theme and beautiful yet effortlessly composed language, *The Barbarian Parade* makes a striking debut for a novelist of daring creativity and passion."
—EDMUND WHITE

"A soulful excavation around the foundation of a young life teetering but still standing, with all the requisite familial heartbreak, busted balls, and self-inflicted wounds that would tumble lesser erections."
—MARK RICHARD, *The Ice at the Bottom of the World*

"Gann's exciting debut, a brave and buoyant bildungsroman, tells one Kentucky boy's own story, with balls and heart and a fiery, hell-bent prose. Rousing and brutal, tender and wise, *The Barbarian Parade* is an original—a picaresque novel of and for our time."
—ROBIN LIPPINCOTT, author of *Mr. Dalloway*

"An evocative, gripping, and fearless first novel, one that peers out of the eyes of a child upon a very adult world. If you have ever watched a tornado snake out of a dark cloud, or a skydiver fall with a tangled chute, then you know what it is like to be utterly transfixed; Gann's novel holds the reader in much the same way."
—LEE DURKEE, *Rides of the Midway*

The Barbarian Parade

or, Pursuit of the
Un-American Dream

For Stephen,
Fellow comrade
in the good fight!
I hope you find something
to enjoy here.

24 March 2004

By ~~Kirby Gann~~

Kirby Gann

Hill Street Press
Athens, Georgia

A HILL STREET PRESS BOOK

Published in the United States of America by
Hill Street Press LLC
191 East Broad Street, Suite 209
Athens, Georgia 30601-2848 USA
706-613-7200
info @hillstreetpress.com
www.hillstreetpress.com

Hill Street Press is committed to preserving the written word. Every effort is made to print books on acid-free paper with a significant amount of post-consumer recycled content.

This is a work of fiction. All names, characters, places, and situations are either products of the author's imagination or are used fictitiously. No reference to any real person, living or deceased, is intended not should be inferred, and any similarity is entirely coincidental.

Library of Congress Cataloging-in-Publication Data

Gann, Kirby, 1968–
The Barbarian parade, or, Pursuit of the un-American dream / by Kirby Gann.
p.   cm.
ISBN 1-58818-065-4 (alk. paper)
1. Fathers and sons—Fiction. 2. Soccer players—Fiction. 3. Young men—Fiction. 4. Kentucky—Fiction. I. Title: Barbarian parade. II. Title: Pursuit of the un-American dream.
III. Title.
PS3607.A55 B37 2002
813'.6—dc21   2002025043

ISBN # 1-58818-065-4
10 9 8 7 6 5 4 3 2 1
First Printing

For my mother and father

If anyone feels like attributing motivations to the actions listed in this book, he's at liberty to do so. Wherever I myself had even an inkling of my reasons I gave them, or tried to. Certainly you wouldn't want invented motivations long after the fact. . . . Why formulate questions if action gives the result more quickly?

—Paul Bowles, in a letter

As long as we're young, we manage to find excuses for the stoniest indifference, the most blatant caddishness, we put them down to emotional eccentricity or some sort of romantic inexperience. But later on, when life shows you how much cunning, cruelty, and malice are required just to keep the body at ninety-eight point six, we catch on, we know the score, we begin to understand how much swinish-ness it takes to make up a past.

—Céline, *Journey to the End of the Night*

Contents

Prologue 1

The House of Toure 19

The Favorite Game 51

The Barbarian Parade 113

Cripplefears and Everything After 197

Acknowledgments 241
A Reader's Guide 243

Prologue

The day the freight train hit my father, I was eight years old and in grave contemplation of our maple tree's crown, shielding my eyes from the sunlight speared there. 1976, hot summer afternoon moving on to evening; Coldwell Godfrey and I were climbing into the tree and then back down. We'd been at it an hour when I bet him I could make it to the last split of branches at the top—a yawning, chancy wishbone we had christened Eagle Point long ago, though neither of us had ever seen a wild eagle before.

—Gaby, your mother will kill you if the fall don't, Cody said, gazing upward.

I hauled myself up through the lower limbs, leaky sap from where our shoes had gored the bark gumming my hands and T-shirt. —You're a coward is all and I'm looking forward to proving it, I said back.

The phone rang in the open window of my parents' bedroom, not five feet from my perch on the middle branches, and we both turned to look. Mother answered; she grabbed for cigarettes and sat on the bed with the same grace as if she had fallen there. I did not shout or scare her; she had an air that said, *not now.* I waited until she hung up. She jumped, startled—her head skirted side-to-side and behind her; she looked again at the phone before moving to the open window.

—Coldwell Godfrey you go tell your mother to come over if she can. I need her to watch the boys tonight.

—I get to spend the night at Cody's?

—I'll call her now, is she home?

He told her yes and she was on the phone again and her voice shook through *accident,* and *Ray;* her back faced the window and she was bent over as though her stomach pained her. *I don't know,* she said. When she got off the phone I asked what's wrong. She didn't answer and I asked again and still she didn't answer, grabbing her purse, her Dorothy Hamill hair swinging, keys rattling in hand. Then she shouted: *Get out of that damn tree before I shake you out of it* and *You listen to Mrs. Godfrey and do what she tells you* and *Go find your brother.* We did not see her again for three days.

The crossing where the train hit my father was rural and forgotten, with no railroad arms or warning lights. Large, full poplars lined the tracks all the way to the roadside edge. My father Ray was running late to Pepper Davis' wedding. He pulled onto the tracks to see, looked left, saw nothing; when he looked right he had enough time to shift gears before the train slammed into his car.

He turned away from the collision and gripped the steering wheel, clutching it until the impact sent him face-first through spraying glass, out of the car and into the air. He missed the trees. His body flew in a long grand arc that took him over the tulip poplars and through two parallel power lines and over the street to a gas station, where he bounced off the hood of an LTD waiting to be serviced. He skidded to a halt on his belly, facedown; then he did not move at all.

The car traveled nearly twenty-five yards, following a similar trajectory. We saw it later, crushed like a cola can I'd guzzled in three swallows to impress Coldwell Godfrey, the steering column twisted into a tongue expressing some new, unfounded word. The car hit the side of a flatbed truck and knocked it over. The train, speeding, powered another half-mile before it came to a stop.

This was outside Montreux, Kentucky; there was nothing aside from the gas station and a tire shop and a small cafeteria advertising BEER & LUNCH for truckers who got off the interstate less than a mile away. After the crash there must have been nothing but a powerful silence, an amazement, and the cranberry sky. People would have been too shocked to react, the birds surely flown away, the animals frozen in place, and there would be no more cars for some time on such a distant road. It was just past twilight in that summer hour when bats flush out to tumble wildly in the air, since it is not yet dark enough for them to understand where they are.

My father's life was like the trajectory of a rock thrown hard through a great tree, snapping all branches along its flight. He described that life to me as a sum of accidents and mishaps, catastrophes endured and overcome. *A man understands who he is once he finds what he can survive,* he said.

My mother Olive ordered me never to pay attention to a word my father said if he had a cigar in hand, which he tended to fire up every few evenings and which he called his Havana Romeo y Julietas, although we knew his cigars were nothing but The King's Standard, available in any liquor store. She didn't concern herself with my brother Michael too much because he was studious and quiet, an almost absent figure; but it was a given in my family that I was just like my father, so she worried.

Before she met my father, he raced cars, revving a super-charged 1958 Corvette at regional drag races. He liked to recite every detail of that car: the first model to sport dual headlights, and then the electric convertible top (white), three-speed close ratio transmission, AM-signal seeking radio, grab bar on the passenger side, and two four-barrel carburetors . . . more vivid to my mind was the moniker *Hellzafire* emblazoned on the side in his own hand. His body, especially his hands, gleamed with scars from engine work and wrecks and sometime bar-fights, and he held a story behind each one. I would touch the scar while he recounted. He had been in the 101st Airborne at the very end of Korea and was shot through the stomach as he landed with his parachute. When he came home, healed, he continued in the army until he reached as far as major, but then decided he detested the bureaucracy and left to perform in air shows, skydiving and teaching students to fly and jump. We owned an entire file of Super 8 movies of him falling from airplanes.

In his jump of greatest renown—one we had on film—my father fell to earth without an open parachute. My brother Michael could already walk, but I'd just been born and mother carried me everywhere. We were at an airfield to see my father in a show. He had stayed out all evening the night before with some army buddies who'd come to skydive with him. Olive declared him hung over and a damn fool and made a big show of it in order to embarrass him into stopping, but Ray rarely allowed himself to listen to her; he made jump after jump on that sunny Saturday afternoon and never once landed close to his target streamer. His back hurt from having slept on a friend's floor that night and he couldn't arch into the proper free fall position, so the air whipped him like a rag. He kept pulling early to stop the spinning, afraid he would pass out. On his final jump, he went second in a group of six from 6000 feet. He started to spin again and pulled early, around 4000 feet. The pilot chute drew forward, the sleeve flapping behind it, but he was still spinning as he fell and so rolled into the unfurling suspension lines, causing them to fold over the canopy. Briefly the full parachute slowed his descent; then the friction of cords against nylon began to burn holes through the canopy, and he started to fall in awful, jagged jerks. On film he rushes down then stutters, his legs flailing wildly as he fights the lines above.

He was in full plummet, falling much too fast. Reserve chutes do not have pilots and so must be thrown from the body to catch air—but in his panic he skipped this important maneuver and just pulled the chute from its casing, throwing it into the canopy where the static of the nylons caused them to suck together.

There was nothing else to do. Mr. Godfrey, a pal since Korea, sprinted onto the airfield almost right below him and yelled, *Prepare to land!* to remind my father how close he'd come to earth. He must have heard, for immediately he pulled his feet together and straightened his eyes to the horizon—giving his parachute the chance to open partway—and he landed not on the airstrip as planned but on the island between runways, where a rainy night had soiled the earth into a swampy bed, and for that he was lucky.

Once, while I traced my finger over the scar where his femur had come through his thigh, my father told me he hit the ground at nearly forty miles an hour. He broke both legs and a clavicle, burst a disc in his back, and punctured his right lung. They kept him in the hospital three weeks. He planned to start jumping again until Mom put her foot down. *Two boys, Ray, two boys,* she said. *Stop thinking of yourself. You've no right to leave me to rear them alone!*

He admitted she was right and Gosh he was sorry and that summer he sold his Cessna and all of his chutes and took his first job as an insurance salesman, a position from which he liked to point out the ironic turns a life could take.

Pops believed his accidents came at peculiar, prophetic times; he said he didn't like to but always he had to prove himself; a man should not have to suffer certain doubts, he said. He only knew how to do that—the proving—physically. Then he added: —You're the same thing, too. Don't forget that. A survivor. See it plain as the scars on my hands.

He would point me out to mother as if noticing me for the first time and say, *Look at this one, doll—born rascal, got too much of that family fire in him* and she would stop whatever it was she was doing to look and then answer, *No no he's a good boy* and it was as though Ray would try to look at me then in a suddenly different light, only to remain unconvinced, saying *I tell you, he's got born rascal written all over him,* and my mother would throw up her hands as if shielding a blow from above, shouting *Goddammit Ray what are you trying to do to the boy?*

Ray would look at her, then back at me, and just laugh and laugh.

We passed that entire summer without my parents. Essentially my brother and I moved in with the Godfreys, which was fine since Cody was my best friend—much closer to me than Michael, who was three years older and quiet, perceptive, a thinker: my opposite. Adults called Cody and me Frick & Frack, or The Two Awfuls, because you couldn't separate us. We were both small for our age and had blond, almost white hair. We could both be very loud, and for whatever reasons, this made us proud.

Not that we didn't have conflicts. The June of Ray's accident gave into July, and Coldwell often challenged me that I'd never climbed my way to Eagle Point. —Get up and do it now, Cody taunted, —if you're not a wuss.

—I'm not scared—

—You haven't been up there yet, he shot back.

A truth. I looked over the scabs on my legs and the fifteen stitches on my arm forming a sneer below the elbow; I'd wrecked my bike landing wrong off of a homemade ramp. Olive had come home with the muscles in her face twitching fury, her skin pale as she hadn't been out all summer (usually she was dark from the golf course). She shouted that she couldn't be everywhere at once and was it her fault it was Michael the only one male in the family with any sense and could she help it if she couldn't take care of everybody at the same time and never mind her own needs. . . . She started to cry then, lit a cigarette with hands shaking. Why couldn't I help her out? Couldn't I see I had to behave more as a grown-up? She knew it wasn't fair but life could be like that, and she needed to be able to trust me, especially now.

It made me feel awful sore and selfish, a feeling underscored by my brother who began to list how much mother worked for us and cleaned up after our messes and drove us everywhere and just because she wasn't around much recently did not mean she never would be, so I might consider thinking ahead. I promised it would be my only accident that summer. This was hard to put out of mind while gazing up at Eagle Point where the branches joined at one thin space near the top, the branches too young to sprout full leaves, a place which even now trembled slightly in a breeze not felt on the ground.

I couldn't tell Coldwell Godfrey I'd promised my mother no more accidents—that would have been all there was for me. I ran my fingers over the aching stitches in my arm and realized there would be a scar there, a story for my father when he finally came home. Robins chose to nest further below that yawning where there wasn't even any real shadow, the birds disbelieving the sturdiness of those pale, reaching branches. —What do I have to prove to you for? I asked, knowing it would be hardly enough.

—My goodness gracious you are *too* scared to go, wait till I see your brother tonight, aren't we going to have some things to talk about, your brother and me. . . . He made this into a song almost.

—Okay okay okay, I said, —What it is is that I promised my dad (promises to fathers being so much more grave than to mothers) not to get hurt anymore until he's better because he wants to be the one to take me to see a doctor and not your mom and dad, who he says have been put out enough.

—Look at you lying. You haven't talked to your dad all summer and I know it, he can't even talk is what I hear, my mother says he's so sick he's gonna die.

—Die?! I yelled. —*Die?* Cody didn't have the chance to take it back. The sunlight seemed to fall very low and white into my eyes and the waving in the leaves filled my ears and I was already on top of his little body, much more frail than mine, thrashing away at his bony ribs and pouring cherry Kool-Aid into his blond hair, his hair the exact same color as mine.

Afterward, we broke into my house. We didn't want his mother to see the damage done to him. He rubbed his ribs, tried to straighten his hair—but he wasn't getting any apology from me. The most he could hope for was what I was doing right then, breaking into my house with a screwdriver against the bathroom window to undo the latch, so he could clean up without his mother seeing.

Cody changed T-shirts and washed his hair in the kitchen sink. Since we were there we made sandwiches and more Kool-Aid. The Super 8 projector remained on a chair from the night before, when Cody's father brought us over to watch a silent version of *Planet of the Apes*. I turned it on and got out Ray's old jumping films.

—You weren't even born when this was made, I told Cody, as if that fact alone should shame him. We watched Ray fall, kicking at air. He asked if that was my dad. I answered *Hell yes it is* and threatened him with a fist again, my face bursting with purple anger. Coldwell asked to see the movie again. We sat quiet before the gray flickering image of my father falling 6000 feet without a full parachute, my father a small gray speck in the sky growing into a flailing rag doll on the white basement door, the rattling projector making the room's only sound. Once it was over, we sat in silence until finally Cody said, *You're right, he's not gonna die,* and we could be friends again.

That night I imagined myself in my father's place, thought of all he had said those many times: how when he looked at me he saw his own father, saw himself. *A line of brothers in calamity,* he called us. And me, I put myself in the driver's seat of a 1958 Corvette convertible, *Hellzafire* flaming along the sides; I could see into those tangled lines and hear the wind rushing in my ears and the whapping flap in the nylons above; felt the rough-worn cords in my hands, the length of them flexing loose then taut as I pulled for control; patches of blue sky burned through my canopy. I tried to imagine the sound of a freight train bearing down only feet away. And it seemed a simple thing.

Tell me where to find another father like my father in all the world.

In early August Coldwell and I were riding our bikes far from home. We tried to ignore the heavy thunderheads that furled and reeled across the sky to the west, blackening what had before been softly overcast. The stale air began to liven, and soon neighbors started to call their children indoors. As we pedaled farther, the street clattered with the clack of windows opened and shutters locked fast to sidings.

—Maybe we should go home now? Cody suggested. But rain had yet to fall. I convinced him we could ride a while longer.

Our bodies awakened as the hour cooled and darkened; grains of dust and dirt began to pepper our faces in the upraised winds; it made me feel strangely giddy. We continued to ride further from home, until soon the wind became nearly all, with its rustle-shushing leaves and bowbacked trees; sheet lightning burst on the horizon, far away and inside the clouds, all the more noticeable for the discreet absence of thunder. We ran into patches of mizzling rain.

—Gaby, we should get on back to the house, Cody said now, the flutter of playing cards thwapping the spokes in his wheels.

You kids get yourselves inside, someone yelled from the safety of his porch, *we're in for a hard one soon.*

I waved to him as though we couldn't hear. But one look at Cody revealed his nervousness; his eyes were cast downward, staring at his front wheel. His teeth worked his bottom lip. —What, you hear your mom calling? I asked, teasing him. Only then did he look at me. Instead of answering, he slowed his bike enough to make a wide turn in the road, turning back toward home. I said something nasty to him. But a heavy curtain of rain was there not far ahead of us, rushing down the street, the smell of it filling my nostrils before overtaking me, then Cody; I turned to join him, and at that instant the blare of the emergency siren wailed high over the city to signal severe weather. The two of us cranked our bikes as fast as our legs would allow, hollering with surprised joy at being caught in the cool summer rain.

Within minutes, though, my feet slowed on their own, slowing until I simply coasted. Soon Cody was far ahead of me. I had never seen—or never noticed before—the raw transformation of the world into storm: rain became hail; the air surged with an electric tang; above me, the clouds roiled in the sky, their shapes changing so quickly that an image came to mind of the creek behind our house, muddy water rushing through it with flood. The certainty arose that something was going on, drastic and of a force awful and uncontrollable. I wanted to be *in* on it—not safely watching from a basement window in Cody's house.

My bike made a steady arc, turning back around. Cody did not see me go. Or, if he called to me, I didn't hear. The sky now glowed oddly green; I felt almost visited by it. Slashes of lightning greeted me like invitations.

This is what my father would seek: the paint of houses glimmering brighter; the stout grass of manicured lawns bent with the wind. It was difficult to control the bike. I had no set path to follow; movement was my only concern, and the rush of that harsh gale on my face and arms. The sirens continued to blare, far away and then suddenly just over my shoulder. Beneath the shrieking there churned the powerful noise of a train passing, yet no tracks were near me, I knew—a thought that set me to shivering. The green leaves of trees overturned and shuddered white, raging then shushing around me, emphasizing brief moments of stillness. But I saw nothing more.

One lone porch light shone brightly unique in the afternoon's strangely bruised light. And then I saw, passing over one of the wide main avenues between subdivisions, that what I'd believed to be a train was not one at all, but a funnel cloud scoring the land several blocks away, moving toward my school. *There*—and the bike directed itself on its own, rushing.

By the time I got near, the neighborhood looked as though a drunken giant had gone to it at his whimsy: one house stood untouched, and the next two or three had lost a roof or wall; beds and furniture, bicycles, piecemeal dolls lay strewn over yards, the street, the roofs of other houses. Fire bellowed clogs of tarred smoke from a second-floor window. Dogs scurried in tight circles, smacking slavering maws, whining in high pitch. It had turned so dark, the only thing that kept me from believing day had leapt to night was absence of fireflies. Flashing red lights washed the surroundings—hard red, soft red—as firefighters arrived and began to unharness their hoses. I stopped to watch that urgent, serpentine unwinding, felt awe before the heavy power of those huge trucks, wiped my nose at the bite of diesel exhaust.

One fireman rushed me, blood-eyed, face streaked with char. His voice boomed through a burgundy beard of whorled whiskers: *What the hell you doing outside? Go home to your momma, boy!* Then he wheeled round to strangers rising from hidden basements and demanded they get back to their houses, the storms were not yet over, they could be hit again at any moment. But nobody listened to him roar; the winds ripped away his voice like some frantic captain lost at sea, the bluster in the trees whipping us with the howl of the lost, and even the rain now fell as more of a spray.

The people shuffle-stepped in a kind of astonishment, not speaking, rubbing foreheads with sweating hands, smoothing down wild wet locks of hair. As a group we stared at one faceless home, the façade torn clean away, nothing touched inside. A doll's house—framed photographs remained propped on table tops, unshorn posters clung to the walls, and furniture sat in place; empty stairways led to quiet rooms. The same fireman pounced on me again and ordered me home, the reproach in his voice pitched at near-fever, his tenor scathed angrier now in a throat turned savagely hoarse. I pedaled toward school to escape him.

The weird battlefield look of the school fields bewildered me: a sea of crabgrass covered now by a matchstick meringue of tree trunks from Bluegrass Park, torn siding boards, and shutters peeling paint; roof shingles, spindles of brush—entire trees, leafless now—and a red car door stuck upright in the ground, one jagged star broken into the window. As though the tornado had picked what it wanted from each subdivision and then dumped it here in the fields. I couldn't bike through for the debris; even parts of the concrete embankment curbing the field had been pummeled, shattered. A dirty mist rose everywhere. Telephone poles foundered or else were completely gone, and one which still stood near the façade of the school had been impaled by the fender of a car. I saw the hind legs of a dog buried beneath refuse. I saw the still form of a large doll lying beneath a tangle of wood and wire.

No, not a doll, but a boy. He lay on his stomach with his right cheek flush to the ground, his arms stretched out overhead, palms down. His face was a purpled bruise, with eyes clenched shut as if he expected somebody to hit him. His skin felt colder than mine. I said *Hey, Hey kid you all right?*—quietly at first, whisperingly, then louder as I shook him by his sleeve. His hand felt glued to the ground; a light rip sounded when I moved it. His fingernails were torn, dirty; one long laceration striped from the bridge of his nose between his eyebrows across his forehead into his hair . . . I knew, vaguely, he shouldn't be moved, in case he was broken inside. I knew, sitting down in front of him, my ankles crossed and elbows on my knees, that he was not alive anymore.

But death made no sense to me; I didn't know what it was. I shook him by the head, snagged his arm, and turned angry: *Look at you!* I shouted, staring at his thin features, the crinkled, pale eyelids. This was just the kind of thing that could happen to Michael or Cody. I stomped around in my shoes, glancing back to see the boy still there, not having moved. I started to run back to the burning house, but the idea of seeing the fireman again frightened me.

You deserve this, I told the boy. *Somehow, you deserved this.*

It had turned mostly quiet again, with the rain falling in broad brushes. The wind eased to a faint whistle. I poked the kid with my foot, but he would not move. The tall hillside butte of Bluegrass Park glowed darkly against the sky, the trees fallen in a long yanking downward, a wood-sculpture waterfall. The gray stones at the summit, bare and somewhat incandescent in new nakedness and storm light, made an appeal, a lure: ESCAPE TO HERE. Daniel Boone stared off over the Ohio Valley with his rifle held across his body; it looked like he had cleared the overgrowth of trees so he could see the city again. George Rogers Clark stood pointing between a groin of branches. The boy still did not move.

His hair looked a lot like my brother's. I tried to budge the debris off of him, straining my shoulder against the weight of it, but it was too heavy. Somebody should stay with him, I thought. Somebody else—in the next instant he was left beneath the trash and I moved toward Boone, half-pedaling, half-pushing the bike up the clogged horse trails.

And Michael? And Cody? It would be just like them to get buried under a house. They would cringe until crushed. Climbing the hillside, long searches over my shoulder gave onto our landscape poled by sharp columnar light bolting through clouds, desolate in smoke and fog and streaks of rain. So many disjointed and broken angles in what I'd believed was permanently settled, eternally planned—torn and turned inside-out and upside-down, or else completely erased. It made no sense. And my family was out there somewhere? My father, sleeping soundly in some hospital. I strained to spot our neighborhood, the rooftops sur-rounded by devastation, and felt horrified; yet also seduced, in the way boys like to destroy wasps by pricking off their wings.

A faint twister spun its way down from the sky, not a half-mile away, drilled one corner of the school and tore open a few houses, then pulled right back into the swirling clouds. My ears whooshed and rang and I screamed until the funnel disappeared.

Whatever stores of energy left to me were squandered reaching the summit of Bluegrass Park. I collapsed there at the foot of Daniel

Boone. A long time passed before I straightened myself and looked over the wide vista encompassing Montreux. No trees were left to inhibit the view, and our small downtown skyline appeared untouched, but entire streets lay razed, bordered by brush fires and simmering ash pits; my eyes traced long, wide, erratic paths torn in every direction.

After another hard rain the air calmed again. The darkest sections of sky moved eastward, and sometimes a few hints of blue patched overhead, until, soon, the full sun blazed through as though God had opened his breast to shower his heart upon the world. A light so incandescent I could look nowhere but down, and my gaze fell to the boy hidden in the fields. I wished I had not come after all. And yet I felt certified in some way, confirmed in that Ray, who indulged catastrophe, was indeed my father. I did not understand why I was out there, but Ray, somehow, would.

He came home the last week of August. At the sound of the car in the driveway I was at the gate of the chainlink fence—mother had instructed us not to rush Pops because he was still weak, and she reminded us of this as she shut her door and went around the car to help him, the engine fan kicking in just as she crossed it.

His dark hair had gone the chalky flax of decayed bone. He had lost at least the equal of my body in weight, which made me think exactly that, of my body cut from his, leaving him hollow and frail. It made me want to run to him, to reconnect by way of a summer's-absence embrace—but the look of him, the fact of his being in such a state before us, and for all to see, stilled me. I held motionless long enough to realize nobody was moving. His shoulders sloped, and something had changed in his face: the slack mouth, or the nose bent in a dramatic curve, or the eyes that merely hung open; maybe the forward tilt of his head that bore the likeness of sleepwalking. He moved in baby steps and held my mother's hand like an old man long

tired of, but resigned to, necessities. Mother spoke slowly, and loud: —
Ray, I'm going to leave you like this just a second while I shut the car
door and get your bags, okay?

All hesitated, waiting, while he seemed to think for a long time.
He gave a barely perceptible nod.

—Somebody open the back door, she said, and a hushed flurry of
movement spun around him as we all moved deliberately in hopes of
becoming useful. But it required only Michael to open the sliding-glass
door. I moved my weight from foot to foot, smiled at my father,
followed my mother to the gate as if this was needed of me. Slowly
we all wound down again and the afternoon seemed to settle, and a
hoarse whisper came out of my father, quiet enough that I wouldn't
have been sure he said anything if not for everyone else leaning
forward: —Hello, boys. . . . He did not look *at* us but around us, with a
shiny crescent sheen reflecting off his wet lower lip, drool dammed
behind it.

—Hi Dad, my brother said. —Man we're really glad to have you
home again.

His eyes closed; he smiled. He could have gone to sleep right
there. He nodded with a little more force, and when he opened his pale
eyes he appeared to survey the three of us boys—murmuring my
brother's name then, his head dancing a little. With a weak sigh, he said
my name, and raised one hand to lay atop Cody's blond head, gently
ruffling the stiff hair that grew straight except for the cowlick at the
crown, just like mine. *Glad for me, too.* . . . is what we think he said, and
then he spoke my name again, touching little Cody's head, and I looked
down at the patio with eyes burning.

—You boys be quiet out here, mother ordered as she shut the gate
and took my father's hand to lead him into the house. —Ray needs his
rest. Coldwell, go on home and tell your mother I'll call her tonight.

My brother, being the oldest, carried the small suitcase she had gone back out to take from the car. They went inside to help my father to bed. When I turned away from the closing door, Cody was already tearing across the backyard toward home.

Alone on the porch, the hot tears I fought seemed unjustified, and shameful. I was being a child, and infant-foolish—as my father would say. My mind even conjured the word *Daddy*, which I hadn't used since I was in diapers. He was not yet completely there; at eight years old even I could see that. His eyes had been hardly open, much less focused.

Still, I ran. I hurdled the fence and tore out of the driveway at full sprint, determined, set with rage. When I turned the front corner of the house I did not stop running until my feet were off the ground, my hands around the lowest branch on the old maple, hauling me upward.

Leaves throughout the wide canopy rustled with the pull of my weight. I grunted to vault my legs higher, faster, pushing off shavings of dead or dying bark, ignoring the small cuts in my hands and the irritable throb in the stitches of my arm—stitches which were supposed to have been removed days ago, but forgotten. My parents' bedroom window passed without my turning to look. A chattering went up through the birds on the house and power lines and soon they were swooping down at me, attacking with tiny claws bared and then banking away, squawking all kinds of noise. Pausing only long enough to swat at them, I saw a small nest with sleeping, bulbous-eyed chicks, and in my anger kicked it free and did not listen as it tumbled from branch to branch. My goal shone above me, and close. Two more quick pulls and I had to slow down with care; the trunk split into several directions there, and the arms of the tree were weak with green.

I caught my breath in sucking gasps. I was above the transformer on the telephone pole cornering our driveway, and could see where squirrels had built nests beneath the antenna on our house. The birds left me alone. In the distance, early evening sunlight starred off the windows of downtown skyscrapers, and the buildings there appeared quiet and still.

A few inches higher, and at Eagle Point my weight overwhelmed the tree. The maple whispered through its leaves and started to lean. I clutched at what I could. Someone on the street screamed *Oh Lord.* The gray-plank siding of the house whizzed past as I hugged the thin trunk tightly with arms and legs, the canopy protesting with loud cracks, until after a sharp bounce my back took a line parallel to the ground, my head slightly lower than my feet. My body hung just above the sill of the bedroom window, but the blinds were drawn. The skin of my hands ripped. The transformer was at a level above me again, and all the birds were circling away in great reeling masses.

There, I thought, dangling at the anchor end of the weakening, warped bow. *There,* I grunted aloud, the sprung stitches in my arm popping tiny splashes of blood onto my cheek, my heart mad with pride at the thought of this scar taking ages to heal.

The House of Toure

1

We're playing basketball. It's October, cool, and dark enough to turn on the floodlight, but we won't interrupt the game. We blow into our chapped, red hands, and warm them beneath our sweatshirts. We smell of milk and sweat, and the ball's tangy echo leaps from the driveway and rings in the air, mixing there with the heartless teasing of boys at play.

The large white car pulls in, the kind my brother once convinced me had to be made in shipyards. It stops at the far end of the drive. But my brother and I never took much notice of strangers, as people often came to visit my father—friends from old days before we were born, or else potential partners and business associates. Ray was a popular man; mother often complained we could never go out to eat without Pops running into somebody he had not seen in fifteen years.

Two men in matching Kentucky Wildcat polo shirts and tan slacks stepped out, cold and white-lipped. One wore bronze aviator sunglasses even though the early evening was overcast. He asked if our father was home. We paused the game then, long enough for Michael to answer. —Yes sir, you just go on in the front, he said.

—All right though boys how about giving me a shot at that ball first? The sunglassed man asked. He didn't take off his glasses. He dribbled meditatively a moment, shot from twenty feet out, missed the rim. No one laughed even after he cursed and demanded another try. He missed again off the front of the rim and was about to chase after the ball for another try, but his associate urged him to forget that and come inside. We turned back to arguing over who had how many points and who should get the ball; we were deep into our game again and did not see Ray leave with the two men.

It got cold enough that our noses stung and our lungs ached, so we called it a night. Michael and I went inside and were surprised to find the house draped in a queer, wrongful silence: the kitchen glowed in spare, first-moonlight darkness falling through the window; clusters of cigarette smoke drifted through the blue shafts of it. Up the stairs, at the narrow counter where the family ate dinner, mother sat alone, staring at the cabinets on the wall, fidgeting with her legs and hands.

—What's for dinner, mom? Michael called out, thumping the basketball on the living room carpet. Usually this brought grave threats from her, but tonight she said nothing.

—Oh I'm sorry boys, God I'm really sorry. . . . Did your friends say anything? I had no idea it would come . . . that this would happen—we thought it was a bad joke. . . . She did not look at us. She pushed the ashtray back and forth before her, a small ceramic bowl which gave off a dim scraping sound. We didn't know what she was talking about. We said as much and the scraping stopped. She exploded: —What do you mean what am I talking about? Are you boys blind? *Humiliation* is what *I'm* talking about—*public humiliation*. Where have you been?

We stared, dumbly. Michael mentioned we'd been playing ball in the driveway, couldn't she hear us? But Mother answered as though he had said nothing.

—Your dad, your dear old man that you two . . . *revere* so much . . .

he was arrested tonight. How did you miss that? Walked out with two damn DEA agents is what he did, *handcuffed* in front of the whole goddamn neighborhood to see. Your dad's in jail, boys. I don't see how you missed it.

But we did. We were playing ball. Nothing else mattered.

—Thank god for small favors, then, mother said. Her voice shallowed. She had been crying. She ordered us to our rooms and would not tell us more: she insisted that at this point she knew nothing. —He'll be home tomorrow, she said. —Or the next day. Or maybe the day after that, I don't know.

When I imagined criminals, I pictured the murderer Gary Gilmore and the photographs of his shackled hands and feet, his wry scowl staring out from behind steel bars—a man who'd recently argued for his right to execution. That had nothing to do with my father. Pops was the man who, having discovered Michael had lifted a pack of gum from a general store, forced him to return it, his hand crushing my brother's neck as he ordered an apology to the owners. Then he docked his allowance for five times the price of the gum. This was the man who carried us to church every Sunday where he taught Sunday school; who prayed at the dining room table each morning in candlelight before the rest of us awoke—a ritual he began once he could act by himself again, after his accident with the train. Here was the man who sang folk songs to the neighbor kids in summer while we waited for homemade ice cream to mix and freeze. Jail was for the enemies of society.

That night, Michael opened his books to study, but I couldn't begin to think of such things. Mother's worry sponged the entire house of whatever contentment had lain there, and we watched happiness retreat to a moment of our past.

Ray dabbled in so many different things at once that for most of my childhood I could never explain exactly what my father did for a living. But recently his main concern had been with a medical-supplies office he owned: surgical instruments, hospital beds, wheelchairs—whatever a hospital or clinic needed, Ray could get. He also took part in a group-ownership of cattle and racehorses, and spent much of his time at the track watching thoroughbreds train. He liked to gamble—the kind of guy who understood all the information given on a racing form—and played poker or gin rummy with buddies every Thursday night. On Saturdays he got a kick out of giving his sons a few dollars at the track to place bets on our own, to see who came out on top at the end of the day.

—Don't tell your mother, he would say, grinning through his explanations of the figures in the racing form: who looked good in which race, which jockeys were well-known, which studs or mares could be worth a raised eyebrow. It was too much information for me. I would forget everything he said and bet on the horses by the simple allure of their names. I rarely won, and this tickled our old man. He ribbed me about it all the way home, teasing me for my losses while reminding us not to tell Mother about our wagers. However, I didn't care about winning or losing; it was all about being with Ray, and walking behind him as he strode ahead in his stylish brown fedora, the brim never turned down, through the stables along the track's back side, shaking hands with trainers and owners who always seemed glad to see him. Voices called from the shadows of side-glimpsed stalls, *How about that Smilin' Ray!* He laughed loudly, called every woman *hey good-lookin'*. Someone even named a horse after him—*Smilin' Ray*—and that the horse never amounted to much was a source of great amusement to that crowd.

Typically Ray wore a red sportcoat and gray slacks with snakeskin ankle boots that zipped up the inside. We trailed in his wake like deputies to some politician come to greet his people, and the farm hands, trainers, walkers, even jockeys, flocked to him. They led us to the paddocks to present a certain horse, serving us over-sugared lemonade as they praised who had been training good all week, which ones were sprinters and which could hold in the long race . . . I'd listen in concentration, frowning at the effort and rubbing my brow, and almost forget to ask if I could touch the horse's nose—which I loved to do because the flesh there was so surprisingly soft and tender.

Smilin' Ray preferred to watch races from the rail along that back stretch, where the horses stormed past huge and frightening and furious. On rainy days the mud splattered our faces as though we were riding ourselves and Pops would laugh out loud and slap his thigh, pronouncing, —That's it, boys, *now* we're racing. . . .

The afternoons held boredom, too. With Ray caught up in long discussion, my brother and I could turn restless, tracing shapes and designs into red dirt tenderized by scores of hooves, listening to the splash of hoses spraying horseflesh, the pumping clump of sprints down the back side, and all the different radio stations clamoring softly from the stalls; I'd sneeze from the dust and dander off the animals, and someone would come with a wet cloth for me to cover my face with, while Michael would try to trick me into stepping into piles of manure.

Often Ray employed my brother and me to provide relief from the tedium of those back-side spring afternoons. In the trunk of whatever recent-model Cadillac he currently drove, he kept two sets of child-sized Everlast boxing gloves. Skimming a handful of cash for himself as he rounded up stakes, my father marked a ring in the soft dirt with the heel of his boot, for the boxing matches staged between his sons.

Kegs of beer sat in iced barrels by a huge grill piled high with burgers and bratwurst, the smell of grilled meat heavy and still in the close air. People got out folding chairs, beer in one fist, a shot of bourbon in the other. They called themselves The Boilermakers. The crowd would watch us fight for six two-minute rounds—no more than six because Ray didn't want our mother to see us too beaten up. Michael hated these matches, and often we had to wait while Ray went in search of him; my brother, so quiet, had a talent for disappearing. My brother, reclined in a way so that his book shaded his eyes, feet propped on the edge of a steel bucket, mentioning offhand how Canada gave NASA a mechanical arm for retrieving satellites. . . . *What do you care for?* I would ask, mystified. *Come on, it's time to fight.*

I loved the fights, and usually won. I was stockier, and Michael could not hit very hard. Still, he was intelligent and planned strategies, analyzed my habits: if he remained patient and dodged my blows, the afternoon heat would wear me down and he could win on points. Such considerations evaded me.

—You don't think, he said, on those rare days when he could gloat. —You're just a brute.

I believed him. But this was not too hard to accept. The back-side circle celebrated the physical; they suspected intelligence. A summer-hard afternoon, stink of stables settling in the nostrils, and I'm in yellow-leather, mink-oiled boxing gloves, thumbless to protect our eyes, shirt tied around my waist. Out into the ring enclosed by a line of familiar strangers, thin-boned Michael pale and waiting in his tentative stance, his gloves up around his face—a hard jab to his ribs and the stance falls apart, the gloves come down; punch his jaw and the gloves are up again, then he goes for the clinch. Ray referees. He pushes us apart and the voices of the crowd are everywhere: *Cover up, Mike! Not so low next time, Gaby! Take it in there now!* We tap gloves to restart, and then it's a suckerpunch slalom of one trying to dodge the other until Crush Hadley breaks his beer bottle against the iced barrel and sneers in his cheery way, *End of Round One!* We head to opposite sides of the circle for a frigid cola. Two-minute rounds, two-minute breaks.

The adults celebrated the winner for the rest of the day—men who were friends of our father and so I made deals with God for their approval. Michael did not seem to care, preferring to seek out a bale of straw to sit with his book. But it meant everything to me. With the match ended, two or three Boilermakers would come to the winner and help you off with your gloves, pat you on the back and give you a smelly horse towel and tell you to call them *Uncle*. I had more uncles than any boy in Kentucky: Uncle Crush, Uncle Orkney, Uncle Blister. . . .

Uncle Crush was an old hand in the horse business. He was only five years older than Pops, but already in such poor health that he looked much older; *I's destined for a short life of trouble,* Crush said in a sing-song voice; *it ages you, boy.* He was only a few inches taller than Michael, maybe five-foot-four. His hands were meaty and red; his palms yellow calluses veined by dry white cracks. He was the one to call me the little Ram of the family, and gave up his belly for my punching exercise:

—C'mon boy, give it a little effort, make me give up a little hey-hey, he ordered. When I began to punch hard enough he'd allow himself tiny yelps, *hey! hey!*

Whenever I won, Uncle Crush would slip me a taste of his beer, which I didn't like, or his bourbon, which I *did* like, after some time on ice. The sunny and humid afternoons would blur and Pops would ask why I was acting such a fool. Although he treated them all as close friends, he did not trust any of them—in other company, he referred to *horse people* with shaking head, and his voice turned low in a disapproving rasp. Still, these people gave him joy. When Crush would tell a dirty joke, —Hey Gaby you know why they call your dad an oyster man? . . . Pops would grunt *ahhh* as if disgusted. But we could see his eyes laughing. —Now what you have to remember about Uncle Crush is that he'd rather climb a tree to tell a lie than stay on the ground speaking the truth. . . .

Pops did not like to be seen as human in front of his boys; he was aware of his hero-status with us, and encouraged it. But he *was* human, and he *did* make mistakes, and it was two of his associates from this horse-network of friends who landed him in jail.

Ray owned horses in a partnership with two hospital pharmacists named Lionel Nelson and Grady Tate, head pharmacists for the hospitals General and St. Sebastian. These two invented a scheme to make money by faking hospital orders and paying the invoices themselves. They sold their pharmaceutical stock to other pharmacists around the state at a discount from the usual price, or else—later—distributed popular drugs like Dilaudid, Valium, and Dexedrine on the street.

They began by contacting old friends from school or conferences, then spreading word-of-mouth. They would place a $50,000 order for themselves—worth twice that at market value—slash the asking price by $20,000 and come out thirty grand ahead. By doing this several times a year they were making quite a lot of money by mid-seventies Kentucky standards. They funneled the cash into the horses. It made an excellent scam, until they tried to find the worth of the drugs on the street. For that they had to contact a back-side regular, Pepper Davis, who sometimes worked for my father.

Ray called him his *go-to guy*. Whenever he needed someone to make a delivery that he couldn't make himself, he called Davis. Ray learned Davis had a legitimate CPA and hired him to keep the books. Davis earned a retainer for the accounting, and commissions on whatever deals he brought in, until Pops was hit by the train. Then Davis worked full-time to help mother get acquainted with the business until my father was well enough to work again.

So Pepper Davis had access to the company cheques, and the authority to cash them himself. With no one around to keep his obsessions in line, Davis began to write enormous cheques to himself. He drove a new car (on the company), and started to place bigger and bigger wagers at the track. He began to buy into the Tate & Nelson pharmaceutical scheme—with company money, the name on the cheques stating simply *Toure Enterprises*. He started dealing directly to the street, because the money there poured in larger amounts for the Dilaudid, morphine, Valium, and cocaine. Eventually even the police discovered this; they paid a visit; Pops was not yet off his prescription for Tylenol-3 for the pain of his wreck.

—Yes it was just like the movies, mother described to us while we three sat alone around the kitchen, recently notified that Pops wouldn't be home until tomorrow (maybe), —and so corny I didn't take it seriously; I thought it was a typical prank by Ray's friends. I looked at the guy with his gun pointed to me and kind of smiled, then began to go through the mail again when the officer yelled *Goddamn lady what part of FREEZE don't you understand?* and smacked one hand down on my desk. I looked at your father and could see this was no joke.

Ray had given away $110,000 to Pepper Davis while recuperating in the hospital. Much of the money was already borrowed. All accompanying debts came to him alone.

Caught, Davis promised to return the money as quickly as he could, and even went so far as to give $5000 up front. Ray reclaimed the car (already damaged), and through lawyers they worked out a plan of repayment which Ray admitted he had no idea how Davis could adhere to—but he wanted Davis to stay out of jail; otherwise he'd never see any money from him.

Maybe Davis *was* trying to get the money back, I don't know, but he quickly got himself in real trouble through his drug distribution, and there he discovered a way out: he cut a deal with the DEA and named Ray Toure as the ringleader behind this distribution of pharmaceuticals, and had convinced the agents that crashed the office that they could expect a huge confiscation of contraband.

Two agents remained in the main office with guns leveled at my parents, while six others tore through the small inventory room. Nothing there. They emptied all drawers onto the floor, kicked papers around, found nothing. They went through closets, the car, cabinets, the bathroom—nothing. Boxes of supplies emptied on the floor, sofa cushions strewn and discarded, desk drawers emptied on the desktops and abandoned; in the end the only drugs they found were in the prescription bottle on my father's desk for Tylenol-3.

—Think you're slick, Toure? an officer grumbled after the three-hour search. The agents had brought vans to cart away the loot, and mother said she could see them getting frustrated, the curses getting louder, the threats less respectful. They confiscated a roll of postage stamps, emptied the refrigerator of cola and beer. Then a detective named Griffin arrived, a glimmer of hope as my parents recognized him from the Horse Chestnut Club where they played golf in summer. He said nothing as he toured the offices with one of his agents; he told the two guarding my parents that the guns were no longer necessary. He sat down in front of my father on the corner of his desk.

—What's going on here, Mr. Griff? Ray asked, using the man's nickname at the club, a feat my mother thought brave.

—Mr. Toure, Griff nodded, scooping up the prescription bottle and pointing it at Ray, —Let's get this much clear: I don't like you. Never have. You swagger around with your hick friends, always bragging about when you won this, how much you paid for that, and ruin the club for the rest of us . . . the rest of us who deal above the table. Let me assure you, sir, you are in trouble now boy and I am going to employ the full extent of my abilities to make positive you receive your punishment to the last letter of the law. I got a man in a ballbind too afraid to lie his way out, and he has you fingered for some big-city work here . . . you a big-city man?

—What the hell are you talking about, Griff? Who has me fingered?

—The witness is my business, not yours. You'll find out at the appropriate time. But I'm looking at a caught man. Smart enough not to stash anything here, I'll grant that; but caught.

He slid off the desktop and straightened his suit, looked at the prescription bottle and pocketed that. He made a motion to the other agents. They confiscated all the accounting records, and left. Griffin waved as he departed behind them. —Hope you got a good lawyer, pal. Wouldn't want to see your pretty wife on the street . . . and kids, too, right?

Now Ray was not stupid; he could guess what was going on; he knew where his partners were coming up with the money to invest in some powerful bloodlines. Immediately he phoned Tate, then Nelson, but they were unable to take his call. They would never be available again, having received similar visits the same afternoon. Mother began to clean up the mess left everywhere as he phoned around, asking for a recommendation of a good criminal lawyer. Within a day he had moved all of the family's assets into our mother's name. The evening after that he was arrested at our house, and thirteen months later, January 1980, he was serving a nine-year sentence.

He was my father, so maybe my version is difficult to believe. The family view is that he acted on bad legal advice. But it was Ray's fault for mouthing off once too often; the only other time he spoke with Pepper Davis, the man was wired.

Nearly a year had passed since the office raid, and we were beginning to believe no indictment would come. Then Davis visited Ray at work, saying he had a payment for him. The taped conversation goes like this:

> **DAVIS:** *Just trying to pay what I owe, Ray. Sorry I been so late with it but you know how it goes.*
> **RAY:** *I don't want to know where you got it.*
> **DAVIS:** (laughter, then garbled; 67 seconds silence): *Hey listen, I hear from Tate they've got a shipment coming in from Mexico—that true?*
> **RAY:** *Give me a break.*
> **DAVIS:** *Listen now Ray, I gotta know, Ray, got to . . . those punks owe me money and I aim to get it back. You don't know what all went on when you were out. We're not square, no sir, they owe me . . .*
> **RAY:** *That's between you all, then. . . . Go ask Tate.*
> **DAVIS:** *But if you know something about it I go in and say*

I know too, see? You're in on it too . . . no fooling. Come on, man, I know we're not square but I was doing business with them while you were in the hospital and they owe me. . . . I know it doesn't look good with all the money but I want to pay you back. . . . I do. Ray, I got out of hand, okay but everybody's human and I can still be the go-to guy, right? I'm sorry Ray but I can still be your go-to guy. . . .

There's more haranguing from Davis, more denials from Ray, until finally Ray says:

RAY *. . . Sure. It's from Mexico and it's supposed to be big.*

Davis thanked him and was out of there.

Ray said he was mouthing off just to get the man to leave, which is fully in character; or maybe he *did* know. Regardless, the tape existed. It made the papers. The prosecutors wanted to go to trial.

The lawyer of the accused cannot be present before a grand jury; our lawyer sat with Ray and Olive and coached him on what to say: nothing. —You just answer, 'I refuse to answer on the grounds that it may incriminate me', Ray, and hell we'll go to trial if we have to but I don't think it will get there.

That was the plan. Thing is, you answer all questions before the jury, or none. You cannot pick and choose. We stayed at home with mother—our lawyer said it would be best to keep away because there would be serious mudslinging and he didn't want her to get upset—but Ray realized how unprepared we were when he heard the first question:

Mr. Toure, is it true, as a witness has stated, that you have put out a contract for the assassination of a Mr. Rodney 'Pepper' Davis?

Pops said he may as well have been hit by another train. He clenched his fists and shouted, *What?* The prosecutor merely repeated the question, adding, —Please answer the question if you so wish.

—I did the only thing I knew, Ray told us. —I had no idea what they were going to ask me next; and if I answer one I've got to answer them all. So I said, *I will not answer on grounds that my own words may incriminate me.* . . . Shit, one old woman *gasped* and put her hands over her mouth. I knew it was all over then.

He passed fifteen minutes of questions with the same answer. I imagine my father standing in his best suit before a mob of twelve, his hair cropped close, distinguishably silvered from the wreck, pleading the fifth to outlandish charges. Our lawyer called with the news, and told mother, —Olive, I know you won't agree, but I've advised Ray to plead guilty. Here's why: all evidence is circumstantial except for that tape, which I think we can beat in court on entrapment but whatever, there's always the possibility that we won't. It'll be a jury trial, and if the dice come up snake-eyes then it's twenty years. If he pleads guilty he gets five and sees only three to six months of that. It's the best way out I can see.

Michael and I were not told until Pops came home, crushed, leanly tobacco-faced, smaller. The advice had been wrong, and he would end up with the nine-year sentence.

—I couldn't put you all through a trial, he said.

Already we had a number of articles pasted in a photograph album ranging from assassination contracts and drugs in exchange for sexual favors to illicit gambling. He did not want to see the album grow larger.

I could not grasp what all this meant, but again the word *humiliation* bounded about our living room—filled with neighbors, track pals, the priest of our church. Gary Gilmore came to me again, with his hard scowl. I tried to replace his face with my father's, but it would not fit. The adults were talking quietly; mother was crying. I left to take my place midway up the maple out front, and gazed over the rows of houses to the few downtown skyscrapers some brief miles distant, desperately wishing for the power to call down a score of tornados to scour this city away.

2

Time became an essential value. Moments turned palpable and worth clinging to, strained with the effort to make each a lasting memory, meaningful, as they were now freighted with the weight of future loss, and could not be wasted. In the kitchen mother kept a monthly calendar which she used in place of a diary, scribbling over the days with appointments and notes (June 17: *spoke with sis for an hour— her bill. Ray. 2:00 P.M. DENTIST APPT FOR G, ask about braces?*). I used to page through the calendar during summers to count the days until school began again, but now the calendar held a different meaning.

One morning, before we were to go on a retreat to Mammoth Cave with our church youth group, mother found me looking through the few months ahead, the days left blank until the black circle around January fourth. She heard me counting out loud, trying to do the math without paper or pencil.

—What's up, kiddo? she asked, cigarette in one hand, the other cupped below to catch spilled ash, —you should be getting your things packed.

—Hold on or I'll get lost . . . forty-one, forty-two, forty-three. . . . That would make eighty-seven days, minus the six we're gone, but then he'll drive us today so subtract that and when he picks us up add another, that makes. . . . Michael! That's eighty-three days, almost three months!

Her face closed in question, then opened again. When we returned from our trip it was days before I realized the calendar had disappeared.

We packed into my father's car, greeted by the odor of cigar smoke in the upholstery. He started the engine and slipped in an 8-track tape at the same time. As we backed out the driveway, a deep baritone voice announced: *Hello; I'm Johnny Cash*, and the familiar guitar riff started in.

I ain't seen sunshine since I don't know when . . .
. . . Time keeps draggin' on . . . .

—That's a king-size I AM, isn't it boys? Oh man is he something else. This song bother you?

We answered No, in unison.

—You know, your mother can't stand him. But no worries now, that's the deal. You boys are going to have fun.

—Are you having fun, Pops?

—It's always fun when I'm with my boys.

Solidarity reigned high: A man and his boys! The Man in Black! Outlaws on the lam! We boasted of bold deeds, ribbed one another over obvious lies. We reached the church and just waved, shouting that we would see everyone at the caves. It was just us and the 8-track, and then, once we settled into the ride, the smoke of Ray's Partagas cigars; gifts from Uncle Crush. It was a well-known signal: we were in for some stories.

—Tell me Gaby, you like this song? (Cash was singing "Give My Love to Rose.") —You should, and I'll tell you why. I was singing it the hour you were born. Not too proud of that, no sir, but not too proud to admit it, either. Your mother was ready to spit nails being left alone in labor. I didn't know! Hell, Gaby, she was about to start her tenth month, I didn't think you'd ever show up.

Ray stopped to chime in with Cash:

He said they let me out of prison in Frisco
for ten long years I paid for what I done
I was trying to get back to Louisiana
to see my Rose and get to know my son. . . .

The three of us lapsed into silence as the song ended, and the road trip began to sink into its own slow rhythm. Ray whistled along with another tune, then thought to turn the sound down a notch and said, looking at the road and not us so that it seemed he was almost speaking to himself, —You two be good to your mother.

—We will.

—Ah, let's talk about something else. And then, quickly: —Shoot, if they can put Johnny Cash in jail for picking flowers in Starkville, I guess I can do some time for getting in with the wrong crowd. But I'm sure glad my Daddy isn't here to see this. That's the first thing your grandmother said to me: *I'm glad your Daddy ain't here, Ray, it would have killed him.* . . . Come on, let's talk about something else. We're having fun now, right? Right!

He puffed on his Partagas a minute, turned up the music and flicked ash out the window, then just as suddenly swirled the music down again as he launched into a memory of the trip he and mother took with Uncle Crush and his now ex-wife to Mallorca. —You two were just little boys, then. Gaby you couldn't even talk.

—Where did he get *Crush*, anyway? Michael thought to ask.

—Well he was a wrestler, you know. You didn't know that? He'd be sorry to hear, he's proud of that time. Take away those years and you find an unhappy man.

—But why *Crush*?

—Well he's small but real strong. You gotta have a gimmick in that business or people forget you. And Crush, he had this bear hug thing where he smothered the other guy, make him pass out. 'Course it's all horseshit. It's acting. He told me they sat around in dressing rooms planning who'd do what and when and then they'd go put on a show. But boy my Daddy, your grandfather, he thought it was the greatest. Time of his life was when the wrestlers came to Bowling Green and he and I'd go down there and he, you know he would get so worked up watching those guys! He spit on them if they passed close enough! One time he got so mad he started swinging his chair and I had to say *Daddy calm down, you don't want us to get thrown out....* Ray laughed, still looking straight ahead. —Yep, that was your grand-papa. He was something.

It started to cool in the car and we rolled up the windows, leaving a crack for his cigar smoke. The hills grew higher as we moved farther south from Montreux, through the Knobs, until they gave to a lolling expanse of fields bordered by three-plank fences painted white or black or chestnut brown, tarred at the joints, marking the paddocks where horses ran and wandered and grazed. In between these stretched denuded fields where corn would grow, in season, as far as my eye could see.

—You two sure are quiet, Ray said then, looking about the car.

—I wish you didn't have to go away, Dad, came Michael's soft voice from the back.

—Aw. Ah, hey, Pops said, then looked over his cigar, nearly stubbed out. He rolled down his window long enough to toss the end onto the highway. The car swerved to the right onto the shoulder, and he took a second to regain control.

—Hey listen, he began again, —I know it's tough, and you guys know I'm not happy about it, either. But I have an insight. That accident put us all through a lot, and I'll tell you honest—I should've died. But I didn't, I don't know why. I think it has something to do with all those people praying for me, and God heard. And that's the big man up there, he doesn't give much for nothing. He set up a task for me, and I believe I'm going to prison to bring his example to those guys there. Now how about that? Doesn't that make sense? I'm going away to do some good work, boys.

Yes, it did make sense. But the sense of it did not matter much to me. Rather than thank God for saving my father's life, I felt as though He had saved him simply to take him away, and I resented it.

But Ray was all optimist; he could find the flower under any stone. In fact he was already talking about something else. My father was a born salesman; he did not like silences. Mother liked to say he could keep a conversation with dirt. He could not sit still unless he was talking to somebody. Even driving, if the conversation flagged—by 'conversation' I mean listening to Pops recount his stories—he would check his mileage, fiddle with the radio dials, search for specific 8-tracks, consult maps, listen closely to the engine, sing, then tell whatever he knew about each small town marked by the exit ramps we passed; swerving about the road the entire time.

He spent most of his life on those Kentucky roads, living out of his car; he knew decent restaurants in even the most obscure hideaways; slept with the front seat laid back to save money on hotels. He would stop in the emergency lane if he saw horses near the fence, talk to them, feed them carrots which he brought specifically for that purpose. —I like to hear them crunch those carrots around in their mouth, he said.

It was impossible to imagine him suffering the sedentary life of prison. Impossible to accept—God's plan or no—that people were safer with my father locked away. What use would anyone have for me, if they did not want Ray? I wanted to go with him, to share his cell.

As he dropped us off, crying out *God bless everything and everybody!* through the open window, I was already subtracting the four days we would be apart. It seemed like trying to imagine four days when I would not exist.

3

Chaney Lawse was the daughter of one of the wealthy families at St. Peter's. She was active in our youth group, and several years older than me—already in her last year of high school, but she skipped a year. She was an accomplished diver for the local branch of the American Athletic Union and enormously popular, something of a Montreux celebrity, having placed highly in the Junior Olympic

Regionals that summer. We saw her face in newspaper articles, on TV; they publicized her as one of the bright young stars of the city, loved all the more for receiving excellent grades at school and for being active in her church. Flawless Lawse, we called her. To watch her move in a white cotton summer dress, exposing the light heft of her calves, was to suddenly embrace Darwinistic truth.

Her eyes were a bright bottle-green in sunlight, a darker blue when enclosed by rooms; her long, straight, ash-blonde hair shot to the small of her back, except when she pulled it into a finely-spun knot for diving, strands of it still shining gold even when wet.

She paid little attention to me at first. Chaney was constantly surrounded by boys closer in age who adored her, or else she was followed by a tight line of girls like a mother with ducklings, each of them hanging on whatever she had to say. When the news of my father became common knowledge, however, she began to take a proprietary interest in both Michael and me. It was terrifying for my brother, taller and only a year younger than she, so that her solicitousness raised hopes that she might be interested in him for reasons other than pity. For me it was more a case of having been ordained in some fashionable sense. When she sat with us at youth group meetings, it threw me into a spotlight of approval. *Everyone* had to accept me, young as I was, without question. A twelve-year-old among teens preparing for college—I accepted my invitation and approval by the older teenagers as a natural progression. Arrogant, perhaps, but I liked most everyone for no reason at all, so why shouldn't I be liked in return? This *mattered*, especially with the prison sentence hanging over the family.

The afternoons wandered past in damp, guided tours of the caves, humid near the surface. We came out shielding our eyes against the light of a late-summer evening. The younger kids in the group were assigned a "buddy," an older member who was responsible for keeping you out of trouble; Chaney shocked everyone by choosing me. At lunch she would compare the similarity of our hair, transformed by chlorine and long hours beneath the sun, and the color of our browned, freckled skin, the burned smell of which we liked. She asked if any girls interested me in the group, or at school, and foolishly I said no (as if to hint I was available). She had recently returned from a diving tournament in Puerto Rico which had left her face blemished, burned raw by the sun there, and her cheeks were peeling in long strips that left eruptions of rose-pink hide over the saddle of her nose, a color wild in contrast to her otherwise mellow skin. She had placed third in the competition, which disappointed her.

—You'll win next year, I said, hopeful.

—I will, she answered, and then burst with laughter. —That's why I like you, Gaby, I'm not ashamed to brag because I know you don't care.

I told her she was the only person I knew who couldn't talk about herself without seeming to brag, since she was so accomplished in everything; then felt my face burn after the comment brought a wad of paper crashing off my cheek, thrown across the table by Coldwell Godfrey. He started to mock my groveling behavior, his voice high-pitched and fawning. Chaney laughed—but it was a comforting laughter, rimmed in a gentle tone that made me warm even more to her.

After lunch a crowd of us went to swim in the swollen lake, warmed by a week's harsh rains. We raced to a float that drifted a hundred yards off the shore, rested there, then raced back. . . . After a few laps I stayed on the aluminum slats of the float and took some sun, alone, watching Chaney undress down to her suit on the beach, the fact of her presence enough to quiet the boys who had been shouting at play the moment before. She arrived with two girlfriends, and they sat on the small wooden dock there with their feet in the water while she tied her hair into the familiar streaked-knot at the back of her head. I waited, and watched, fighting the urge to call out to her, knowing if I did it would bring an awful round of teasing later from Cody and my other cabin roommates. So I waited alone there on the float, shoulders burning in the sun, hoping she would see me.

She looked up from where she sat speaking to Michael, who tread water at her feet. She shaded her eyes with the palm of her hand turned upward—a weird gesture—then waved. A word to the girl next to her, and in the next instant they were both in the water, swimming toward the float.

Her strokes were masterful, placid, the calm swell of the surface before her moving gently to the sides to accommodate her body, the flat lake surface powerfully chopped in the wake behind as she wove her way toward me. The other girl did not approach as fast, although she seemed to work even harder, slapping at the waves. I couldn't help smiling as Chaney pulled to a stop several feet before me, her eyes winched against the sun, her legs catching the greenish glow of the light penetrating the water, as she asked in a voice full of concern, — Gaby, you all right?

—What? I'm fine, I declared, surprised.

—I just thought you might've cramped from coming out so soon after lunch; you ate so much, you know.

Only because she ate so slowly and I didn't want to abandon her unless she instructed me to.

—Want company? she asked, and I moved over on the slats, ignoring the pain of a screw pricking my hand.

We passed through pointless conversation as my eye traced the fine rib of muscle where the front of her thigh locked into her hamstring; she mentioned how her face itched from peeling, and we probed the topic of skin cancer; she asked how I was dealing with the prospect of Ray leaving us. I acted noncommittal and distant, even when she placed her hand on my bare knee once to emphasize a point. In that late angle of sunlight, an amber honey spilled over the lake and us, and I could not avoid recognizing her perfection. Even the way she sniffed to clear congestion from her nose seemed inviting, and healthy. Then she made a statement that left me stricken: —I can't believe the water is still so warm this late in the year, she said. —It's even warm at night.

—At night? You come swimming here at night?

Chaney hesitated, smiling to herself more than me, as if she felt unsure she could, or should, admit this (nightswimming was banned at the camp) . . . but she decided to nod, adding, —I come here once everyone's asleep. It helps me sleep later. Haven't you ever come down here at night? I thought everybody did.

She said this with a particular inflection that struck me as a veiled invitation to join her. —No, I've never thought about it, I said.

—Well you should try it some time.

The conversation passed on to other things and it wasn't long before we swam back to join the others. My body teemed with spectacular energy; there would be no question of sleep. That night I tried to order my roommates to bed, since we had to rise early for a seven-hour cavern tour. If any of them saw me leave they would either follow or else report me to a chaperon unless I was willing to pay some whimsical price. I got under the covers to set an example, the pillow smelling somewhat of mildew, my eyes pinned to the small digital clock nearby, the time ticking past ten; ten-thirty; eleven. . . . I had given up hope until, near midnight, the rhythm of breathing in the room suggested sleep.

The grass wet my feet until I reached the lakeside trail, where dirt glued itself to my soles and mired between my toes. The night was nearly cold beneath a clear sky of untold stars. The path wound through a small wood, kind of frightening in the dark—enough light fell to find my way but the sounds of the campgrounds at night were unfamiliar and stronger without the shield of cabin walls; they fell closer: the rustlings in the weeds, the whirs of strange nocturnal birds, the trickle of water lapping against the old dock. Giant shadows of everything.

The moon chopped silver light on the surface of the lake. Immediately I knew Chaney was there—a pile of clothes lay strewn near one corner of the dock. But I did not see her until the wood slats were pricking my feet, and the grains of dirt suddenly pressed harder into my soles. She came up for air and began an easy backstroke. Several minutes passed before, with a start, she noticed me.

—It's me, Gabriel. . . .

—Gaby what are you doing out here? Does anybody know you came?

She spoke in a loud whisper. She fell still in the water, her feet planted in the soft muck of the bottom; she appeared nothing more than a dark head floating on the surface.

—No, of course not, I'm alone. . . .

She laughed quietly. —Well get in, then. It feels great tonight.

I got in. I asked if she wanted to swim to the float, but she said it would make too much noise. —We have to be quiet out here or somebody will come down to see.

—It's freezing.

—I know. But it feels great, don't you think?

No, I didn't, but I wasn't going to tell her that. My balls instantly sucked into my abdomen. I said, Sure it's great, even though my body was shivering and gooseflesh had tightened all over me. We kept to the space between the shore and the end of the dock, where the depth did not go more than ten feet, keeping everything but our heads below water, where it felt warmer.

—You know, my mom and I go skinny-dipping in our pool at night all the time. . . . It feels great on your body. . . .

—Naked? You swim naked?

—Of course, silly. Why else would you come out swimming in the middle of the night?

The realization that I was within a few feet of a nude Chaney Lawse crushed me with a caving lightness. I could see no part of her—her usual bathing suit exposed more than what I could see now. Still, the knowledge of her proximity, and that we were alone, shocked me . . . when she asked if I'd ever swam naked before, I felt a rush as I untied my shorts with one hand and then tossed them to her over the water saying, —I have now. . . .

She laughed her quiet laugh again, and swam to the dock to set my shorts beside her clothes. Again she told me I had to be quiet (was I making noise? I froze in place), then asked —How old are you, anyway? Twelve? Thirteen?

—Thirteen, I lied, —but I'll be fourteen in the Spring (some seven months away). As if the gain of a year would have made a difference.

—Mmmmm. It feels nice doesn't it?

—What, thirteen?

—*No;* swimming without your suit on. Don't you feel free? What's it feel like to a boy?

I swam a bit, closing the distance between us, my mind stilled in panic. A phrase of Ray's came to mind: —Swinging easy. . . .

Chaney gave that laugh again, then disappeared beneath the water. She surfaced a few feet farther away, and I didn't dare come forward but remained where I was, chilled to the spine, treading in place. She dove again and I tried to follow her path by the breaks in the water but couldn't for the darkness; then, a hard tug on my ankle pulled me under, and left me sputtering. She came up just behind me, chuckling. —Are you nervous?

—Why should I be nervous? Are you going to do something to me?

—Hah. *Maybe . . .* if you're lucky. You'd like that, I bet. What do you know about girls, anyway?

As soon as words rose to my lips there fell an overwhelming sense of defeat; it was humiliating, who was I fooling? To brag right now would be ridiculous. A part of me understood that the reason she was kind to me was that I was so much younger, so harmless.

—Nothing, really, I confessed into the water. My breath steamed on the surface.

—I didn't think so.

—Well what do you know?

—*Everything*, Gaby. . . . I know pretty much everything.

She moved toward me, and I stilled my feet into the lake bottom. I was about to kiss the most magnificent girl I'd ever known. We were surrounded by the chorus of crickets in the woods, the loud droplets of water falling from our faces into the lake, the echoing slap of the waves reckless beneath the old dock. Leaves stirred on the ground in the dark; a fox, maybe. Through the trees fell timmers of light from the cabins up the hillside, and the moon that night shone low as she turned and rose slightly, enough that I could see the top rounds of her breasts—they were covered by a strapless suit. It snapped the reverie. —Hey, I thought we were skinny dipping, I protested.

Chaney giggled. —Oh Gaby, I'm so sorry, she said, and her giggles came more fluently now, sinking me with a horrible understanding. The stirring leaves in the dark turned to shadows darting onto the dock toward my clothes; the night seemed to cave in. —You didn't! I shouted. Chaney started into a full laugh, joined by squeals and laughter from the shadows scurrying over the dock, her usual gathering of duckling followers. I turned to grab her, but Chaney was already up the incline of shore to beach, soon fully out of the water and beyond my grasp. The other girls ran to join her, my clothes in hand, their laughter echoing over the lake.

—You can't, I said. They stood in a line ten or fifteen yards away, silhouetted by the cabin lights up the hill. They cooed to me; teased me; they wanted to see me come out of the water. They thought this was the funniest thing.

—Gaby, please don't hate me for this, Chaney said. But she was laughing, too. I searched frantically about me, looking for some object to throw; all I could find was the freezing mud from the bottom. Throwing it brought only more jeers and laughter.

They tried for a long time to get me to come out of the water, but

I refused. They told me they were mad that I wouldn't come out into the light. I rejected the idea. They complained that it was a shame I could not see the humor in their trick. I told them I hated them, and to give back my clothes. In time they seemed to get bored; they left me there in the dark, Chaney allowing herself one long look over her shoulder at me huddled in the freezing lake, chin down, shivering.

The final two days of camp dragged by as word quickly spread, Cody jumping on the event and inventing details of how he caught me naked and puckered trying to sneak back to bed. Even Michael thought it was funny. —Why did you think Chaney Lawse would want to get naked with you, Gaby? he asked, over and over, before anyone. It caused all kinds of hilarity.

When Ray arrived to pick us up, I fairly ran to him. I had everything packed in the car—Michael's bag, too—within minutes. Ray felt like lingering, though. He spotted Chaney walking near a cabin in a sun dress and sandals, alone; he watched her through the windshield, hands folded over the steering wheel. —Whoa, boys, that Lawse girl is something else, isn't she? Look at that. How old is she? Sixteen? You know in my day we would have had her a mother with another on the way by now. . . .

Michael was getting into the back seat, already laughing, starting in with a 'you wouldn't believe what happened' to Ray, but one hard look from me shut him up, and our father continued to list the ways in which young girls were beautiful.

For once I barely listened to my father, keeping quiet the entire way home, my head allowing no other words but her name, underscored by my rage. There were actual silences in the car which Ray announced must have been due to all the fun we'd had that week; but for me there was only that night in the lake with Chaney, and the ridiculous belief I had held that something special was about to happen to me—her body beneath my cold hands; our breaths rushing out onto the water; the shock of the water on my skin. I thought that by losing my father I'd gain something else. I was wrong.

—Okay now but listen to this, boys, something big happened to me while you were gone. I had a revelation. You know I've been worried sick about what's going to happen while I'm away. I can't escape the fact I'm abandoning you two when you need your father most. It sickens me, it really does, and I've been praying about it a lot. Well yesterday this question was weighing particularly heavy on my mind, don't know why but it was just there when I awoke with the dawn, and when I went downstairs to light my prayer candles I opened the Bible to find a passage to meditate upon—see that's what I do, open the book at random and read and then pray over that. Try it some time. That morning God sent me reassurance. I opened the book and my eyes fell upon Isaiah 54:13: *All your sons will be taught by the Lord and great will be your children's peace.* What do you think? I'd never even read Isaiah before. So no worries about the future, boys. You're going to be taken care of. I hope that makes you feel as good as it does me.

But I was hardly listening, hardly aware of his speech as it faded to a faraway cadence in mind.

4

His sentence began the same day we returned to school from Christmas vacation. It snowed heavily overnight. We awoke to a silent, veiled Montreux, and crowded around the radio in hopes of finding the county schools closed. But the reports kept saying they would remain open, and Pops told us to go on and get ready. He would drive us to school in his car, then meet Uncle Crush, who would drive him to Marion County for his reception there. Michael and I believed we should avoid school that day to accompany him, and to give Crush somebody to talk to during the drive back. Ray would not have it.

—I don't want you all to be kept from normal life by all this, he said. —Don't look for excuses. If you keep at your day-to-day it will all go by faster.

He made us pancakes, and eggs browned with Worcestershire sauce, whistling joyfully the way he would before a business trip. Mother remained in bed.

It was still dark and snowing when we left; the snow fell without wind and piled on the trees and power lines. Our footsteps, our voices, fell close, like they were being pushed back upon us, as if the snow did not want its peaceful descent disturbed. There was the peculiar shine of the white within all that darkness, the street lights sparkling millions of tiny crystals in the unspoiled surface of small white dunes, and the air smelled of the simple cold. Stacks of newspapers yet to be collected by delivery boys formed abstract totems at street corners. But it was a powdery snow and not icy, and Pops' Cadillac maneuvered through the neighborhood toward school with ease.

—I wish I had something profound to tell you guys, he said, his voice soft and rueful, —but I don't. Never have thought that way. Are you all scared?

We both mumbled, No.

—Sure, it's going to be tough, but I have faith in my boys. . . . Don't be too hard on your mother, she's got an overstacked plate. I'm sorry, real sorry, you know. . . . His voice cut off, and he twisted his lips as though searching for something caught in his teeth. He drove with one hand—red and callused, mapped by any number of dated scars— on my knee, tapping it from time to time. Michael sat back with his eyes closed.

—Don't let anybody give you a hard time over this, either. But don't go looking for fights. I'm not going to be there to bail you out if you get into any. . . .

—Pops, we're going to be fine, Michael interrupted, leaning forward through the break between the seats.

—Yeah, I know.

The heater buzzed and rattled with debris trapped in the air ducts. We could hear the lazy crush of our tires over the road. At the entrance to our school, he leaned over the console to hug and kiss me, held me tightly and for a long time; then the same for Michael over the back of the seats. The three of us sat silently for a moment while other kids dashed by the car to go into school, screaming with laughter, dodging snowballs. The sky now appeared faintly in crepuscular gray, the snow turning blue as it passed through the beams of headlights, street lights, the lamps above the school doors.

—Just remember what I told you: Isaiah 54:13. I'm not worried cause I've already turned us over to the Lord, and he knows better what's going on than I ever could. Keep that in mind. Now go on in and hold your heads high. You got nothing to be ashamed of.

Okay, dad. . . .

—Go on! he urged from his window, watching us until we reached the large double doors of reinforced glass at the entrance. We all three raised our hands to wave at exactly the same instant.

When he pulled back onto the circular drive I ran to where he'd been, my body half-hidden by the corner of the school to watch him go: his white Cadillac soiled around the wheels by blackened slush; the car moving slowly forward, away; the snow lumping a dull silence over the land. His brake lights glowed red (pink where the snow piled on his rear bumper) as he slowed to an aching roll at the end of the drive— *Never come to a full stop in the snow, boys; people here always getting stuck because they don't know how to drive.* A turn to the left, and he was gone, shielded by a row of capped firs. I turned to Michael, waiting at the door; he shrugged, raised his eyebrows, set his face with resignation. I set my own face in a mask of indifference, and followed my brother inside. The hallway stretched before us empty and silent. The warning alarm had already sounded to begin the day; we hurried to join the others, to where we were expected.

The Favorite Game

1

We called it the World's Most Beautiful Game because Pelé did, although none of us would have been able to define what made the sport beautiful. We knew not to touch the ball with our hands, and that was all. Ray had been gone nearly a year by the time I played for the first time, just before I turned fourteen, in a YMCA recreational league. Cody Godfrey talked me into joining. He said you didn't have to be good, they accepted everybody; which was a key factor, since this little ram made a less than auspicious debut. The coach recognized my complete lack of skill and positioned me at wing defender. There, I immediately cottoned to the running, the constant action, the mob mentality that overwhelmed us on the field—twenty mad kids chasing a ball over yards of turf.

In Montreux we had no local professional team, so we did not see the game's artful side: how there were plans of attack, styles to master, a method of building momentum from the back, moving forward and crosswise, a flow to aspire to. We groped in darkness. In these leagues the larger, stronger, faster boys excelled. Some improved dramatically from season to season, attending camps at Indiana University—NCAA champions—and thus learning more about the game, improving through articulate drills; but with Ray gone, the camps were an impossibility for me. We rolled coins to pay my league fees. Electricity bills had priority over wished-for soccer camps. The responsibility of improvement fell to me alone.

I rented videos from a nearby sporting-goods store that carried classic matches and highlights from legendary careers—all from Europe or South America, a world apart. I'd watch in awe, then take to our backyard to try newly-discovered moves and feints against Michael, a tree, garbage can; anything. I passed hours kicking against the back of the garage, trapping the rebound, driving the neighbors insane with the noise long after dark. By season's end, the coach moved me from defender to forward to capitalize on my gift for speed. After scoring my first goal and feeling that incendiary rush, I knew I'd found the game for me.

—Ah, I wish I'd been there to see it, Ray lamented over the phone. He asked me to describe it again, which I did, and we could hear him slap his knee as he bellowed, *that's my boy, that's my boy . . . you take it to 'em.* From the background there came a faraway voice: *What you laughing at, Smilin' Ray? You out of here?* to which he shouted back: *No, better than that, my boy scored a goal. I told you, I've got a helluva young athlete back home. . . .*

Thus began a long period of solitude and ambition, in place of growing up. My father's enthusiasm charged my own; it became my conscious goal to make myself not just the best player I could be by the time he came home, but the best player, point, end of line. I wanted him to return not a shamed and chastened ex-convict, but bursting with pride to see the amazing accomplishments of this product from his loins. Every time I took to the field—either alone or with the team—his words served as a stoking brand against my heart: *I wish I was there to see it.* Someday, he would, and it was my duty to make that day spectacular.

I can barely imagine the difficulty of these years for Olive. Often I heard her say, to Michael and me, to her mother or Pops on the phone, or to herself alone: *I'm not prepared for this, I'm not ready, I never asked for any of this.* By nature she was an over-achiever: Captain of the cheerleading squad at Western Kentucky, named Miss Cheeks there for best ass on campus, she was beautiful when she married Ray—inky black hair and blue eyes, prominent cheekbones and a small nose, fine lips; she was social and gregarious by nature, and always eager to throw a party or attend one. She was blessed with exceptional intelligence and an independent spirit; refusing to follow the well-worn path of her peers in Paducah, she didn't come home from college with a husband—didn't seek one—and by the time she met Ray she was twenty-seven years old, an old bird by hometown standards. But she had wanted a life of her own. Once, rolling coins together at the kitchen table for league fees, I remarked upon how easily she corralled the change into the paper wrapping. For every one I finished, she had three or four.

—I worked summers in a bank, she explained. —One time the manager told me—she was some old widow—'you're really talented, Olive, we'll be glad to hire you after college. I'm sure you'll go far. . . .' and I thought *no thank you,* no way.

For Olive and Ray, Montreux, the thirty-seventh largest in America, was the big city.

She took a degree in Education, but her real strength lay in the more mundane labor of Motherhood. She was an extraordinary mother, early on. Fiercely loyal, her capacity to fight any perceived slight against us was frightening to behold; one time, called into a conference with my second grade teacher on account of my disruptive behavior in class—I talked too much to Coldwell Godfrey—she made a scene arguing with the teacher in the hallway: if I was speaking too much in class it was only that I was bored with the trite busywork the teacher offered, rather than being *taught* anything; one held children's attention by *interesting* them, not by handing out dittoed exercises by the handful. The talk turned vehement and nasty, with overtones of race (our teacher was black). In another week I was transferred to a different class.

Still beautiful despite the defining cigarette lines around her mouth and eyes, Olive had two healthy boys to raise, a good starter house, and a charming husband who supplied her family with a higher standard of living than she knew growing up. She was committed to making sure we reached swim practice on time, or choir practice; she lounged by the swimming pool at the Horse Chestnut Club all summer long, bragging about her boys as she simultaneously kept an eye on them there. The tenacity of her cheerleading for the swim team resulted in a new award created at season's end, presented at our celebratory banquet: *Rah Rah Mama.* On holidays she made crafts with us, boiled the eggs we painted for Easter, rolled the dough we cut into shapes for Christmas cookies to leave for Santa, scissored-out photographs from magazines so we could create our own Valentine cards to exchange at school. If she missed dinner at home, she was leading the PTA meeting; if she missed a swim meet, she was shopping for the team party to be hosted that night. Then Ray got sent away.

Immediately after the sentence began, our house brimmed with siege mentality and family loyalty reigned at its height. But Michael and I were still young boys, and the taste of freedom—did it really matter if we were in the house by seven? if we washed dishes right after supper?—the lure of liberty, of being left completely to ourselves, was too seductive. We had nobody to answer to: me suddenly fourteen, Michael at the edge of eighteen.

Each afternoon I sped off to the YMCA fields to practice alone, and as the days lengthened to summertime, my attention to the house shrank proportionately. It wouldn't become too dark to play until 10:00 P.M., even later in the high point of summer, and if hunger did not call me home to dinner, I didn't go. I lost track of everything as I fell into a world of imaginary stadiums, opponents, the whistles of referees. Ray watching from the sidelines. In my head I narrated the action like an announcer, the crowd's applause sung by nearby crickets and cicadas. I faked injuries to play through. I became a marked player to be hacked down by my opponents, and so attempted a fantastic number of free kicks—the ball set at the foul—and tried to master placing spin on the ball, hitting it with enough pace so that its trajectory arced around the defensive five-man wall placed between me and the goal. My mouth grew salty and dry; my back ached from the strain of starting, stopping, pivoting one direction before darting the other; the fresh-cut grass and snowing pollen tickled my allergies. Dinner passed, as did promises to Olive to be home on time, promises to Ray to go easy on my mother. I was too busy leading the United States to its first World Cup victory, scoring a hat trick in the finals over Brazil. I'd found what I wanted; what trouble could it cause?

Olive saw the case differently. Some evenings passed without conflict—but they became increasingly rare. More often, as dusk came bathing the fields and white goal posts into a light blue sealike hue, her small white Toyota—what Pops christened the "eggsucker"—would careen into the empty YMCA parking lot, and trouble had arrived. Leaning across the seats to roll down the window she shouted: —Claude Gabriel Toure if I have to get out of this car and put you on that bike myself, you're not going to have the legs to kick another soccer ball again. I'll give you ten seconds. . . . She slowly counted down, ticking off her thumb first from a clenched fist rather than with her index finger like anybody else, —10 . . . 9 . . . 8 . . . *Give me that ball!*

I wouldn't have time to change from cleats to sneakers, humiliated before the teenage nihilists who hung out near the dumpster behind the YMCA building smoking pot and drinking tallboys. Their laughter gnawed as I scurried to drop the ball into the passenger seat, fearful I wouldn't see it again. Mother would drive maddeningly slow behind me, the road glaring before us in her headlights, honking if she believed I wasn't pedaling fast enough.

Once home, the real combat began. The ball remained in the car, our sliding glass door rattled in its tracks as she let fly a string of curses and complaints while simultaneously hurling her purse to the couch, her keys chiming as they shot through the air to end with a ringing crash against the china cabinet. —Look at these dishes! she shouted. —Look at the dust in this house! and she wiped one finger across the nearest surface to present me with the evidence. —Don't think you won't pull your share around here! Inevitably she would storm up to her room to come down again with the latest report card and call off the classes marked with C's and D's and demand that I do better, that I follow the rules or else I'd be out of that house and on the street. —And don't you dare give me that look, you boys think because your father isn't here I can't tell you anything? That soccer ball is a *privilege,* young man, and starting tonight you won't have it back until I see you've got the maturity to handle the responsibility. I won't have this conduct in my house, I will not have it!

—Mother come *on*—

—Don't you ever talk back to me!

She let fly with a punch to my face, shocking me silent. She was a small woman with a tight build—by the time I was twelve we stood eye to eye—but she had power. I went off to my room, chastened, disappointed in having disappointed her . . . angry, too . . . Olive concocted her cocktail of ginger ale and bourbon while continuing her tirade more quietly to herself. I shut the door to my room and tried to read. But beside my bed I kept a few tennis balls, and it was not long before I started rehearsing moves again, rolling a ball between my bare feet, getting wily with it.

Later, Michael joined me in my room, book in hand. He sat on my bed and we discussed how difficult mother was becoming (not recognizing how hard her day must be, or how we might be behaving less than cooperatively—me more so than Michael); she couldn't take the time to see things from our point of view, we thought. —I'm not even doing anything, he said. —Listen, you've got to be more aware. I catch the fallout.

—You're the man in the family now. I know, I heard.

His smile was a thin, musing one; between the two of us, he *was* the thin, musing one. He lay on his back, staring at the ceiling. In such moments it struck me how impossibly different we were, and looked: he had mother's blue eyes, her hair; I have the darker blue eyes of our father, but otherwise share no likeness to my parents or Michael. My brother had very pale skin, the kind that peels in summer without tanning; he was a full six inches taller than me at nearly six feet; his shoulders had a narrow spread while mine were wide. And our interests dramatized two diametrically-opposed minds: while he thought, I acted; as he watched, I talked.

—It's only a few years, he added, locking his hands behind his head in a ruminative, philosophical pose, —and we'll laugh about this some day.

For a while we dealt with our problems by invoking this phrase to one another, a reminder that crises were temporary and that one day it would all pass, mother would relax and return to normal, Pops would be home, and we could get on with our lives. We thought—*hoped*—we had entered into a floating-chamber of time, and that these years didn't count. When Pops came back I'd still be twelve and Michael fifteen and we'd carry on from there. But we *were* getting on with our lives; we were already older than when he left; time was passing. By the time Ray came home, neither my brother or I would be living there anymore, and Olive would be somebody completely different than any of us could have ever imagined.

2

I practiced at the YMCA alone, but within range of a small crowd of hooligans who hid behind the dumpster, drinking beer, smoking pot, scrawling their names and loves on the old trees. Sometimes they rode a loud motor bike along the trails winding through the narrow woods that split the grounds from a dusty cement factory. I was often more aware of their presence than of the ball at my feet. They threw taunts, and insults; their challenges of mock applause made it hard to concentrate. But they had a girl among them, and she came to initiate me into their company.

Her name was Angela and we called her Angie, everybody but me at least—for me she would be Angela always: thick chestnut hair, almost roan, finished red in sunlight; pink lips she kept glossed; chewed fingernails and scabby shins, and skin as pale as my brother's. She smoked and had a loud, screeching laugh, standing while the boys sat, almost performing as she talked, kicking off her pink plastic sandals to lean barefoot against the oak tree teeming with the names of rock bands, signatures, and declarations of love.

The group lazed stoned in the withering heat, the motorbike silent, broiling on its side beneath the sun, the day Angela approached me. She stepped cautiously, with frequent pauses; I saw her coming. When she came close enough, I casually passed her the ball, and she burst out laughing. The ball bounced off of her softly.

—Don't you know to come in out of the heat? She asked.

I shrugged, but did not answer. We kicked around. She held out her cigarette with one hand, her giggling punctuated by short bursts of *ohmygod's* every time she touched the ball, showering me with declarations that she didn't know anything about soccer. Her embarrassment broke my shyness and I began to coach her in earnest, showing her how to touch the ball correctly, how to trap it, speaking in an undammed rush everything I knew, I was so thrilled to tell *some*one. In ten minutes she was exhausted. —How can you stand this heat? I'm dying already.

—Would you like some water?

—Hm, you're cute. Why not come sit with us in the shade a bit? I need a cigarette.

I said sure, okay, but a glance to the boys waiting there showed them staring intently at us, their faces void of expression, lions on the plain lazily gazing at wandering gazelles. An alarm of caution sounded in my head. She must have felt my hesitation as she said again, a few steps away, —Come on, it's okay . . . you're invited. What's your name, anyway? I'm Angie.

I told her *Gabriel,* thinking *Gaby* too sweet and childish. I wanted to seem older. I followed her into the shade, bringing my bike, ball, and water bottle, careful to give her a lot of space.

—Hey, it's the soccer star, a boy said as we arrived. —I've been watching you play out there for weeks, man. You suck.

His voice exhaled smoke and as he finished his sentence he laughed himself into a choking cough.

—Ronnie, stop teasing, Angela said, and then introduced everyone. Ronnie was their leader. He did the talking. The others automatically deferred to his authority on such matters as the controversial meanings to heavy metal lyrics and album covers, the true workings of the everyday world which was for losers and bullshit, the stupidness of the YMCA employees who ordered them to clear out every now and then. The oldest at sixteen, Ronnie was skinnier than Michael but tanned, and the motorbike was his—a gift from his older brother. He had wisps of reddish facial hair over his lip and chin at odds with the mousy-brown hair on his head, which limped to his shoulders though he styled it often with a big plastic comb kept sheathed in his back pocket. When he asked to see the ball I tossed it to him, and stood against the tree near Angela, trying to appear unassuming.

—First problem you got is that you play a sissy sport, man. Ballgames you gotta play with your hands.

He launched into a series of basketball moves, agile and surprisingly quick, using a space on the wall as if a hoop waited there, then jumping toward a low branch of the tree as a rim to dunk over. *Hoooo!!* he shouted with each jump. *Hoooweeyeah!* The other boys egged him on, asked him to have a try with the ball. A kid named Berle said he wanted to see my bike, could he ride it? and before I could answer yes he'd taken off over the fields, breaking onto one of the trails beneath the trees, darting out through weeds and brush to skid haphazard arcs on the grass. I did not say anything. It was as though my arrival had been a catalyst they'd been looking for, previously sedated there in the shade—now there was a pandemonium of action and gestures and whoops of boys at play, and all with the things that I owned and was beginning to fear I'd lost for good.

Angela must have guessed my thoughts for she reassured me suddenly, saying —They're only playing, Gabriel, don't you worry, they'll get tired soon, which they did, coming back to collapse in the shade and draining my water bottle, tossing it away so that it thumped emptily against the dumpster. Then, as if the thought just occurred to her: —Hey listen, do you get high?

—Sure. Of course, I lied.

—Well Ronnie has some great stuff, don't you Ronnie? Have some great stuff? And do you have any money, Gabriel? Sometimes he's not so friendly to share. . . .

—I don't know what you're talking about Angie, Ronnie said.

—Listen you brought him over here, he's probably a narc.

—A what?

—Hey, he's no square, Ronnie, I can tell. Where're your manners boy, that's right I brought him over here and he's invited. For Pete's sake. He wouldn't tell anybody on us, would he Gabriel? You wouldn't tell anybody to get us in trouble, would you?

—I don't want to cause any problems. . . .

—See how you're making him feel unwelcome Ronnie? Gabriel's no square, now you be nice and roll us a fine one. And then, in a hushed voice to my ear, —You know you don't have to do anything if you don't want to. You need to stay in shape, I know. I don't care what Ronnie says, I think you play soccer just fine.

—All I can see is his mother driving up while we're in the middle of a jay, Angie, and you know, no thanks, that's all I'm saying.

—Leave my mother alone. She works real hard, she gets worried, that's all.

—You think my mother don't work? You never see her tearing out over the parking lot telling me to come home . . . you're a momma's boy, that's what I'm saying. I didn't invite you here.

Angela, eager to keep the peace—Ronnie was now standing over me, the other boys leaning forward hungrily on their elbows, all smiles and accelerated heartbeats—said, —So you say your mother works, Gabriel, what does your daddy do?

I remained seated on the ground, thinking Ronnie wouldn't throw a punch if I stayed there. —He doesn't do anything. He's in jail.

Such words draped a warm, strange curtain of interest over me; a brief reprieve. Ronnie frowned for a moment of unbelieving silence. As Angie trailed off with *Ohmygod what did he do?*, he murmured —Your dad hain't in no jail. . . .

—He is, too, I insisted, the disbelief setting off a tirade in me. —He's at Marion County nine years, six if he's good, and he left January, 1980, and I rushed into the entire saga starting with the wreck and the horses and even adding in Pepper Davis, who I knew nearly nothing about other than it was all his fault. Details I didn't know were either glossed over or made up from the pastiche of what I'd overheard between my parents and the lawyer. It must have made sense; the rest of the boys crowded closer to listen, and the leers slid from their faces. I told them everything I knew, everything save for the fact I believed my father an innocent man. Defiance is best when one feels uneasy. Humility and caution before his charges put Ray in jail—obvious!—and so I looked straight at Ronnie as my tale unfurled, my anger rising to the point that if he *did* want to fight I was ready.

Once finished, silence came, save for the echoing splash of waves and children playing in the pool behind the wall. The story left an effect: the entire group turned quiet for several minutes, the boys kicking absently at my ball, Berle turning the cranks of my bike with his hand, watching the roll of the gears; even Angie's voice shallowed and withered to nothing, aside from a sadly mumbled, *God.* . . .

Ronnie raised his eyebrows in calm, convinced surprise, strangely smiling to me as if he had been the one to make the secret confession, as if he and I were the only ones there. He slumped back into his spot against the wall where I'd originally found him, and kept his eyes on me. After another moment's reflection, he brought out a small plastic bag from his pants pocket to prepare a joint with masterful precision. The atmosphere relaxed, the shade cast by the tree seemed actually cooling now, although it took me some time to realize it; I'd been deafened by the pulse at my temples. I looked around as if ready to throw out a longer defense, feeling ready to keep talking, to stay on the attack. But there was no need. The joint made its way around to me, and the only existing pressure was to lean my head back against the warm bark of the tree, feel the smoke's sharp flowering in my lungs, and let the drug make its effect. I'd never realized having a father in prison could advance me in some social circles.

Angela, I had decided, was definitely not gorgeous; the closer I got to her the more impossible it was to avoid it. Her face was pockmarked and heavily rouged, her eye make-up a silvery-blue; the green feather tied by rawhide to a roach-clip which she kept clamped to her hair, curled like a chartreuse banana following the curve of her face, gave her the air of an ugly, sweating peacock. Still, I liked her. She seemed within reach; something I needed after Chaney. As the pot hit, the conversation turned to sexual jokes directed at her, and never once did she seem upset, or even mildly surprised; in fact, when the discussion turned to the breasts of women—spurred by porn Ronnie had brought along—Angela offered us her own, smiling as we touched her through the cotton of her tank top, our faces now in sudden, serious concentration. This only fed our curiosity, and some of the boys grew feisty, more demanding, grabbing at her crotch through her cut-offs and snapping her bra-strap against her back, hoping to undo the latch with a lucky flick. All this made me laugh. She got mad, though, lamenting, *Where are your manners?* But just as she stormed off, Ronnie fired up his dirt bike and caught up with her, saying he'd take her home.

I became strangely attached to Ronnie. It felt natural that he was the leader; he seemed to wear an official badge as Public Outcast with a certain dignity—a dignity that, by proximity, was endowed to the rest of us. Within the course of one joint, I'd changed from a younger boy uneasy before Ronnie's mellow bravado to the group's undeclared agreement that we should all defer to him, unjudging and innocently accepting of a spontaneous hierarchy.

My daily routine changed to accommodate my new friends. I stopped going with Michael to the Horse Chestnut Club in the mornings for swim practice; instead, I took my bike to the fields and trained until Ronnie and Angela and their cronies appeared with the loud rip of the dirt bike. After a few weeks my training took second place to just hanging out with them and getting stoned and doing nothing. It was late spring when we met, and I was playing four or five hours a day; this changed to two or three hours, then one, then I stopped bringing my cleats and ball altogether.

Ronnie brought us magazines to peruse in sedated silence, magazines like *Hustler* and *Juggs* and *Penthouse* that we passed around as we made comments. They teased me for bothering to read the articles—always some scandalous exposé against government abuse in the army, or the secret yearning all women had for anal sex—while Angie looked over my shoulder and took the magazines herself to study with frank curiosity. She compared her breasts to those in the photographs, asking our own opinions, and examined the different coifs of pubic hair as unself-consciously as if she were looking through the latest *Cosmopolitan* in search of a new style. Pubic hair was a popular subject of discussion in that group: Ronnie liked the thin ribbon which rose inches from a bare vagina, saying you could feel the inside of a woman better when she was trimmed that way; Berle declared bald cunts the best. We noted every style: heart-shaped or flared like wings; tattooed with two red lips puckered for a kiss; the trim beard of three-day's growth.

—So what does yours look like? we asked Angie, and she shuddered in false modesty, told us maybe she would show us someday if we were nice. Then she touched my knee and winked as if the comment were directly pointed at me.

—Well I already know, Ronnie boasted.

—Ronnie! That's nobody's business!

We begged Ronnie to describe Angie's crotch to us. *Don't you dare,* she admonished him, *don't you dare,* —Not while I'm here, at least. *Hon*estly.... As he opened his mouth to say something she cut him off by shouting, —Ronnie Smits, you start describing my pussy here in front of everybody and you'll never see it again!

He snickered, mimicked a frightened, trembling face. Then he said, with a confident, royal air: —Angie, I'll take that pussy of yours anytime I want it.

She answered with nothing more than turning her face away and raising a petulant shrug. We all knew he was right and saw no point in denying it. Ronnie was also the only one of us who could claim, without reprisals for proof, to not be a virgin. He described the sensation as like sticking your cock into a jar of oily peanut butter—a description of such stark allure that I often stopped at a nearby convenience store and gazed upon the rows of jars on the shelves, mouth parted, tongue resting on my lower lip, as I stared in strange hypnotic reverie.

Sex was his domain, and we wanted in. We crowded about the magazines he brought from a tattered nylon book bag, tossing them to us and showing no particular interest himself as he knew the real thing. He belittled us for our rhapsodic attention to the photographs. He told us of his adventures, tales which made Angie giggle and laugh, chiding him each time for being so nasty and shameless. —Don't y'all get any ideas from *that* story, that's not about me, she would say. To ease the tension that mounted in us, eventually she would let us touch her breasts again, allowing us to pinch gently at her hardened nipples, sometimes grabbing our crotches through our shorts and pronouncing her amazement at how hard we all were.

All this worked to attract me strongly to Angela. I longed for the chance to be alone with her. And when she told me of a midnight party, I knew it was my time.

—I want you to meet my girlfriends, she said. —You can come tonight, can't you? Please come tonight. It'll be worth it, I promise.

Her words fed a determination in me to escape our house that night at any cost. By the time I made it home that evening I was angry for having to sneak out in the first place—that was Ray's way. Michael could hear nothing about the idea; he would try to talk me out of it, or betray me to our mother or, worse, ask to come along. I planned with blistering concentration how to steal from the house undetected.

Step One: Leave the bike behind our garage rather than in the basement, so a getaway could be made without the opening of doors. Done.

Step Two: How to get past mother? Though she felt no need to safeguard us, Olive was still crafty; the slightest mistake on my part would instill instant suspicion. But I had options: she tended to fall asleep watching TV, the noise of which could cover my descent down the stairs past her room and out of the house. Our bathroom was on the first floor, and if caught, I could easily suggest I'd been going there.

I took care not to go to bed any earlier than usual. Mother complained of a hard day, and went upstairs to watch the ten o'clock news, leaving her door open a crack. I told her good night and waited, my body lit with anticipation.

In my bed, fully dressed, I imagined the party getting started . . . I didn't even know where it would be. Ronnie said he would have beer. Girls would be there . . . it promised to be a real event—the beginning of which exploded over me at the first hint of mother's snores in the room across from mine. I bolted from the bed and shot barefoot to her door, my sneakers held behind my back: there, feet crossed at the ankle, thin hands folded on her belly, the yellow nightgown rising and falling with each breath, Olive's face settled into the bitter frown her face made in sleep. A cigarette burned in the bedside ashtray, the smoke pluming into the lampshade above; a half-filled glass of pale ginger ale and melting ice beside it, a bottle of bourbon standing open on the floor.

I darted into the warm wild night; through the pathetic hedge fencing our backyard, pedaling up the creek bank beneath a thin mustard moon. Each barking dog quickened my pulse; the murmuring creek made me hear voices. But soon I was on the road and soaring.

Angela waited where she said she would be, alone against the dumpster, a small shadow pinned by the red glow of her cigarette. She started at the sound of my bike on the grass, then laughed as she saw me, saying, —I didn't think you'd make it. . . .

—Where is everybody?

—Inside. Come here and sit down first. I brought a beer for you.

I did as told, popping the tab with one hand as if I'd performed the task a thousand times, although in truth it was my first; Uncle Crush always handed me his foamy beer in a paper cup. But beer cans are like soda cans and so I felt manly and confident . . . the beer tasted a little cold still, sweeping bitter over my tongue. I held my breath at the smell, which brought to mind the bitter and sharp odor of the pools of horse urine on the backside of the race track. —You say everybody's inside? in the pool?

—Ronnie swiped a door key last summer. You can't get into the offices, tho, that's another key I guess. You just jump the fence there.

—Let's stay here a while.

She nodded, and the smoke from her cigarette rose blue and chalky above us. Her hand lay palm down on the inside of my thigh and I was already hard—my thoughts landed briefly on Chaney Lawse and that whole humiliating catastrophe, so I searched about the shadows for any sign of witnesses. There was nothing but the moonlight. And Angela looked prettier in blue moonlight. . . . the cake of her make-up faded in the darkness, and the acne-peppered face appeared smooth, childlike . . . her hair was stacked and pinned on top of her head, taking some of the roundness from her face. She never stopped smiling. I took this as an invitation and reached for her breast. She pushed my hand away.

—Aren't you quick, she said with her usual giggle, a bubble of air tapping through her lips, —I thought you'd be romantic.

I mumbled through an embarrassed apology, one hand clutching a wad of painful crabgrass in frustration.

—Let's at least lie down, she said then, and the night lit up again.

Her tongue pushed thick and heavy into my mouth. It tasted awful, stinking of cigarettes and beer . . . it did not matter. I could feel her breasts beneath me, the rise of her pelvis on either side of my abdomen; in my excitement at the depth of our kiss, my saliva poured over the corners of her mouth and onto her cheeks, following the line of her jaw to her ears. She didn't seem to care and this aroused me even more. I tried to unhook her bra but couldn't—first attempting it one-handed, like in the movies; then with both hands, Angela rising slightly off the ground to give me room; but no luck. Patiently she performed this act for me, and I pushed up her top to be struck by how Angela's breasts spilled tiredly over her ribs; stretch-marks mapped the skin near her breastbone. Her skin seemed already old and dry, yet she was no older than me. Still, she was there. It did not matter that she hadn't jumped from the photo of a magazine. I slurped and sucked at her; thrust my hand down the front of her jeans and fingered the mess of hair, my motions violent and ridiculous as I tried to picture what style she had shaven down there. She told me to slow down, be more gentle. *Right, right,* I mumbled. *Sorry.*

Her own hands lazed on my back. If her touch glided to my hips I turned in a way to put my sex within reach, thinking she'd clutch it hungrily, but she kept moving elsewhere. My cock strained against my shorts and I pressed the swelling into her side, rubbed it into the softness of her thighs, the pale softness of her belly, turning again so she could have me, shouting in my head *God just touch me,* but for whatever reason she would not dare. When I started to unbutton her jeans, she stopped my hand after the first one, and I dropped onto my side to take a breath.

—Don't be mad. . . .

—Who's mad?

—I really like you, she said, as if that changed anything.

She began to talk about her life, her single mother, but my head was too busy with my own thoughts to listen, and the brown steel façade of the dumpster glowing oddly in the leaf-flecked moonlight, the crabgrass in my fist again, became more compelling. It seemed as though a strange, teeming spirit had taken hold of me, anxious, impatient—what I wanted from her had nothing to do with liking one another. She must have understood that she was speaking to herself, and soon stopped; for the next few minutes we sat in silence and neither moved, listening to the insects around us; an owl cooed in the tree above but we couldn't find him. The time passed with interrupted touches as we finished our beers, and she another cigarette. What did I mean to her then? Why did she want me here? I would never know. These thoughts brought me a sadness. I thought to try to touch her again, to get her to lie back, but when we kissed she turned slightly, away from me, and said, —You want to see what's going on inside?

I yanked the grass from the ground and threw it aside. *Sure,* I said. *Why not.* We climbed the fence together, and I tried not to hear her soft apologies for making me angry.

We met the bark of wilding kids, the rush and slap of water against pool walls; then the chlorine biting sharp in our nostrils and eyes. Young, half-naked bodies swept and swerved over the wet macadam, their high-pitched voices echoing into a thick morass of winsome noise. The spirit that had saddened me outside was sucked away into the recklessness. Angela already had her top off, standing beside me in nothing but bra and panties; Ronnie's silhouette enjoyed two girls in the pool shallows, one hanging from his mouth, the other holding on as though afraid of drifting away. His skinny chest, pale, farmer-tanned, looked ridiculous without his shirt, and his long straight hair, matted to his scalp and shoulders, made him appear smaller, mongrel-like.

Angela screeched and jumped into the water. I needed time to get acclimated. I walked into the darkened sauna, where two couples had completely disrobed and were groping one another. I wandered in, wandered out, wondering what had I gotten myself into? even as I wished to join everyone at once. Who were these kids? Where had they been hiding? The Y had transformed into a hormonal volcano in full eruption. I cracked open another beer and forced two swigs, and the alcohol went to work on my body. . . . Eyes adjusted to the dark, I re-entered the sauna, where someone lit a spliff, and I cradled a girl's bottom in one hand while toking lightly with the other. Somebody mentioned they were tripping and felt scared and we laughed, goofy and unconcerned, the joint making its way between five of us cramped inside this tiny room, the smell of pot hanging musty and thick in the squalid heat, making my body rise and shine . . . *hey is this laced or what?* . . . giggles and sighs, a murmur half-stifled, the smack of two tongues working against one another . . . *no, hold it like that, like that, but harder . . .* the slip of a thigh scooting over on wooden slats . . . *did you bring a towel? I'm scorched over here. . . .* What's your name? —*I'm a friend of Ronnie's . . . Can I have a sip of that beer?*

Sure. . . .

I leaned against the fogged window in the sauna door as sweat poured out of me; peeling off my shirt a girl murmured *mmm, nice,* and I fell into the crack of her smile, almost startled to find her small breasts in my hands. I had no clue what she looked like; she still had her underwear on, soaked through and clinging, and her mouth moved all over me as another girl said *hey welcome the new guy,* our bodies rubbing and slipping together, her mouth on my neck, my chest, my stomach, until finally my crotch. I gasped at that new sensation, not caring about the close, hissing laughter . . . no time for thought or consideration, it was all movement and stimulation—*doing* was all. . . . Back to the pool to find two guys spraying graffiti over the walls, *Fuck* and *Cunt* and epithets I'd never heard before. We sang and shouted, we hollered. We played water games, the girls taking to our shoulders to wrestle one another down. Hours passed, I've no idea how many; chlorine burned my eyes, water sizzled my sinuses; I didn't care. Laughter brought gulps of water into my throat, and I choked and coughed . . . somebody said *look out I'm taking a piss* and we eased away from him.

The mood heightened still, nearer to frenzy. Boys ran naked on the pool side, bony and red-armed; girls wandered without anything more than panties which we could see through from being soaked with sauna-sweat and pool water. A stack of Styrofoam kickboards tumbled to the ground and some guys urinated over them.

We were having such fun until the police arrived. The lights came on and there they were, all black jackets and mag flashes and night sticks. *You kids having yourselves a party?*

Yelps of panic rebounded with that flat, slap-back echo of a pool room. Everyone made desperate moves toward the doors, but they'd covered the exits. . . . Within minutes the police had us set in a line against the wall.

Everyone except Ronnie. He remained defiant until the end, smacking the water to splash the nearest cop, shouting, *You can come get me, motherfuckers!* as he waded quickly to the middle where he couldn't be hooked.

His resistance shocked all of us. It was an impressive display. We looked to him for an idea of what to do; perhaps he could somehow get us out of this. Then again, maybe he was hoping we could somehow help him out. One cop answered Ronnie in a solemn, tired voice, *Son, the last thing you want is for me to come in after you.* His flashlight fell onto the middle of the pool and he added, *Is that you, Ronnie Smits?* Ronnie's name brought laughter and shaking heads from a few of the officers. —Well this is a pleasure; you're in the three-strike zone, aren't you boy?

Ronnie's only response was to wring himself about in the middle of the pool, looking for an escape. He stretched the farce as long as he could. But he knew he was trapped, and so did we. We watched him turn round and round in the pool, keeping to the spaces where he couldn't be reached, the police waiting calmly and not reacting to his hysterical insults. We giggled stupidly at his antics as though through him we were just as defiant, and the cops indulged us by saying nothing for a long time. Instead they spoke quietly to one another with inclined heads, radios cackling into the early-morning air.

—Take all the time you want, son, one said. —We'll still be here when you get out.

When he finally sulked his way to a ladder, Ronnie pulled himself out with taut, snappish tugs, making jeering faces that made us cronies proud, until he was greeted roughly by two officers. He spit at them, raised his arm as though to fight, screamed *fuckin' don't touch me fuckers!* The police answered by clubbing him repeatedly with the night sticks. That silenced the entire crew of us. The last I saw of Ronnie Smits was in a police car's spotlight, showering upon his mouth pulped and crimson, eyes clenched shut, nose running blood, wrists cuffed behind his back.

Whatever spirit there had been to cradle me all night quickly drained away with such speed I could almost see it flit off over the water, laughing at me: *sucker. . . .* The party was over.

A few people stood outside on their porches, back-lit by house lights, applauding as we were led into the cars. I felt hated, a menace, and scared; yet even then shared a powerful solidarity with my new friends, as though we hadn't been arrested for anything more shameful than a heroic protest. With no idea what lay ahead for me at the station, but knowing exactly the furor that would erupt at home, I hardened. *This is who I am,* I thought, and did not care. Ray would have been defiant.

Pulling off, I caught Angela's face—puffy-eyed, her make-up washed away—and felt a brief need to apologize to her. But the urge frittered off with the touch of my forehead against the filmy glass window. The headlights of the patrol car swept the area as we turned, and I just glimpsed the handlebars of my bike on the ground behind the dumpster, suspecting that it would be the last time. I didn't care. I was up to this. Fear comes from what you've never seen before, and I knew where I was.

3

Mother decided it best to wait to come to the detention center downtown. She instructed them to lock me up for the night to give me a taste of punishment, and to have time to think over my stupidity. Before she came to reclaim me, two days later, I weathered a few cafeteria beatings. I was very angry at her for that—so angry that I looked forward to our upcoming fight, to flashing my black eye and tenderloin lip into her face. But once she did appear, and I saw her quietly signing the papers to take her son home, my anger collapsed before the defeat in that face, the fatigue and worry etched there; it collapsed beneath the sorry tone in her voice as she gave humble apologies to the officers for my behavior.

Instead it was Ray who went apoplectic at the news. His wrath set off Olive's, and they shouted furiously at one another on the phone: — What would you like me to do, Ray, keep him under lock and key? He's *your* son . . . you never wanted to punish him and now look. . . . Don't you yell at me, maybe it has something to do with having a father in prison, Ray, have you stopped to consider that? Okay well I'm at my last nerve trying to keep together the mess you left behind so don't you use that language with me!

Once finished, she slammed down the phone so hard that it rang again. She picked it back up to see if there was another call. —I could spit nails! she growled into the empty receiver.

Something had apparently gone wrong on the phone: she heard no dead line: it wouldn't hang up. Ray's calls were long-distance affairs, made collect to our home, and so any added time was damaging to our already-short purse strings. Quickly mother passed from mild irritation to balls-out frantic. She hung up the phone softly to assure it set in place, waited, tried again: it still sounded as if the line were open. *Ray?* she asked firmly, *Ray, are you there? Hang up the phone!* She did the same thing again, then three times, at a loss as to what else to do. *Dammit! Michael!* —You fix it. And when he couldn't—what did he know about telephones?—we both set to performing the same careful act as she had just before, returning the receiver to its cradle, pressing it down for a moment to make sure it was securely bedded, then raising it again in search of a dial tone. Still we heard the open line.

Olive turned hysterical. She threw her keys about the small kitchen, she tore open cupboards and slammed them shut again, she burst into tears. Her face drained of all color except for splotches of wild rouge in odd places, and she held her hands out before her in the form of claws, chipped-red nails gleaming in search of an object to tear. A litany of curses poured forth, blaming the conspiracy against us, the bureaucracy of government and, by extension, large phone corporations, each curse blending into the lament *I need a break, Lord, I need a break, what is it you want from me?* Michael stared at the criminal phone. Suddenly he struck upon the idea to visit a neighbor's house and use their phone to call us; when mother didn't answer him, he took her silence as a yes and bolted outside. Within minutes the phone rang, breaking or overriding the other problem. Still, even as relief settled back into the kitchen, Olive remained rattled sick with tension. —Ha ha! she cried in mock gratefulness, —Our little blessing for the day!

She confined me to my room pending further punishment, *Until I decide what to do, **damn** it!* and she did go so far as to have a lock-bolt set into my bedroom door.

Olive never confronted me with the question *why.* She was smart enough to understand there was no reason, that I hadn't thought anything through. She told me she would never trust me again, and that I should take this time spent alone to consider what I'd done along with the extent of its ramifications, to dwell over the shame I'd brought the family—*at least your father can claim innocence!*—and most of all, to meditate upon the rupture I'd created in my relationship to her.

—Be clear on this point if on nothing else, Claude Gabriel Toure: until you straighten out, you are my *enemy.*

The level and sustain of her anger amazed me for its awesome force alone. I expected a huge bawling-out once back from the detention center, a couple of her weak punches which I was now big enough to fend off, loss of certain privileges, et cetera—but then a gradual relaxing of the atmosphere once the rhythms of home grew normal again. This did not happen. Not yet two years into Ray's absence, my mother's whole demeanor changed; her shoulders curved inward like an old woman's; her eyes and mouth narrowed with bitter wrinkles about the edges, taking more of the characteristics of the chronic smoker's harsh face; her yellow hands shook over the most menial tasks. And though all of these characteristics show signs of a body fatigued and weakening, her maniacal will to keep control of that house, to defy the possibility that her youngest son was growing into a hooligan, struggled to overcome them. Any perceived slight to her command would now be swiftly and ruthlessly punished.

I blamed myself for the changes in her. It would be a long time before we made the connection between her transformation and the bottles of bourbon kept open on the kitchen table. Alcohol had always been around the house and so it didn't seem terribly wrong that she added a full double-shot to her morning coffee, or that her cocktail with ginger-ale never left her grasp in the evenings—sometimes keeping two or three glasses ready-made in separate rooms, forgetting she'd already mixed one. Each room had its own bottle. I wasn't looking for deeper meanings (not yet) and took the world at face-value, only noticing the ferocity of her rage against my uselessness, when before she used to praise me to the stars; how sarcasm became a permanent edge in her voice; how the punches grew wilder and easier to dodge, if one stayed on the lookout for them, for they seemed to come now from any situation at all. That's how it became between Olive and me. I blamed myself.

Michael had his own way. He was older, and had the added responsibility of acting *the man* of the house—whatever that meant, for it wasn't like he could go out and get a job. He turned away door-to-door salesmen, took phone messages, set the bills out to be paid, kept a watch over me. *The family disruption,* he called me. But also he was a teenager simply trying to get through with the least amount of damage. Whereas I bashed my head into obstacles, Michael considered his from an ironic distance, wadding them up in his mind until they became discardable. He avoided Olive when he could, and did his chores on time. He kept to himself or, once he began to drive, spent time with his few friends, discussing books.

Michael loved the absurdist writers. Seventeen years old, and already my brother had secondhand volumes of Ionesco and Camus and Beckett standing in neat piles around the house—the neat piles hiding the creased covers and ratty pages. He liked the outright weirdness of these texts, and found a certain solace there. For him, *The Myth of Sisyphus* was a self-help book. Once, "guarding" me in my room, I found him staring at me with intense, amused eyes; when I asked him what his problem was he said, —I'm trying to imagine you with the head of a rhinoceros.... (I had no clue to what he meant.) If I said, —It can't go on like this, something has to change, he would answer: —Neither of us can go on like this, but you know, we'll do nothing and yet keep going....

He even tried his hand at writing absurdist plays. It started as an assignment from school, but one which he took to with his casual fervor. Sitting with Ray in the Visitor's Gallery in Marion County,

Michael would read his newest "text": most likely a play without dialogue. A single man alone, sitting on a stool beneath a single spotlight, beginning in the same intense position as Rodin's *Thinker*. Progressively his body reflects one now bored with his thoughts, then intrigued by a new line of meditation, now despairing, now lying folded on the floor. . . . Michael said he was unsure if at the end the man was dead, or just asleep.

The family sat quietly for a few minutes after he finished. Olive watched the other visitors, smoked a cigarette. Pops alternately smiled and frowned at his hands folded between his knees. —That's great, son, he started. Then, —Well, it's above me. What's it supposed to be?

This, my brother proclaimed, was Art. Suddenly Olive found herself having to defend an educational system as though she were the one to have invented it.

Most of all, however, Michael found refuge in music. Again, obscurity was his aim; he felt exalted when converting a listener to his own tastes. Michael took a certain pride in listening to bands nobody had ever heard of; if one of his groups came close to popularity, he stopped liking them. At fourteen he had found Pops' old Martin guitar, and Michael had a gifted ear, learning a few chords from Pops before he left, then learning songs off of records, and it wasn't long before he tried his hand at composing his own tunes. His friends picked up instruments, too, and it wasn't long before they were passing their weekends holed-up in the basement of the drummer's house, Michael on bass (nobody else wanted to play it) for Fifty Foot Sister, recording their own songs on a simple tape recorder set in the middle of the room.

This set a precedent for the man he would become. Fifty Foot Sister had no desire to learn songs to play out at parties or dances; they wanted, from the start, to play only for themselves. As science drew Michael into the insipid excitement of quiet research—it would be his major at the University of Georgia, which he chose solely for the fecund music scene there—music would balance him creatively. He passed his time alone, collecting more and more technical equipment to better the quality and range of available sounds, going into serious debt to record music that never left his apartment or car stereo.

In this way our paths would diverge even further: as I set out to surround myself with as many people as possible, Michael burrowed further into the basement of somebody else's home. I could not stand silence or being alone, but Michael would refuse to keep a phone in his apartment, saying disembodied voices unnerved him. His ability to converse soon abandoned subjects of books or movies and even science, which he found too painful to discuss with those who weren't already familiar with the difficult terms, and revolved only around music. I came to think of him as a disappearing man, a ghost, too distracted to keep the company of other people, until finally we lost contact altogether—two lost brothers standing to receive our mother's ashes in an urn, then two total strangers fidgeting beside the hospital bed of our dying father. Oh, there's so much more to tell.

4

Angela got probation, I heard; Ronnie, on the momentum of past arrests, would serve three years and matriculate from juvenile when the time came. Myself, I landed 150 community-service hours, to begin immediately. This meant wearing stiff orange jumpsuits in a crowd of other juveniles as we scrubbed graffiti from office buildings, picked up highway debris, and scoured the used condoms and picnic garbage from Montreux's parks. It sounded awful when the judge explained my sentence—after each short article glancing up from her desk to ask, *do you understand* and *do you have anything to add?*—but in fact these hours became moments of relative freedom for me, as all privileges at home were now denied. My memory of this time is of brutal sun; disgust at the waste stuck to my hands and the misery in an aching back; fatigue, thirst, and brooding indifference to the taunts and insults thrown from passing cars; the uncomfortable silences of clearing gay trickers from the public toilets so we could disinfect the place. But you can't keep kids down, and so this was also a time of irresponsibility and corrosive laughter which flourished within the constant joking around of delinquents. Although we were all supposed to have been chastened by the public's view of our punishment, nothing could have been less serious.

Nobody was guilty. That's the main thing. Each of us polished our crimes to a brilliant shine, and nobody felt remorse for what they'd done; only for being caught. Crime was not of moral question, but of bragging rights:

> *I hit the bitch three times before they pulled me off her—elbow to her face,* **bang!** *She sucking off my best friend? I woulda killed him next with half the chance.*

> *I was so drunk I didn't even know the party'd been busted, man, and I was outside taking a piss on the tire of a car not even seeing the blue light flashing on top. . . .*

> *This old lady had a thousand dollars in her purse when I took it, baby—a thousand dollars! Now what kind of bitch goes around with that kind of cash in hand? By the time they caught up with me I'd been flying for days. . . .*

This brought boundless glee and high-fives from the entire crew. None of us denied our crimes, but neither did we claim any responsibility for them. It was all the fault of a system *out there;* we were victims to a bureaucracy which kept us in scratching-hot orange cotton which bled through with our sweat, stained with the sweat of others before us. We were powerless beneath a manner of rule which denied us the freedom to be ourselves.

I didn't plan to hurt nobody, every one of us said. *I'm the victim here!*

At the end of the long day Michael would pick me up, a cassette of Fifty Foot Sister's latest practice session vibrating the windows. Since we still had a few hours before Olive came home, he would let me watch TV or listen to music—his—while we kept out a careful eye for the specter of her Toyota rolling onto our small court, when I'd rush up the worn carpet of our stairs to my room and shut the door.

—He's been quiet today, I think they're wearing him out pretty good, Michael might say once she entered the house. With no words between us, I'd hear her wearily mount the same stairs I'd scurried up moments before. Beneath the jangle of keys there would come the firm *slat* of my lock slipping into place, and a huff of contentment at the action done. *There.*

But Michael could not be held responsible for me all the time. Once school began, reinforcements were called in. Olive couldn't keep me confined throughout the school year—the logistics were just too complicated—and so Mama Sarah, Olive's mother, took the bus from her small western Kentucky town of Guthrie to live with us in Montreux.

A bad tactical move on mother's part—*Gabriel* had been Mama Sarah's maiden name, and even though it was her policy to spoil all of us equally, her behavior made clear that most of her attentions would focus upon me. But with Mama Sarah's arrival came a short period of temperance. It was she who convinced Olive to allow me to play soccer in the recreational leagues again: —He's still such a young boy, dear, and you don't want him to come to resent his own mother, do you? She asked, her voice still lightly tinged with her immigrant's English accent.

—I don't care how he feels, Mom, as long as he obeys. As long as he lives under my roof, he doesn't have the choice but to follow my rules.

—Yes, but a boy needs exercise and as many friends as he can muster, especially now with Ray . . . absent.

Mama Sarah paid for my league fees from her own social security check and made the calls to the mothers of teammates to arrange transport to practices and games. —I quite like football myself, you know, she told me; —My father and I used to watch Aston Villa's matches every Saturday, but my mother could not stand the crowds.

My grandmother revealed a world of which I'd only read accounts in the soccer magazine I lifted from a nearby bookstore: a world where my sport was not a scorned and ridiculed athletic match but a passion excelling religion; where sold-out crowds chanted songs and threw firecrackers; where the enormous desire to see a match firsthand caused collapsed stadiums and crushed spectators. She set me to dreaming about an escape not just from this house and Kentucky, but the entire United States, in the hope that one day I could play in Europe.

In the evenings she regarded me as I juggled the "English Football" beside the garage while she sipped a small gin martini (she considered gin a lady's drink), with only a touch of vermouth. I loved to show off for her, excited to find somebody interested in the latest mastered tricks: balancing the ball on my forehead, or else the Rainbow, a feat that required rolling the ball up the back of one calf as you step forward, flicking the ball over your head so that it landed again in front of you. I longed for the chance to use it in a game, confounding a helpless goalie as he watched the ball sail languidly—the move demanded a deft touch—over his head and softly sighing down the back of the net.

Mama Sarah brought our house some calm. When I was the single frosh on the varsity squad she baked chocolate chip cookies from scratch; if we watched TV together at night, she let me rest my head on her lap, or else traced her strong fingernails along the soles of my bare feet, which I liked; she didn't knit, but practiced needlepoint, and in that year the house slowly filled with small, decorative pillows, and framed settings of flowers or mother's beloved cardinals. Once, for my birthday, Ray sketched a portrait of me from memory; although I was fourteen now, the portrait made me look as though I'd frozen at the age of ten or eleven. Mother took this especially hard, musing over his work with tender drunken melancholy, freshening her ginger-ale with the ever-ready bourbon after each sip. —Gaby you hold onto this forever, boy, do you understand? she said to me with raw, swollen eyes. —Don't you ever lose this, it would crush him. And me. You don't know it now but this will be one of your most cherished possessions some day.

My grandmother quickly made a needlepoint matting to set it upon, bordered at the top by the Gabriel Coat-of-Arms, and we hung it in my room. The art of needlepoint formed a distinct bridge between Olive and Mama Sarah. Each new work readily accepted the weight of becoming an immediate family heirloom, *Priceless,* as Olive would say. Before Ray's sentence began, she used to make her own designs, stitching intricate figures on shirts for Michael and me, and belts for Pops, and Christmas stockings; although now she didn't have the time to set herself to the hobby anymore, at night she sat with her mother at the small yellow kitchen table, discussing the merits and faults of various patterns in catalogues, choosing the next project, filling the air with cigarette smoke—Sarah might smoke one for every ten of Olive's. The murmur of their evenings together would climb calmly up the stairs to my room, drift faultlessly through the air ducts, and as a wary peace seemed to slowly descend on our house again—a night having passed without argument or threat—I'd pass off into sleep, always too exhausted from training, my community service now a memory, to dream.

For one year we lived like that, with these rhythms. Calm, peppered by occasional outbursts of antagonism: the usual family life with everyone getting on each other's nerves. Boredom, and (for me) time uneventful. I longed then for a defining moment—be it calamity or triumph. That moment arrived just as I entered my sophomore year, with the appearance of a glossy poster on a wall outside the school gym: *Professional Indoor Soccer is Coming to Montreux!* In another two weeks the team would be there to give a demonstration and clinic.

Even though I was bused downtown to school, meaning I'd have to take a city bus after the demonstration, meaning I wouldn't be home until late in the evening as we had to make two line changes in order to get home and the wait took forever, I talked it over with Sarah and she gave me permission to go.

About forty or so boys hung around the gym, all from the varsity and junior varsity teams. Five members of the *Montreux Tornado* arrived in a van marked with the new logo, and in the hush that swept over us as they filed out, I was struck by the first *real* soccer players I'd ever seen in the flesh, so purposefully opposite of the two-inch figures I followed on the TV screen at home. Their bodies radiated the spring-like tension and confidence of animals, a calm bearing that did not hide the readiness for action—this despite the tired pallor of unshaven faces and fashionable, shoulder-length hair. Immediately we boys were awed; these men became our idols before even setting foot to ball. We noted the make of their shoes; we remarked on the coolness of the crimson and gray striping of their uniforms. We straightened ourselves on the floor in anticipation, already trying to mimic their stature.

The demonstration was an event at once inspiring and demeaning. Inspiring to see talented players caress the ball with such mastery, each blessed with a soft touch that made a quiet *whup* as they brought the ball off their feet, passed it around between them, displayed new tricks with foreign imagination, acting with an unfamiliar confidence. Beneath the gym's fluorescent light, mixed with the dusty glow of the sun streaming through huge caged windows on the far wall, the ball took on a distinct balance and measure, seemed to be a different ball than the type we used. (It *was* different, made of handsewn leather rather than the glued plastic thing we smacked around.) The ball was an extension of their thoughts and intentions, and not a singular object with a will of its own. . . . And so it felt demeaning, too, since despite excelling in Kentucky leagues, I'd missed out; I was already behind. None of these players were local; they all came from the Northeast or West; one hailed all the way from Yugoslavia. It seemed impossible to reach such a plateau of play. The failure meant everything.

They put us through drills on the hardwood floor. The quiet echo of professional touches disappeared beneath the hard, nervous smacks from our less-talented feet. They pointed out what we were doing wrong—everything—and urged us to relax. There were so many angles to consider, more than I'd ever fathomed before: the idea of *vision,* most of all. They had us dribble in a circle around one stilled pro; we had to avoid knocking into each other and at the same time call out the number of fingers he would silently raise. How could you dribble without looking at your feet? Every new drill showcased yet another facet of the game I had yet to consider, or even imagine.

Then some varsity players scrimmaged against the *Tornado*—who duly embarrassed us. We were intimidated and the score was depressing after fifteen minutes. We stopped keeping count of the number of times the ball passed between two orange pylons marking the goal we were to defend.

Still, despite my nervousness I managed to score with a blind, angry rip; the only one on our team to do so. The scrimmage ended there. And then we listened to an announcement from the coach that sent us reeling:

—To help encourage the sport of soccer and your participation in the community, I'd like to tell you a bit about our special Youth Project. We're going to choose two players from each high school in the Greater Montreux Area to form a junior team. This team will practice twice weekly, scrimmage against the professional squad when our schedule permits, and finally travel to compete against the youth teams in all the other cities in our league. Next summer our team will travel to France for a tournament there, and this will give you a chance to learn how you measure up against boys who have been playing from the cradle!

Throughout the long bus ride home in a chilly October night, I folded myself in my seat and dreamed of this glory that would have to be mine. I imagined the crimson-and-gray uniforms, and how I would wear the jersey to school . . . sleep in it and eat in it and train in it and Sarah would have to steal the shirt while I showered in order to add it to the day's laundry . . . that jersey would be an emblem worthy of admiration, envy. . . . I saw myself scoring goals against older, supposedly better players. My sunken confidence at how far behind I was from where I needed to be paled before the grail of being selected to this team. And then there was the luminous star of France circling in the distance—I knew nothing of lavender fields or Notre Dame . . . no, to me, France was the legendary midfield of Platini and Tigana and Fernandez and Giresse, the figure of a goalscorer in the frothy-haired Didier Six. It was the memory of the indefatigable Blues in the 1982 World Cup, losing in a semifinal to Brazil on overtime penalties. I would excel overseas, too; they would ask me to skip college to accept a contract with the celebrated team of Monaco or Paris St. Germain. . . .

My reverie rose to such intensity that I missed my bus connection. I had to doubleback and wait as the hour lengthened and the sun had long gone down; the stars were scratched out by city lights so that above there stretched a cursory wipe of black. Those bright lights on the city streets only accentuated the carbon-arc lamps of stadiums in my head; the tedium of waiting for a bus behind schedule only length-ened the time I could imagine maturing into a body as strong and confident as the players I'd watched tumble into their van after the demonstration. Any refuse at hand—small chunks of pavement, wadded newspaper, discarded cigarette packs—I kicked with tireless concentration.

It was past ten o'clock before I returned home, passing under the maple tree in the front yard, pausing for a moment to gaze up to that summit Coldwell Godfrey and I never did reach. It was thicker now, approachable, and the coming autumn had cleared enough leaves so that I could see stars through the branches. It occurred to me to try the climb now—but immediately following that thought came the memory of once playing war with Cody, me in the lower branches getting shot through the chest, so lost in my reality of the game that I allowed myself to fall, and broke my arm against the ground. The memory made me smile, shaking my head in disbelief at my capability for idiocy. I felt happy opening the door to our house.

I entered a foyer bristling with strange quiet. The radio played very softly beside Mama Sarah, who looked at me, forced a thin smile, and looked away. She leaned closer to the radio to hear the classical music lilting there. Light TV chatter fell from mother's bedroom.

—Olive would like to speak with you, my grandmother said.

Of course: Olive. What good would the day have been without a bitching awaiting me at its end? Mounting the stairs, I wandered among the possibilities of what I might have done wrong—any recent lies told which could be discovered today—but found nothing. Olive waited in her tattered yellow nightgown; the drink lay pressed between her thighs; a cigarette sizzled in the ashtray beside her. The company accounting books lay spread out on the bed before her as she worked with an adding machine, noting figures. Head still inclined toward the books, her eyebrows raised at my entrance into the room: —Fun clinic? she asked.

I warily played down my joy. —It was all right. . . . Where's Michael?

—He's in his room studying. (A squeak edged out of her mouth as she sucked hard on the cigarette.)—I'm sure you haven't eaten yet. There's leftover stew downstairs. Eat it then go to your room. Do your homework and then go to bed. Now.

And that was all. Her tone was stern, but quiet. Not understanding what I had missed—the tension teemed especially in that room—I was happy to get away. I didn't *want* to know.

That night I lay in bed with the door partially open. It was impossible to sleep even if my body felt tired . . . my head continued to create future scenes in my soccer career. But near midnight I heard the plodding, weary gait of Sarah climbing the stairs to Olive's bedroom— rare in that she had awful arthritis in her knees and hips and so kept to the bottom level of the house, with our small Lhasa apso snuggled into her lap. Through the opening of my door I watched her stop before

Olive's, pause, then carefully push back the weak particle-board door, which shushed against the thickness of the carpet. The yellow light of the room enveloped the front of her; in that spill of light a furl of smoke smoothly tumbled out and swamped into the darkness of the hallway. Sarah remained in the doorway without moving, save for a nervous rubbing of her hands pressed against her belly, below the heavy weight of her breasts.

—Olive? she asked, —Olive, I. . . .

—What do you want, mother? in a voice drowned by an impatient sigh.

—Don't you think we should talk?

The TV murmured softly. I hid behind my own door, listening.

—I don't see what there is to talk about.

—Olive, we've never argued like this before.

Her weight shifted from foot to foot like a child chastened before an angry parent. Mother's bed creaked.

—You openly defied me, mother! I'm the one running this house, not you! If the boys want something they come to *me* for permission, do you understand? It's not your place to grant privileges in my house, it's up to me! Not in *my* house!

—Olive, I'm sorry . . . you're right and I've told you that. I did not see what harm the boy's going could have done but you're right, I should have told him to ask you. But he was so excited. . . .

—Are you trying to undermine me behind my back? Don't you come through that door yet, you stay where you are. Are you trying to turn my boys against me? Answer me!

—Olive? . . .

—Answer me!

—Of course not. Olive, I . . . tell me, what is it you want me to say? What can I do to make this right?

—Nothing can be made right. What's done is done. Apologies never change anything.

The TV again: strong laughter from the Late Show. Big band music. The crinkle of plastic from a cigarette pack, the brusque scratch of a lighter. Olive inhaled deeply and the end of the cigarette popped with oxygen. After a long time she spoke again, exhaling:

—Look, you want forgiveness? I'll forgive you when you get down on your knees and crawl over here. Then you can ask my forgiveness. And you can have it hell, I don't care.

Now I stood fully within the opening between my door and the frame, disbelieving. Sarah's hands were white at the knuckle—oh, they were white anyway, you could see the blue and green veins through the skin. She had the air of a deflated bag. She opened her mouth to speak, but nothing came out but the snap of dry spit as her lips peeled from one another. She turned her face away from the light, toward me, and the wet pools of her eyes split in half by her bifocals made the bottom half appear enlarged and gaping . . . she did not see me. She turned back to mother hidden in her room, and stood there for a long, long time, long enough that the Late Show broke for commercials and then came back on again with the band swinging. *Could Michael hear any of this?* Sarah's face took on another expression as though to ask, or plead, but the silence—flat and heavy—won out. She looked at the floor and dropped her hands to her sides; paused again, and then raised her nightdress just an inch to begin the weary effort of kneeling.

My grandmother was on one knee before a tiny gasp slipped from inside the bedroom, then mother's tearful voice croaking: —No . . . no. Come here, Mom, come here.

Sarah rose and paused again, her face twisted with a muffled sob and her eyes taking an air of horror or revulsion—she looked like she had tasted something awful. But finally she entered the room.

—I'm sorry, Olive, I am so sorry, she groaned, her voice smothered by their embrace. Olive did not raise herself from the bed.

I hurried to the shelter of my covers. The room glided about me and my heart sped and my breath came hard; by the burn in my nostrils

I realized I was crying and asked myself *why are you crying?* Soccer and the new team escaped my concerns. The night appeared darker than usual, the lamps lighting the street outside had extinguished. I growled into that darkness, *Wow Pops, I sure wish you could come home. . . .* and began to think of him as the lucky one. At least he was *out of here.* It was with the image of him sleeping soundly in the solitude of his cell, certain in the words of his Isaiah 54:13 (*and their bones shall not be broken*), that I finally made my way to greet him there, falling to sleep myself. His verse was wrong; something inside me *had* broken. The night passed in a fitful sleep, one full of sweat and confused hard-ons and longing that left me exhausted by morning. Awoke to sunlight, and an uncertain end to allegiances.

5

Mama Sarah did not last much longer at our house. Michael fled to the University of Georgia. That left mother and me, and the disembodied voice of Ray over the phone each Sunday evening—but at least he was calling with welcome news.

—I got a judge out there reviewing my case, he said. —You want to see the power of faith, son? This judge is all about me now because of all the parishes sending letters. On our behalf. I might get out of here soon.

Naturally I was excited to hear. But my father had been away four years now, and we were weathered by this time and held few illusions. Bureaucracies move at such a glacial pace—it took them over a year just to *indict* him, and they had actively *wanted* that. We told him that yes his faith was right and our fingers were crossed, yet we also slipped the hope a few spaces away in mind. It made a brief topic during our phone conversations and that's all. Ray must have sensed our reservations; at our next visit to prison he did not talk about the possibility. We found other subjects to discuss.

—You're getting fat, Olive chided him gently.

—Ah, don't I know it. It's the ice cream. Not much to do around here, either. They tell me you gain five pounds each year here but after a while you level out. Hope I level out soon, he said smiling, patting his belly. —Hey Gaby, listen to this: I'm working in the confectionery nowadays, and you know what the black guys call Neapolitan ice cream? *Napoleon.* Or *Metropolitan.* 'Hey baby! give me some of that Metropolitan ice cream!' they say. He chuckled. I stared at him.

—Well, Gaby, give your Dad the big news, Olive said then.

—What news is that? He asked. —You got something to tell me?

I had made the junior team. —First as just an alternate, Pops, that means I practice with them but don't dress for games, or travel. But then two guys got injured and they're like, done. So they called me up. Don't you think that's great? I mean, not for them, but for us?

That was how my father and I always spoke of our lives—events never happened to just me, or him; they happened *to us,* good or bad.

—I can't say I understand the way God works, he said.

—Fifteen years old, he's the youngest on the team, Olive said.

Ray beamed with pride. He said *that's my boy* a few times, and then, because he was Ray and it was his nature, my few accomplishments sparked his own memories, and he bragged, —You know your athleticism comes from my side of the family. My Daddy didn't get past sixth grade but he was a strong man, you got to be to tar roofs, and he was built a lot like you, Gaby, thick chest, big thighs, not too tall. . . . I had the state record in the long jump for a couple of years. Daddy was sick and didn't get to see me do it. I hope I don't have to miss it whenever you do something great.

He stared at me with his blue eyes wandering in a bloodshot field of white, yellowed in the corners, his face tired but honestly merry. Even his white hair appeared to have yellowed at the ends, which he said was due to all the cigarette smoke every hour of the day. —Well what do you know, he said in one of the conversation's long pauses.

—Pops, you get into any fights here?

—No, they leave me alone; kid me a lot, though, ask what the hell I'm doing here, call me Smilin' Ray, just like the track. . . . His eyes, however, admitted he was lying to me, and he knew that I understood that. With a wince to Olive, he acknowledged, —One time some guys tried to rough me outside the bathroom, some black boys who wanted to teach the old man a few tricks, you know? See, son, it's all about hierarchy. But these guys, they're only tough in gangs. Remember that. Get them one on one, bust up the first, and the others think twice. So I rushed into a toilet stall and the first guy came at me and bam! I got him dead on the bridge of his nose with my elbow.

—Ray, don't give him any ideas, Olive said. —Gaby it's rough in here and your father has had to defend himself, but that doesn't mean you need to go looking for fights. You should be more quiet like your brother.

—It was only that one time, Olive! (And then, lower, to me): —Word gets around and they leave you alone. . . . But your mom's right, you stay out of trouble. You got a great opportunity. Wow! France, you said? I've never been there. But you won't have problems with punk blacks marauding you outside.

Pops never said the word "nigger" unless it was required for a bad joke, and even then he had to squeak the word out, embarrassed. Still, he did not like blacks—didn't like welfare recipients or labor unions, either. Pops believed all of them morally inferior and responsible for their own troubles, yet always blaming it on everyone else. *They complain about not getting enough Respect but they never try to earn it, see. I hate that.* But he liked the blacks who took part in his Prison Parish; he loved their voices, too. Once, when I asked why he was always insulting black people, he frowned, said he didn't realize he was doing that, he didn't really have any problem with them. —You have to understand, Gaby, I'm here with the worst—whites, too—and that's my only experience with their culture. I guess my view is a little *colored*. . . . The pun brought the old cheerful sparkle again to his eyes, but just for an instant.

After an hour we readied to go. His words to me when we left:

—Hey! Keep your head up, boy, and make your father proud. . . . I'm up for a twelve-hour furlough in another six months—can't wait to get me a decent cheeseburger! I nodded, turned, and almost forgot to kiss him, wanting to leave there as quickly as possible now before tears came into my eyes. Ray didn't need to see that, for sure. But it's despairing to say goodbye to everybody all the time. Despite making the team, a gloominess was struck about me, emphasized every time I came to a prison to see my father. At home there was no more Mama Sarah to plead my case, no Michael to calm me down. I was your average teenager kind of down in the mouth. Saying goodbye to everybody. . . . Everybody but Olive.

6

I did have my sport to disappear into, and through that, Myer Bruck, who changed my perspective. Mies life struck me with the force of revelation. He was not especially impressive the first time I saw him play—he did not exhibit any particular flash or flair—but gradually I came to recognize his influence on the game; how he directed the style and pace of his team.

I had seen very few full professional matches. Most of my experience lay in endless reviewing of videotaped highlights: either goals scored or goals miraculously saved, stars in the brief instant of inspiration, or luck, in fleeting instances of gifted improvisation . . . they dribbled through three or four players, weathered a brutal tackle, feinted one way and shot the other. The most impressive feats always involved one against many, and thus my style matured in highlights-imitation: I did not simply want an undefeated team; I wanted to *take* my team to a season without losses. I wanted to be Johann Cruyff, Pelé, this young Argentinean Diego Maradona whom all the soccer monthlies were raving about. I wanted my name to stand out in the annals of sport, to be remembered and recalled in a wreath of thunder, my name like a champion thoroughbred's, a horse that ran and won.

I was selfish with the ball.

—There's no *I* in TEAM, the coach of our *Tornado* Juniors barked at us.

Myer Bruck perfectly embodied this philosophy. He had the skills to shine as an individual, but rarely flaunted them: more important was his team keeping possession of the ball, to make the ball do the work—moving it forward through long lofting through-passes, or else a quick series of tightly woven one-touches resulting in a shot on goal. Although the action constantly circled about him, he rarely touched the ball more than once or twice at a time. He preferred to play intelligently rather than brilliantly.

Mies came from Seattle, turned twenty-four in Montreux, and lived the life I longed for, having left college at eighteen to begin a two-year contract in the North American Soccer League. —They paid me $20,000 a year, he told me, —I was making more money as a teenager than I'm making now . . . how you figure that?

The NASL folded just after he turned twenty, and he pursued the standard American journeyman's career: a different city each year in the indoor leagues; two seasons as a substitute in the second division in Portugal. A few caps on our national team. All of his belongings fit into his Datsun's hatchback: several pairs of cleats, a hand-stitched soccer ball, photographs, cassettes, and a huge knapsack stuffed with stinking laundry. Soccer players lived like mercenaries, ready to drop all stability for a chance to join the adventure. Poorly paid with contracts that covered only part of the year, they had to work oddjobs off-season. It was a life lived without close friends, lasting relationships having been replaced by an infinite line of acquaintances.

It was a life I desperately wanted. Myer Bruck opened it to me. —You have a lot to learn, he admitted. —You're behind where you need to be at your age. But we'll get you there.

We stayed after practice while he drilled me tirelessly on my touch, my reactions, my thoughts during a match. We would practice until it was time to shut off the lights, and then he drove me home, drilling me even further:

—Check it out, we got a trixie at ten o'clock, he might announce on the road, our windows open to the sharp air to keep our smell from overwhelming us.

—What? Where?

—Have to be quick, Gaby! *Never* stop practicing . . . develop that midfielder's vision! Out of my blindness I'd find the 'trixie' he meant, passing my window now, a tight-hipped young blonde in short skirt slinking along the sidewalk.

Olive had her suspicions. Mies was all I talked about to her, when we talked. One night she was there waiting for us, and invited him in. She handed over a beer, asked if he wanted a cigarette (he declined), and then set him at the kitchen table. —Listen, I don't have time to be polite, Mr. Bruck, I work hard and I'm tired. I appreciate your attentions to Gaby but tell me: you're not queer or anything, are you?

—Mother! I shouted.

I was impressed by the calm with which Mies reacted. He blushed; he coughed in surprise. But he had a good nature, and I talked with him a lot about Olive; he knew about Ray, about my arrest and probation, about the times I cut school and passed afternoons chasing a girl or two. And he must have had his own conceptions of what to expect in backward Kentucky. He swigged from his bottle, wiped the curl of black hair from his eyes, and said, —Queer, me? I'm not gay, Mrs. Toure. . . . Why? I'm not even sure I've ever met one.

—Sorry but I had to ask. You spend a lot of time with Gaby and like I said I appreciate it, but he has a habit of getting himself in trouble.

She smiled then and invited him to eat dinner with us. *I prefer to know my son's friends,* she said. He told us of his family in Washington, his sister who married a lawyer, living now in West Germany; how he grew up playing soccer in the rain, because it always rained in Washington.

Olive relaxed and became chatty, more so than I'd seen her in a long time.
She was close to flirtatious. And Mies made a good game of it for her:
laughing at her jokes and puns, lighting her cigarettes, which she took as
a form of gallantry. Me, I was enthralled by the whole spectacle, and
barely spoke at all. I couldn't believe it when she said she would go with
me to the game that Sunday.

—I'll leave you a ticket, Mies said, to which she replied in her best
mock-Southern manner, —Why Myer Bruck that would be mighty
white of you. . . .

Sunday afternoon cool and crisp and nary a wisp of whisky in the air—
by this time I took notice of the liquor only when it wasn't around; you
get so inured to the daily drag of what annoys you, angers you, that
when it's absent, the surprise is enough to be disappointing. When
mother skipped alcohol, she gained patience, so it didn't frustrate her
too much to learn she couldn't smoke in the arena. After each period
she bolted out to the surrounding corridors for a quick smoke, joining
in with the other furtive, scowling types, and returned each time with
corn dogs and a coke for me, beer for her. —Would you just look at the
size of the beers they serve here! she marveled. —They ought to be big
for the highway-robbery prices they charge. Making up for the small
crowds, I guess.

It was true. Despite the enormous number of kids enrolled in
recreational soccer leagues, the attendance at *Tornado* games was hardly
huge: 1500 to 2500 people at a time, maximum, lolled around in an
arena designed to hold 8000 screaming spectators. But mother caught
the fire of competition early on with the sudden strike of a quick
Tornado goal, scored by Myer Bruck himself, and her old *Rah Rah
Mama* character was reborn. She yelled; she hollered; she stood on her
seat to applaud, then groused to me at how dead the rest of the crowd
seemed.

—Is it always like this? she asked. —What's the point in paying good money if they don't want to act any more lively than before the idiot box at home? Don't they realize these boys need our support? It's sinful!

A couple more beers warmed her up. I sunk somewhat in my seat, getting quieter as she turned up the volume. She led the small group of nearby spectators in a series of cheers. Whenever someone on our side touched the ball, she asked quickly, —Who is that? Number twenty-seven? Where're my glasses. . . . Then: *Come on, so-and-so! Do it up right!* If the other team hit with a particularly nasty foul she could not contain her fury: *What kind of game you watching here, ref? Throw the bum out!* Even the announcer noticed her, remarked on her, encouraged the rest of the crowd to follow her lead. The place got noisy, and I was laughing, waving to my other teammates who wandered by, shaking my head in wonder at this strange lady beside me; it would only be a matter of time before she had the crowd doing the wave.

After the game, Olive assailed Mies outside the locker room: —What a pretty goal you scored! You know I've never seen the like before, it's poetry in motion, I can't remember the last time I had so much fun, didn't you have fun, Gaby?

—You played a great game, Mies. . . .

He grinned and thanked her as she went on, raving happily. He introduced her to other members of the team, all flushed from effort and with their hair soaked from showering. She beamed with each new handshake, readily accepting the new attentions thrown her way, and the coquette sprang out of her when someone asked: —That was you up there in the stands? This led to the inevitable details of her cheer-leading days, and how sport came so naturally to our family, how she'd been the squad captain in both high school and college, —Even if you can't see it now, boys, she said.

—She's really something, your mother, Tourbie, the coach mentioned to me.

And, for the first time in a long while, I could see that she was.

7

We forged something of a truce that day, my mother and I—but it began to falter as soon as pressure was applied. Just before my sixteenth birthday, we learned the review had changed nothing, and Ray's sentence would be upheld.

He gave us the news on one of our visits. I had tried to stifle the notion of his returning home sooner than planned, but it was still there, buoyant and waiting. Mother and I met his flat statement—*Well, we didn't get it*—with a drawn silence; then she began a stream of muttered curses through the straight line of her mouth. She left the table in a sudden rush. Pops did not look after her, but stared mournfully at my chest.

—I'm awful sorry, son, his hands flat on the tepid surface of formica that separated us. —Now I wish I didn't even tell you they were reviewing the case. Except it seemed so promising. Look now, don't cry. . . .

—I'm not crying, I insisted. Until I blinked, and tears ran rivulets over my pimpled face.

—Come on, let's talk about something else. Tell me how the soccer's going.

I could not think of a single word to say. I could only stare at those powerful hands, stitched together by scars, the meat raw, scalded. They could give me nothing and seemed to know that about themselves, folded over the table, clenching, stretching out again, the thick fingers tapping a quiet rhythm, searching for use. When he turned his palms upward, I was nearly surprised to find his hands empty. They seemed to have nothing to do with me anymore and had become the hands of a stranger, someone I had to think about, be awkward with, only because we were sitting together at the same table. Sitting together, surrounded by discomforting shadows.

We did not remain throughout the allotted hour. We couldn't. Riding home in a car radiated by silence, nothing appeared worth doing anymore. I felt caught in a flux of events around me, my body in the center, static, unable to move forward or backward, forever in the same place. Mother stopped at a roadside liquor store and sipped canned beer all the way home. She said nothing when I opened a can of my own, not wanting or even liking it; it seemed the only thing to do, and proper. We fathomed our bitterness quietly. She said nothing when I took one of her cigarettes and smoked it, feeling the peaceful nausea breathe over my body, spread through my shoulders and flush down my legs as I stared out the open window watching a dead spring landscape. All that beauty! But we may as well have been driving through the night. The green had no purpose; the trees were simply vast roots above the ground; the roadside rock formations where the highway had been dynamited through appeared ominous. She looked straight ahead at the empty road as she smoked, and did not glance once at me.

We fell apart for good after that day. That's how I remember it. In our anger and disappointment at our powerlessness to change anything—Olive returning to work the next morning, to that office she described as her cave; me to school, all that interminable waiting—we channeled it against each other. It was the only way to get through. When the world conspires against you, you need an enemy to focus on, to thrive against. Someone to blame. Otherwise you go nuts.

8

That spring, the *Tornado* management realized they had less on the books than planned; they were budgeted for a season average of 4000 spectators, yet cracked that number only twice. The tour to France would still happen, but players needed to come up with part of the expense themselves.

Initially we sought support from the public. A drive was launched to raise money: *help these young men become ambassadors for Montreux,* that kind of hype. We staged a "game-a-thon" at the indoor arena, playing in shifts for twenty-four hours against all comers willing to pay a fee and added donation. We couldn't fill all the time slots and the idea went bust. We tried corporate sponsorship, but the banks said they were tapped out supporting the professional team. By May, when the money had to be there, each player was still required to come up with $600 to cover meals and touring.

—I don't have it, Olive said. —What with your brother in college and the house isn't paid off, I've got enough problems.

I was teaching swimming lessons to preschoolers at the same YMCA of my arrest, but that was just weekend work that covered the cost of teenage living. There was no time to find another job to come up with that kind of money. I had about thirty dollars to my name. Uncle Crush said he could spot me $200, then asked why I never called. I got industrious, canvassed the neighborhood in search of lawns to mow, gutters to clear, pools to sweep—anything. But the money was not there.

Except . . . except for one small account in the family savings. See, Olive had a dream: she wanted boys with perfect teeth. This was a small, driving obsession; to her mind, boys without overbites or gaps or gnarled rows equated success in life, proof that the boys she had created and carried in her own womb were a level above all other boys in the world. She wanted beautiful smiles, she said. High-class mouths. It would give her something to brag about to her decreasing circle of friends. She cut out advertisements with the smiles she had in mind and stuck them on the refrigerator door as inspiration. Michael got through with braces and a retainer, but my teeth posed a more intricate hassle: my upper plate was too small for my lower jaw; it had to be widened by a bridge which could slowly expand by the key-turn of a tiny tension spring every morning. The bone would gradually crack and then heal, and *then* we could worry about forcing my teeth into proper line with the aid of braces.

It would be an expensive process, over $2500. Olive had a thousand in that account specifically for the glory of my mouth. To me, the answer appeared obvious. Who needs perfect teeth? It sounded like torture anyway, and for the sake of a secret beauty nobody would notice—only a dentist (and Olive) could see my teeth weren't every-thing they should be. What difference would it make if we waited a few more years? The surgeon said that if we waited long my bones would mature and fuse, and he would have to break open my palate to insert a wedge. —I can chance that, I said.

—No you can't, mister, Olive argued.

Oh, how I begged. I *pleaded.* I got down on my knees as I believed that's what she secretly longed for from everybody. I humiliated myself, gave up all pride, swore to every kind of increasingly absurd oath I could imagine. No more sneaking out at night! Higher grades! More respect toward my mother! No more lip from me, you can count on it!

—The answer is no, Gaby, mother said. —You don't seem to understand, the subject is not open to discussion. I've been saving five years now for these dental aids, I've worked my finger to the bone and that's all there is to that. One more year and I'll have the money and a beautiful boy, even if he doesn't appreciate it. You will when you're older.

—You said that about piano lessons, and I still don't care that I can play *The Little Speedboat.* I don't even *want* to have my teeth fixed!

—That's not the point. This is what I want, and I say what goes around here. I know you're disappointed but honey that's just life. Get used to it.

But I couldn't get used to it. . . . The only one to stay home. I saw them off at the airport in their shiny new warm-up suits, maroon with gray striping down the arms and legs, matching sandals; the air buzzed with jokes and pranks, the slap of new sandals against the soles of socked feet. They flirted with the woman taking tickets at the gate. I received thumbs-up signs, some regretful looks, references to 'next time, Tourbie!'—but in the end they didn't care that much, even if I was the second highest goalscorer on the team; they couldn't care about me because they were going.

Even Mies went. He was going as assistant coach, but also had workouts scheduled with the team in Auxerre, a possible contract there. In my selfish heart, I hoped they wouldn't offer him anything, so he would stay in Montreux. I did not feel bad about it, either, and told him so. Mies only laughed. He left me a list of drills he wanted me to continue with during his absence, and then, as the plane began to accept passengers, he gave me a final surprise:

—Listen, my roommate went home for the summer and there's no one at our apartment. Here are the keys. The fridge has beer and the liquor is above the sink. Just change the sheets before I come back, okay?

—You're a pal, Mies.

—Don't make me regret it.

No way would I. He lived far enough away from our house that I needed a car to get there and so had to rely on friends. Coldwell Godfrey had a jeep, and even though we had little in common aside from childhood and a kind of wildness, we began to spend time together again. I told him No parties, that was the deal. We brought girls around, pushing them as far as they would allow us to go, but otherwise kept the apartment a secret. I told Olive I needed to go over at least once each day to feed the cat, which didn't exist, and tried to let those six weeks pass without incident, keeping track of my team's journey through France by a published diary in the daily paper. The teams in Europe were slaughtering them, lending me to a certain morning glee over my breakfast, a guilt-free relish.

9

School finished for the summer. I passed my mornings teaching swim lessons at the Y, and spent afternoons mowing lawns in the neighborhood or running through Mies' drills.

I liked teaching the preschoolers. The first session began at eight in the morning, its cold water shocking me awake, but still this was a good, fun job. They paid you to be a kid again. The kids needed a clown to keep their minds off the terror of water. So every task became an act of imagination; we made up songs to sing together; invented seafaring legends and tales; every boy was a shipwrecked pirate, every girl a beautiful mermaid.

Inevitably one in each class would become my favorite. I couldn't help it: a girl's sparkling laugh hinting at the knockout she will become; a boy full of willful energy who reminded me of myself. Specifically I made friends with a little boy named Brad Rapagna, a skinny, petrified runt—he was only three years old—who had the same glittering blond hair that I once had, the same determination to trust his own instincts before anybody else's. —Ah, you can't pull the wool over my eyes, mister, he repeated in a tiny voice that had not fully mastered pronunciation. He howled and screamed his first day; he cried and clutched his young mother; he insisted she remain in the pool area where he could see her. Usually we didn't allow that as it's too distracting to the children, but I made an exception for such a cute, little terrified kid. Besides, the biggest distraction his mother posed was to the teachers: she looked thirty at most, and showed no signs of having carried a child to term, a fact we could all see as she tended to wear tight tube dresses that stopped short on the thigh.

Eventually Brad learned to trust me. He switched from clutching his mother to clutching me, but at least he was in the water. We called each other Dude and became great friends. When his parents continued his lessons for another six-week period, he refused to follow any other teacher but his great good friend Gabe-dude. It helped that he lived around the corner from our court; when I mowed lawns nearby he came out and followed me from behind, pushing a small neon-plastic lawn mower, sometimes bringing out a quart of iced tea his mother had made for us.

His parents were not divorced yet, but separated. His mother,

Catherine, turned out to be thirty-three. She worked as an aerobics instructor. She'd once been a model—nothing as glamorous as New York, but she did appear in the local catalogues for years, and still looked breathtaking. She was something of an adventurer: neighborhood gossip whispered that she sunbathed topless in her backyard (though I never saw her), and in her spare time she was accumulating hours for a pilot's license. She had refused to take her husband's name when they married—*Rapagna is too rare a name to let go,* she insisted—and as we became more acquainted she confessed she didn't care if she received anything else but the house from the divorce settlement; her parents had both died before she was twenty, in separate car crashes one year apart, and they left her a sum of money that she could live on without working, if she watched her expenses. She taught aerobics part-time to have something to do, and she planned to leave it once her pilot requirements were filled.

Velvet eyes and the brassy blonde hair of northern Italians, that was Catherine Rapagna. She was beautiful and had money. She spoke languages, as comfortable in French as in Italian, and played opera on a new CD player, loud. She said she was impressed by the quickness with which Brad attached himself to me, and her voice, the authority of her eyes directed at me as she spoke, made me glow. And I assumed that glow to signify love; to this day I'm unsure if Catherine loosed me into the world, or ruined me forever in Olive's eyes.

By the time the team left for France, I was doing odd-jobs around her house and sometimes watched over her son if she wanted to get out for the night. One evening she came back late, after midnight, humming Rossini and smelling of cigarettes and alcohol. I was mad at the time. We had agreed that she would return by ten, and I'd made plans to meet Coldwell and some girls later at Mies' place. But she came in all smiles and no apologies, saying *You know I don't wear a watch.* Pissing me off was of little concern to her.

—Listen Gabriel, I don't have any cash to pay you, she said. —You don't mind driving me to a money machine do you? I'm not sober enough to drive. But let me take a shower first.

So I sit there and wait, thinking *well this night is blown*. She doesn't bother to fully close the bathroom door. The shower starts up, and I hear the rings chime along the rod as she pulls the curtain back; in a moment she calls from the shower: —Gabriel, there's no soap in here, could you get me a bar from out of the closet? and I'm fairly thrilled to do that, her naked arm reaching from behind the shower curtain patterned with green water lilies, too thick to see through but just transparent enough to guess at her outline. Just knowing she's behind there, bare, rubbing her body, is enough to set my imagination reeling. I stand there dumbly, unable to move, considering green water lilies fluxing with the spray of water from the shower, my eyelids dripping to repose while bursts of steam rise from the tub. —I'll only be a minute; there's beer in the fridge if you'd like to help yourself. Her voice seems louder and echoes in the acoustics of the tiles.

I nod in answer. Later she comes out in nothing but two thick towels, one in a turban and the other, patterned with yellow flowers, wrapped over her body and barely reaching her thighs. I sit there with a bottle of warming beer squeezed between my thighs, and watch as she applies lotion to her hands and arms in the half-light spilling from the bathroom down the hallway. She whispers, —Now that's better, god the bar was awfully hot and everybody was smoking . . . did everything go okay with Brad tonight? I met some of the crudest men you could imagine—*The Dragon Lounge*. What a worn-out dump. Guys wearing silk shirts and gold medallions, sporting new hair plugs. Disgusting! I can't stand being called *baby*.

We were comfortable enough as friends that her appearance there in a towel, though arousing, didn't suggest anything more than that she thought me harmless. But then she sits down on the sofa beside me and says hot showers always dry her out so much, would I put some lotion on her back? She unfolds the towel from behind, pressing it with one hand over her breasts to remain covered, and exposes her entire back to me: sleek and firm, tanned (without lines), dusted with dark freckles along the shoulders, a raised mole to the left of the base of her spine. I start to breathe consciously through my mouth. The lotion is cold and smells of flowers; she jumps when I apply it, but her skin is still warm and humid from her shower. —Here, it'll be easier if I lie down, she says, and she positions her body so that her breasts are bare against the sofa, the towel draping her bottom. I don't know what to think.

—Rub deeply, Gabriel.

Okay. I do as I'm told, kneading her skin, trying not to stare too much at the swell of her breast pressed against the couch. I have no idea what's expected of me, but I don't want to stop touching her, and so even though it takes two minutes to cover her back with lotion, I keep going back to the bottle to add more and more, gobbing it on so that there's too much to rub in. Her skin shines wetly between long strips of pulpy white. I get daring, and push my hands below the curve of her back, marveling. She says nothing; her eyes are closed; she murmurs *hmmm* on a falling note as I keep checking for signs of disapproval. But she reflects only contentment.

—That feels good, she whispers, and I let my touch swash over the side of breast just to see if I can cop a feel. No reaction from her.

—Would you like me to do your legs, too?

—Why not?

Yes, why not? I wonder. I'm getting into it now, feeling brave before the possibilities. I start at her feet, soft, without calluses, her toenails painted red. I baste her firm calves to an oily shine. I push my hands closer, moving up the back of her smooth thighs. . . . How alive I was! The warmth of her crotch brushes the back of my hands, but I stop at the crease where her legs end. She doesn't move; I wait a few minutes more, staring at where her legs meet the shadow of the towel. Gently I push the towel a quarter-inch higher; then another quarter-inch. But I can't bring myself to touch her. As though everything had been understood until now, and maybe she's asleep, and it's okay to just look, but if I touch she'll jump up screaming.

Catherine stirs. She raises herself on one elbow, looks over her shoulder at me with a sleepy smile, and the towel on her head tumbles to the side, letting fall the wet strands of hair across her back. The light in the room casts everything in dark blue, but as she raises herself to her hands now, half-turning with her legs sweeping past me to the floor, I see the melon shade of her nipples, two small points darker than the rest of her. She pushes me down so that I'm on my back and lifts my shirt; she plays her fingernails over my stomach and chest, gazing over my body with never a glance to my face. She smells of soap and lotion. We kiss; we touch; she says, —Come on, let's go to my room. I don't want to wake Brad.

The towels remain behind on the sofa. We turn off the bathroom light as we pass. In her room she undresses me, pushes me down on the bed, and then lies down beside me. *I can't believe I'm doing this,* she murmurs, but it was impossible for me to say anything . . . when she straddles me, finally, she rubs me in tiny circles against her crotch and the only sound in the room is the smack of sticky wetness there. Slowly, she rides down—and I'm there. *Breathe deeply,* Catherine says. *Let it last; relax.* She stops moving when I get too excited, and with more knowledge of my body than my own, presses the edge of one fingernail into the cord of muscle just behind my balls—hard, painfully. —You can't come when I do that, she explains. I nod; we wait for me to soften; we begin again after.

Afterward I had to pull myself from the softness of that downy bed, the cool white sheets warmed on one side by our bodies, the touch of her skin on mine, the smell of that lotion heavy in my nostrils. In gratitude I thanked her, and she laughed, not even getting out of bed to lock the door behind me.

All the way home I skipped like a kid beneath the full moon shivering a clear summer night, just for me. Wait until I told Mies! If I couldn't have France, at least I had Catherine: her operatic melodies, her laugh, her languages. For once I felt happy to be so static as the world swirled its dark dreams about me.

The next morning my ecstasy gave way to an agony of church-guilt, believing I had condemned my soul to Hell. She was *still married,* for christ's sake. Adults would somehow recognize the change in me as though I had been marked . . . I'd given away my one sacred gift. . . . The guilt wavered—if I had set myself up for Hell, it was too late now; I called Cody and told him everything and basked in his congratula-tions. Then the guilt returned. The rest of the day alternated between riotous pride and shudders of fear, between reliving my hour and swearing never to go back to that house again. But I did go back, the guilt and fear adding to my excitement before disappearing entirely; I *did* go back, again and again.

A single woman needs her toy. That's how Catherine explained it.

Splendid things rarely last. How Catherine came to marry Harry Finick will forever remain a mystery; he was a jealous furniture salesman, a fevered control-maniac, who already acted weirdly competitive toward me before I'd ever gone to bed with his wife. At swim lessons, if he came to pick up Brad and heard some mother nearby ask me about soccer, Harry would lean over to spout, —Basketball's my game. Top scorer on my intra-mural team three years straight. Or he felt compelled to criticize my teaching methods: —You're never firm enough, you indulge the kids, he would say. He was very proud to be the first man on the block with a mobile phone in his car—*for business,* he informed me, gravely. I tried to imagine the necessity of furniture-dealing from his Ford, picturing him at full bark into the mouthpiece to make sure oak desks found their way to remodeled offices. The image never stuck.

He still loved Catherine, for obvious reasons, but he was the one who moved out for "the woman who understood him best," a red-haired exotic dancer with the stage name Tuscany. This caused no end of anger and humiliation to Catherine, and when her husband called to say Tuscany had left him for the club's owner, we shared a bottle of cheap champagne while Brad watched, applauding, kicking around a child's soccer ball I'd given him. Apparently Harry discovered us through Brad; he interrogated the boy for information on his mother's friends and activities and my name continued to crop up: Brad couldn't help gushing about his wonderful new soccer-playing friend. Immediately Harry grew suspicious; he started appearing at Catherine's house at any haphazard moment. I felt no respect for him from the beginning; I *wanted* him to find out. I teased him mercilessly if he stopped by while I was there to watch Brad, dropping as much innuendo into our dialogue as possible without going so far as to admit I was balling his wife and loving it. It pleased me to imagine him furious and violent in his car, swearing at some employee on his mobile phone while his head filled with pictures of his wife giving love to some teenage boy.

When he told Catherine he wanted a chance at reconciliation, she said she wanted to push through with a divorce. Any last regrets she might have felt were erased the night Tuscany called, angry with accusations of Harry-harassment, asking if Catherine could do something to call off her husband before the nightclub owner got fed up and got Harry's legs busted?

It all seemed a game to me: Gabriel posturing in the world of adults, where liaisons took on soap-opera dimensions and betrayal ran rampant through the orderly suburbs. But as a true adult Harry bore more respect than me in my mother's eyes. When he caused a neighborhood scandal late one night by breaking through Catherine's bedroom window after spying what was going on down there, bringing neighbors outside to stare and the police to file reports, Olive rained down upon me with more righteous anger than the most inspired preacher: —What kind of shame do you intend to bring into this house! Who do you think you are, what kind of monster have you become? Home wrecker! I don't even know you anymore—don't even *want* to know you . . . these are families, this is their home! Sex addict! You bring police sirens, flashing lights, waking up everybody and their uncle in the middle of the night! Abortion, arrests, adultery . . . where does it stop, Gabriel? Where does it stop?

I ignored her. The situation with Catherine weighed more heavily in mind. I was uncertain what Harry's public barnstorming would bring down upon us, afraid it meant the loss of her bedroom, her caresses, her fascinating thought—she was my gatehouse to the wider world. I wound around the spool of a single question: when would we have the chance to clear up the matter? Olive sensed my preoccupation. She snapped me to the moment with a strike at my head: —Goddamn you son, look at me when I'm talking to you! Look at me, damn your hide!

I followed her instructions: I looked at her. I saw the burst veins in her nose and cheeks, the bitter lines wrinkled early over her lips from endless cigarettes, the rheumy murk in her eyes, the harsh stencil of her hairless brow, her yellow teeth, sparkling rouge make-up, ruined mascara, lifeless hair. I looked at my mother and saw the ravaged, disgraced body I watched every morning near dawn, bleary and wearied by a tumor of fog, the tattered cotton nightgown accentuating the starved aging of her body fed on alcohol, the withered breasts, the way she crashed down on the toilet seat with all bathroom doors left open, thin sagging legs bruised and varicosed, puffing that first cigarette before even a drink of water, that dirty *chink* made by the lighter in the morning stillness, the flatulence emphasized by toilet-bowl acoustics, the bar-smell of the house that greeted me each morning with scratching throat and burning eyes. Yes, I looked at her, I raised my head and gazed upon nothing *but* Olive in her foul grandeur, and saw only all that life could take away.

—You disgust me, I said.

Her face took time to register the new wave of rage. Her leather skin faded to ash; her cavernous eyes bulged, overwhelming that haggard visage; her hands rose level with her head, fingers sprung tight into shaking claws.

—Get out of here you son of a bitch! Get out of my home, you're not welcome anymore! You think you're so smug there well get on out that door into the real world, little boy . . . I disgust you? Disgust does not even approach *my* revulsion—Get out! Get the hell out of my house!

I did not say goodbye. A bus got me to Mies' apartment and I buried myself there for days without speaking to anybody. He would be home in another week, and I had to figure a plan, a means to convince him to let me stay. Initially it seemed a question of Olive's calming down—and myself, too—before we would make up and I would return home; but it did not turn out that way. Without my realizing, I had been launched into a wastrel life of couches and floors and the pose as eternal guest in another's bed; I was making my first uncertain steps into the marching-band rhythm of the barbarian parade, of strangers met and cast away. I was no longer on the playground fields dreaming myself a conqueror; no longer welcome to that palace where the summit of an old maple tree caused rhapsody enough; now I found myself joining the masses raging at the gate.

The Barbarian Parade

1

Mies let me use his apartment as a base. From there I sprang into nights passed with dogwild Coldwell Godfrey. My man Cody—he had grace with the girls, a jeep to run around in, and easy access to his father's guns. He thought he needed to teach me a thing or two. We passed a good year in chemical abandon, huffing ether or drinking beer, firing pistols into the black Ohio River at night.

Coldwell lived with his father off Rootless Creek. His father moved there after the divorce. He wanted to be close to his speedboat, and built a small dock at the edge of their backyard for it. Cody's father managed a trucking company and was away for weeks at a time. We would take his boat onto the river at night, stoned, and water ski in the darkness, often passing out on the thin beach of small, wooded Warren Island. Awake again in hard morning light, we rode the boat back to his house to bury ourselves in basement hours, Cody burning off his hangover lifting weights, the stereo cranked loud. I either watched or slept. Sometimes I spotted him at the bench press.

We looked nothing alike now. Coldwell's body had metamorphosed into a powerful six feet, 210 pounds, a layer of fat covering his thick muscles. A pistol in his hand looked like a toy. That first year, alone, he made my perfect companion: standing with paper cup in hand, a baseball cap turned backward on his head, tobacco chug pushing his bottom lip—confidence arrayed his body as he inspected a stolen car radio, or measured out the bags of pot he sold at school. His confidence was good to have nearby—his violence, too. He played defensive end for two years in high school, and though he quit the team his senior year, an explosive, edgy aura remained about him; a good fight set him in a choice mood for days.

—Got to get the ya-yas out, he said, sitting on his father's speed boat off Warren Island, our feet dangling over the fiberglass sides, the barrel of a .9 mm Beretta in his fist. A half-pint of whisky would set him shooting randomly into the wooded beach there. —It's the *burn*, dog, I'm telling you. You go crazy if you can't get it out. I feel it building up like my pores get all clogged, and—(he raised his arm toward the woods, the pistol cracked with a heavy report)—that's your pressure valve. *Bam!* Thumping some asshole is even better. Here, Gabe, you try.

Coldwell handed me the pistol. I held it for some time without placing my finger on the trigger, turning it so that the black metal shone in different angles of the sunlight. The gun felt good in my hand, felt molded for it. I raised my arm toward a stand of crooked trees and fired, the shot ringing a charge up my arm to the shoulder. The valley echoed, and the fiberglass boat sang for long seconds after. *Solid, Jackson.* I grinned at Coldwell . . . summer heat, a boat on the river, ass-pocket full of whisky and a gun—Cody knew how to take the stress off.

—Don't even call your mother, he said. —Don't even call. I can always hook you up with money, dog.

He was never without a fat wad of cash. Cody had a scavengerlike cleverness in finance. He knew how to jimmy a door; could quickly surmise the worth of goods at a house party; knew the delivery times of beer trucks at various gas stations. Through his father, he'd made a wealth of contacts in the Kentucky grass trade, and he had his own plants growing on remote areas at a number of farms. I never saw him handle bills smaller than twenties.

When the Challenger space shuttle exploded, Cody saw it as a business opportunity. We made Cape Canaveral in twelve hours, the all-night drive punctuated by the Beretta's random roadside blasts. We discovered huge swaths of beach lined off, but there was too much confusion to keep everyone out. At a coffee shop, Cody made good with the waitress, and she convinced her boyfriend to let us forage alongside him on his fishing boat; we dredged the seawater with his nets, scoured the beach for shiny pieces of metal. It was everywhere: scorched wire, a singed glove, crackled gizmo things we couldn't identify, riding on the foam. No one spoke to us that first day. On the second day two uniformed officers claimed us at the dock, but Coldwell—cool, lighthanded—was ready.

—Here, he said, and dumped two heavy-duty contractor bags full of debris at their feet. —We wanted to help out but didn't know who to see.

They let us go, just like that. They even cited our patriotism. Cody gives them two full trash bags and they don't even bother to search the boat. We came away with a small rack of blackened fuses, the letters NA and half of an S paneled along the bottom, and a stash of gnarled steel flecks that Mr. Godfrey would sell on his travels. Coldwell called the cache our college spending money; he said his father would be able to sell the curios for years.

We left with the same wicked satisfaction of two gamblers hot off a Las Vegas swindle, driving home sick with pills; it felt like the tissue beneath my skin had been scraped out. Coldwell kept nodding off. I kept us awake firing the Beretta at highway signs, the sharp clang settling a spiny monotone ring to my ear. Outside of Kentucky, though, the chamber clicked empty. Coldwell stared dully at the road before us for some time before I told him to talk to me until we got home. He sat hunched over the steering wheel, dwarfing it, his heavy forearms steering while his hands hung limply over one another. His face was dry and dirty, his hair tangled. Finally he said:

—You know, that's the way I want to go out. If I could choose.

—What, you want to be an astronaut?

—No no no, he began, and he turned to me, suddenly animated, —but imagine, you're in the cockpit and the whole thing's shaking awesome, and you know *the whole world is watching* when—BOOM!—dust. Christa McAuliffe went out right. Every time I see that film, the rockets shooting out in opposite directions, and just the *size* of that fireball, dog, you telling me they got people inside that?

The image settled in my head. *The whole world is watching and you know it.* We spoke of death a lot on our evenings together, Cody and I, encouraged by weed and ether and alcohol. We saw the space shuttle explode again and again on every diner TV between Montreaux and Cape Canaveral. Often we bragged to one another that neither of us would reach thirty years old as if it were a point of pride.

After a long while there in the jeep, Cody asked what I was thinking. I held the empty Beretta to my temple, smiling at him, then pointed it out the window and clicked the trigger.

—I want to go out in a ball of fire, too.

—I'd take everybody with me! Cody yelled, laughing. He clapped me on the shoulder. He gripped the back of my neck and squeezed powerfully hard. The new day shined splintering off our windshield. He shouted how he loved that Gaby Toure—*Love him, dog!*

Something in Coldwell Godfrey fueled an ugliness in me. Around Coldwell I sought that *burn;* I understood it: this rage demanding relief. If everybody loves you then no one's paying attention, that's what Ray said. We bullied underclassmen from rival schools beneath the stands during football games. We tossed beer cans off highway overpasses and waited for the cops to arrive, bolting along planned

escape routes at the first hint of blue lights. Or, less often, stealing
home to come out armed with a bottle of bourbon snatched from the
cabinets, we chased trickers in the parks. A skinny boy with furious
hair and girlish stance near the bathrooms around midnight . . . I'd
sidle up alone and strike a conversation:

—You on your own tonight?

—Only if I have to be. . . .

—Here, have a drink.

He took it straight from the lip and his dark eyes remained on me,
bottle upturned to mouth, those eyes reflecting nervous trust as I tried to
hide my contempt (*you're different, you're a fag, I hate you*—because I
needed to hate somebody). I tried my best eager look for him.

—Listen, I got a friend at the bottom of the hill. We want head,
you know? You'll follow me?

He nodded, said, —My lucky night, in a dancing lisp that convinced me he deserved what he had coming. He carried the bottle as
I led him down Boone Hill to where Coldwell glowered and waited,
his menacing silhouette, slouched against the hard shadows of flour-
ishing trees, growing more conspicuous in the gloaming light as we
neared. There, I asked for the bottle, and at that signal Cody sprinted
to tackle him. My boxing days swept over me again, the *burn* rushed as
my knuckles burst against the bones of his face, the frail cage of his ribs,
my blood, his blood, it didn't matter, as long as a mess got made. All the
while grunting, —You fucking fruit . . . cocksucker . . . you think you
faggots can take over our park? He put up no fight; they never did; he
crumpled into a self-protective ball and took his beating. He murmured
no, and *please,* and then *please* again, as I shouted —What? What did
you say? between blows to his abdomen and my mad laughter, the
punches raining down harder, then more sparse, finally ceasing once he
stopped saying anything.

Cody and I fed off one another, urged each other on for nothing
but the gush of delirious frenzy, hormones surging amok in our

muscles, soaked in our own unique marmalade of madness. I could say we were drunk, but what would that explain? I could say we were afraid, that we were provoked by our fear of not being men enough to claim a small territory in a minor park in an average city in a small common-wealth of the United States. But what would that mean to the boy on the ground with the torn face?

There's just a meanness in this world.

Afterward, our energies sated, *the burn* caught and extinguished, we stare at the motionless, mussed body moaning at our feet; empty the bottle over the wounds in his face; then ride our rush as far as it can take us, beasts of inspired ferocity, hurling beer cans out Coldwell's topless jeep while I hang by my knees from the roll bar. We shout; we sing; we cuddle dangerously close to another car and piss on the windshield—street lights and headlights a blinding whizz of streaks in the hot night—until we crash on the floor of his father's basement room, coolly abuzz with the memory of our savagery, our barbarous capabilities, quiet and quizzical and confused by our capacity for such rage—yet believing that within a seed of these acts hid the flower of becoming men—until, exhausted, we pass out into befuddled stupors.

2

Out of this life, I was somehow expected to transform into a college man. Thanks to Mies, I'd received the necessary soccer scholarship (he lobbied hard for me) to get me there, but it would take me far from Montreux—to Fairfax, Virginia, and George Mason University. Coldwell planned a send-off the night before I was to leave: we took his father's boat out to Warren Island, bringing grill supplies and a dime bag and a bottle of Four Roses. Aside from Bull, his black lab, we were going out alone, with the hope that a couple of girls who had agreed to meet us there might actually show up.

—Free pot is usually an effective lure, Cody mused, getting ready.

The narrow beach was halved by a rocky rift curving around our site like a collective arm. We built a fire in the sand from dry sedgegrass and underbrush, packed onions and peppers into a wad of hamburger balled within aluminum foil, and threw them onto the coals to prepare dinner. We stared out over the river to the Kentucky side, looking for a sign of the girls we'd met water skiing that afternoon. The river was bare. We perked at the sound of every boat engine, looking for those two blonde heads in the fading light, only to shrug when we realized the craft wasn't coming our way. It's early, Cody said. It was then that he felt the pockets of his cut-offs and realized he'd left his pipe and papers in another pair. In our urgency to set out on the river he'd forgotten them, and so the small amount of pot we had seemed useless. —I can jigger a pipe out of the foil, he offered.

—Whatever, I answered, honestly indifferent. I was to start training with the team at GMU the next day, so I couldn't go too far tonight. We threw a frisbee around with Bull—*the ultimate frisbee dog!* according to Coldwell—and listened to the radio, and did not talk much until our burgers were ready. Sitting down to eat seemed like a further disappointment in an already-weak day, but at least it was something to do.

—Nothing like a scorched slab of meat to get you going, I murmured as a way to break the monotony.

Coldwell grunted in agreement. He threw a handful of burger to the dog, who pounced upon it eagerly, devouring the meat in one gulp and then shooting us a look of needful pleading. Cody laughed, but just as suddenly his face pinched in distaste. —Aw, where are those girls?

—Who cares? I'm not going to see you for a long time, man. I won't have you, won't have Mies....

—You'll make a million dollars playing in Europe, dog. You'll support me and dad the rest of your life.

Europe.... Of course I still sought that elusive carrot—although the idea of attaining it filled me with doubts. If I went to Europe, wouldn't it mean moving that much farther from Mies, from Ray, from Coldwell? I could never tell them that. . . . Life was such an ambition! One molded by eternal quest and faithless pilgrimage, one I didn't want to make alone. Mentioning this to Coldwell would have only provoked a calmly clenched fist, and the response "solid, Jackson" or "no worries, dog." The air whistling off a suspension bridge nearby made a lonely, forlorn sound in the night.

—So three mice are sitting at this bar, see, one-upping each other on who's the toughest, Cody began. —First one swigs down his bourbon, says, 'I'm so tough, I laugh at my landlord's efforts to kill me. I see the trap, I pull up the spring, take the cheese, and break the trap in half.'

—'Ah, that's nothing,' second mouse says. He pours some powder into his drink, swigs it down. 'This is rat poison. A cocktail as far as I'm concerned.'

—The third mouse doesn't say anything. He finishes a shot, scoots back his stool, slaps some money down on the bar, and starts to walk away. 'Where you going?' the first two ask. 'We too tough for ya?'

—The third mouse glances at his watch, shakes his head. 'I'm late. Got to get home and fuck the cat.'

I've always liked that joke. I wanted to be the mouse that fucked the cat.

That my life would take me away from that small island, from Montreaux, and perhaps take me even further, across an ocean, filled me with a hopeful gloom. I didn't know if Cody felt the same or not; I *assumed* it, and wanted nothing to change. When a hush settled over us again, a fatigue, with the rush of cars on the bridge sailing over the rock music spewing from the boat radio, all of us beneath the gory purple clouds furling above the city line, I said: —Jesus, Cody, what am I going to do without you around?

—Good god do you sound like a pussy sometimes.

We weren't of a ruminative stripe. We rose, and the dog jumped up with us, and despite that night had fully fallen and darkness dressed us all in thickening blue shadow, we started to toss the luminous yellow Frisbee for Bull to chase down and catch. The Frisbee coasted lightly on a long arc over the orange firelight glow, the dog's excited breaths filling the air. No sign of a boat heavy with girls. We avoided speaking of any concerns or fears we might have had. The moody fatigue slowed me even more then, and a disappointed anger pinched at the muscles in my neck; I wanted to say *something*, but didn't know what.

Cody remained cocooned in casual indifference. Unlike me, who couldn't *not* imagine and invent paths our lives were to take, those paths stretching before me like the torn trails of tornadoes I'd once watched spinning through our city, pulling us—or at least me—farther and farther until we no longer shared anything of ourselves, Coldwell thought in terms of days or immediate tasks, of the next meeting with some girl, or the chance to make some quick, easy money; the farthest plans he made involved payments on a car or motorcycle, and what kind of stereo to swipe next; he did not worry so much about the future and what it held or who his friends or lovers would be, because he enjoyed that rare gift of believing no matter what happened, he would be all right.

I didn't have such a gift. Coldwell was my only chance at a friend for life. I closely watched him tangle with the dog near the pulsing fire glow, their forms turned to shades flickering against the fire's gleam, like moths, and knew—deeply—you could not change anybody. Immediately upon this revelation my mind jumped to the prospect of those phantom girls again, and I peered back over the dark river for some sign of their arrival. The night was calm, undisturbed.

—Wake up, Gabe! Cody shouted. The Frisbee suddenly appeared before my eyes and bounced off my forehead into the sand. Cody began laughing. The dog barked. I raised the bottle of bourbon to them both as if to show what had distracted me. He came out of the shadows and into the firelight, Bull trailing after, sniffing in the sand. —Man, this is more lame than I thought it would be. What time is it?

—Almost midnight.

Bull lay on his belly, chin resting on his forepaws, whining softly. While Cody and I gazed upward at the midnight sky, at the thin film of the milky way, the dog shot to its feet and stilled there, listening. —What is it, boy? Cody asked. The dog glanced at him, lowed its head, growled again. He was staring directly between and behind us. —He smells something, I said. —Probably a squirrel or something.

Gently I set the bottle down on the stone ledge of the embankment. Cody started teasing the dog, encouraging him to go after what was out there. Bull bucked and hopped, tail wagging. He barked harshly a few times and we howled with him, laughing, clapping our hands to incite him further. In two sudden, great strides, the dog shot from the sandy beach and between Cody and me, darting after some movement in the tall grasses further up the embankment. His foot grazed the bottle and knocked it from the ledge; the bottle shattered on the stone just as my hand enclosed it, leaving me a fistful of nothing but the jagged neck. We stared at the broken glass, dumbly.

—Bad dog, Coldwell muttered. The long grass hissed with the wild motions of Bull in chase, punctuated by his sharp barks.

Our party was a bust. Those long, drawn-out years of waiting to leave rushed with the force of a surging tide behind me, a crushing pressure to make these final hours, this night, count. There was an expectancy in the air; a certainty that tonight should have an impact, a satisfying finish to our seventeen years of palling about. But there was nothing satisfying about it at all. I tossed the broken bottleneck into the fire. We watched it blacken together, in silence, and waited for the dog to return.

Coldwell sighed. —Shoot, Gabe, I'm sorry. That is one serious waste of alcohol there, and this is one fiercely blown night. Not the bon voyage I had in mind.

—Forget about it, I said. In our passion to make something great of this final occasion, we had stamped out the spark we'd been riding nearly two years: the promise of the next great adventure, the next outrageous event, the next adrenaline surge. The night seemed to be begging us to close out with a simpering meekness, to crawl into our beds alone, preparing for the next day, the future, whatever.

—There he is, Coldwell said, nodding toward Bull trotting back into the light. He was panting hard, his tail wagging happily. —At least you had some fun, huh boy? Cody mumbled, running his hand over his head. —Old Bull had himself a big day, didn't he?

He gave me a weak grin. We seemed suddenly sheepish, embarrassed for one another.

It was time to clear out.

3

We buried the fire in cold ash and sand and gathered up our mess into plastic bags and threw them onto the small boat, ready to go. As I started to push us from shore, Coldwell cried a soft curse barely audible over the popping motor: a fuse had shorted; the running lights would not come on. I held the boat in place best I could, my grip wrenched tight over the rope at the stern, my body leaning back against the current as Cody and Bull looked across the wide blackness. We said nothing as the motor sputtered out and gave to the quiet wind and whiss from the distant bridge, the plop of waves around my legs. We listened for the sound of traffic on the river.

—Is it that big a deal? I asked. I knew nothing about boats.

—Well, it's illegal, Cody said, his face uncharacteristically serious. —Out on the water without your lights. We better hide that pot . . . I can't see a damn thing.

It was true. We stared into utter darkness. —One of those lights over there has to be Rootless Creek, right? Wouldn't you say?

—We got two flashlights, Cody answered, the steel handle of a tackle box jangling noisily as he flipped it open. —Fuck it, let's go, it's not that big a deal.

I flung the rope in and hopped up beside Bull. —Just take it slow, I said. I rubbed my fingers into the damp fur on the dog's neck to ease the odd apprehension taking hold of me.

—We'll just have to chance it, Cody said. —I'm not sleeping here, that's for sure.

He started the motor humming again, the loud rumble of which I couldn't imagine another boater not hearing if he happened to chance by. I took a post on one side of the narrow cockpit, holding the dim flashlights forward as we watched for debris in the river and the sign of nearby watercraft, but even with the flashlights it was nearly impossible to see with any clarity in that absolute night; a darkness made more murky by our misgivings, as Coldwell frowned with concentration— something he never did, and so it gave rise to my own nervousness. Bull sat forward and seemed to peer with us, his mouth set in a grin, tongue hanging out, tail wagging joyfully.

The wet breeze pressed our faces. Coldwell opened the throttle a bit—it would take all night to get across otherwise. Again, we'd just have to chance it. I held the stainless-steel railing and scanned the water with yellow light, licking the spray off my lip as it gathered there. —Can you see anything? I called out. He shook his head. He leaned over the windshield, eyes spiked in the effort to see. Then the boat rocked with a loud thump from below, a jarring crack. —Fuck! Cody shouted. —What was that?

We were thrown hard enough that I dropped one flashlight in order to keep from falling. The motor wound down again as we slowed. —Look back there, what's behind us?

I searched off the back side but the vector of light caught only the shine of furling white in our wake. —Must've been a log. . . .

—Any damage?

—How the fuck would I know? We're not sinking, are we?

We looked down at the floor of the boat for signs of water seepage. It appeared clear. Far behind us, the filmy glow of my sinking flashlight looked gloomy as it sifted and shrank beneath a shadowy green; we watched the light sink until it flickered and disappeared, swirled away beneath the foam and wake, looking after it with the same forlorn longing as when the bottle of bourbon had crashed against the stone. Again, Cody sighed. This time I felt that he was impatient with me as much as anything else. The silhouettes of bridges spanning the banks seemed even more immense and somber from our minuscule point of view, stilled there on the water, and the boom of clouds overhead tinged in mauve from the glow off the city, one mile south, settled above. Coldwell handed me his flashlight, said, —Here, take this and don't drop it. He started the throttle forward again while I stared uselessly off my side into nothing but the flat sheen of dark before us.

—See anything?

—No–

And the world erupted into the white.

We kicked backward as Coldwell flung the boat into high gear and swerved the wheel, the motor whining above the heavy wake of a coal barge . . . we ramped a large wave and our propeller screeched against air. My grip slipped from the railing; the floor fell from beneath my feet as the boat crashed down again onto the river; then I fell, too, my thighs banging hard on the boat side—the sound ringing the length of the fiberglass. I bounced; smacked the water back-first, the noise above slipping to submarine echoes . . . bubbles erupted about my head, in my mouth and ears . . . my legs kicked frantically to find up or down, eyes squenched tight . . . and then oxygen again, and the barge spotlight, air cold on my wet face with the speedboat skipping a football field away, the barge horn thundering above me.

Two or three strokes to escape. The heavy waves crushed down and my head turned for a last gasp of air, and then I was under again, my body twisting against the undertow that sucked me down, down deep, down deeper into the murk of the muddy river . . . the churning groan and grind of metal overhead . . . the water darker, colder, my muscles burning weakly. My hands clawed at nothing, feet kicked nothing, my ears rang and lungs tightened and with that engine's *thrum* going in my head . . . *thrum-thrum-thrum.* . . . The sound pounded down everywhere.

The fight went out of me; I choked for air, and the bubbles coughing out my mouth scraped my throat, fluttering against my cheeks and eyelids . . . the river smell of mud and oil, a burn in my eyes . . . I coughed again and it hurt this time, the water seared my throat and tasted of fish tank smell—chest searing—and I let go, felt my body rise with the extinguishing light in my head, the darkness swelling from the base of my skull and tiding forward over me . . . the engines suddenly quiet and distant . . . I don't remember anything else. . . .

. . . mud in my teeth? . . .

4

I did not go out in the ball of fire before a rapt world (as hoped), but in a vacuum of black river. I remember nothing. They found me an exhausted echo of Ray after the train: face-down in mud, one foot lost of its shoe, pale blue eyes dilated to black.

Saved by the laws of physics. The barge engines shoved me down as they passed over, then sucked me back to the surface. I stayed two nights in the hospital, kept cozy by a thermal blanket and one silent, on-all-night TV set. Mies came to visit, awakened at dawn by a call from Olive (Coldwell said he had no one else to call). And then even Olive came, Olive with the shaking hands and permanent frown, coming to run her chipped nails through my tangled hair, her youngest son, his close call enough to bring out the weepy eyes sliding behind her glasses; she was certain this was all her fault—and in my typical selfish nature I allowed her to believe so. Mies stood in the doorway, listening but not looking, his eyes directed somewhere down the hall. She sat by the bed until my release was arranged and ready, speaking in barely audible tones, her small hands clutched on the white, antiseptic bed sheet. Those small hands with the chipped nails—they looked like the dead hands of the boy I saw buried beneath the debris of our disastrous tornado: like claws, almost, as the fingers moved jointly and not individually, the tendons drawn and lined, the skin puckered to the crease of her joints. The flesh there dulled to a yellowish green.

—I wanted to bring you something from home, she said. —After Cody called I looked in your room for something, I don't know what, pajamas—but you don't wear pajamas, do you?—and it's the first time I realized that there was nothing there. You've been gone a long time.

I said nothing. I'd been living away from her a year now, what could any teenage boy say? Another moment and she would be telling me what an awful mother she was.

—I'm a terrible mother. (She said it.) —Michael doesn't come home to visit, he doesn't write, he calls maybe once a month and then you, *my baby*, I kicked out of our own home. . . .

I tried to tell her it was okay. At least, I *wanted* to tell her, but for whatever reason—maybe the weakness left over from dying and coming back—I could not. She cowered weeping at my bedside. I almost raised my hand to touch her, but couldn't do that, either. Mies pushed off the frame of the doorway and disappeared into the hall. —Has anybody called Michael? I asked. —Does he know?

This gave her a small confidence. —Yes! she cried out, and those crumpled hands clawed at my thigh, gaining spirit in this small detail to prove she was a good mother. —Yes, I called him, I talked to your brother, he's very concerned and sends his love and you need to call him as soon as you get home. I want you to come home with me until you leave for school, Myer telephoned the university and they said they understand. . . . Suddenly she was on her feet and gathering my things into an old gym bag of mine she had found in the closet, something she could bring from home.

I did return to the house for a couple of days, although I chose to ride from the hospital with Mies, in his car. He was angry with me. He drove with a scowl and mentioned—quickly—that I was a stupid boy. —I can't always look out for you, Gaby.

—I don't ask you to, I answered, petulant.

—Sorry man, but it's time for a lecture. You're in my car and you have to listen.

He turned off the radio; he turned down the AC to quiet the fan. Then he spoke of priorities and acting like an adult, pointing out that if I wanted to be an athlete, then I had to understand the demands, and the choices—for instance, one might want to avoid risky ventures that can end up getting one killed. Taking care of the body, not partying like a rock star. Living with responsibility toward my health. —I can help you get the things you want, he said, —but I won't do it if you're not pulling your share.

We drove another minute in silence. Tears were in my eyes, so I stared out the window at the passing landscape of fast-food joints, condos, the occasional strip mall. —I'm sorry, I said. He waved me off.

—I'm not looking for an apology. You just need to know where I'm coming from.

He may as well have hit me. He was my hero, the man I wanted to be, and I had disappointed him. I felt like a dog caught gnawing on my master's favorite shoe.

When next I spoke to Ray he yelled, *What the hell is going on there?* He had been summoned from a prison parish meeting and was told only that there had been an accident at home involving me. He worried I was dead.

—Well it looks like you got the worst and best of being a Toure, he said after listening through my explanations. —You skid catastrophe like any moron with half a brain knows not to do, but at least you have the old family luck. Now listen, I want you to take it easy in Fairfax, okay? I want you around when I get out.

And then he had further advice: —You know, Gaby, you should

have died; and if God let you live, it means he has a plan for you. He expects something. So be careful, Pops said, and keep watch.

I said okay and dumped down the phone, somehow angry at him for caring. Between him and Mies, how was I supposed to be a normal teenage kid? The last thing I wanted was extra responsibilities, especially any of a metaphysical nature. For the sake of argument let's say that, angry or not, I believed him. But the thing about life-changing experiences is that they pass. For a time the world takes on a peculiar glow, and every event reads as a code secretly directed to you, transmitted for your particular interpretation. Then the day-to-day takes hold, dims the nerves, fades the eyes, softens the ears, and you forget that anything has changed. An apple tastes like an apple again, and not like a peek into the infinite.

I tried my best to be good, and Mies did not lose his faith in me; not only my hero, he became something of a savior. I played two years at GMU, and hated it; the kids were rich snots trampling an ugly campus, and I was perpetually behind in my classes. Although I majored in English, those professors held it against me for being a jock who missed exams traveling to away games. But after my sophomore season I received a phone call from Mies; he had news: a league was organizing under the principle of melding older import players with American rookies. Did I want a try-out in Washington, D.C.? The owner needed homegrown boys.

Ray was about to be released that year. I was twenty years old, walking into my dream.

5

It was hardly the American Dream, living in city after city on pauper's wages and a free, unfurnished apartment, but I didn't care; $220 a week could have been a million dollars to me. I would be forever broke, and burdened by ragged-out clothes and constant car problems, dirty fingernails and unwashed hair and perpetual jock itch, but there was no greater bliss. We believed the game would explode in popularity and the big money would come later, before we retired. Or we dreamed of Europe. . . . I had no other ideas; had not searched for any. As I stepped onto our practice field for the first time as a full-fledged professional soccer player, it seemed all my life had consisted of nothing more than a trash-strewn highway leading to this lush Bermuda grass, where handsewn leather balls whipped across the pitch and men sighed over knees popped and crackling, like dying embers stoked for one final burst of warmth as they stretched before training.

Why put such stock where the dividends promise so little, you might ask (as did Olive and, somewhat more faintly, Ray). Maybe if I could put you in my shoes—literally: they are Adidas Copa Mondials, supple kangaroo leather sweating from a fresh buff of mink oil, and the cleats clack on the track as you cross toward the grass. You buy the boots a size too small then slip them over your bare feet and walk, wincing at the tightness, into the shower, soaking them daily until the leather stretches and conforms to the shape of your foot. You don't want to have to think of them during the game, because what matters most is the game. It's the wildlife refuge, the proving ground, a playpen all in one; a place apart. As everyone waits for the start you hop in place, already sweating in high afternoon heat, flick your limbs and shrug your shoulders to get loose. But at the blast of the whistle you are taut and alert.

The game begins slowly; teammates move the ball backward from the kickoff toward their own goal rather than launching into an outright attack, spreading the field to lure the opponent out of position and to give the players a chance to touch the game ball, to get a feel for it. You relax after that first touch, pass it off, move forward, noting already where your other teammates should be and which defender has been assigned to mark you; you roll your twice-sprained ankle slowly and feel the tightness of athletic tape supporting it; you ignore the slight pain in your big toe, which is black and hasn't had a full toenail since the season began. It only hurts when you first begin to run on it and then the discomfort fades. You pat the stitches over your left eye from the collision a few days before, smear the Vaseline around on your brow.

The pace jumps a notch and so does your breathing. The offense moves constantly now in a creative flow of exchanging positions, and nobody lets their weight off the balls of their feet because it slows reaction time; you check and recheck over your shoulder to memorize exactly how the other team situates behind you; when the ball comes down out of the air, you back into your defender and clutch the leg of his shorts so he can't jump and head the ball away—make him wait to see what you will do with it first. Nearby mates call out: *Open on your right; square! one touch! . . . man on!* The team moves the ball efficiently, letting it do all the work as each player rarely touches it more than two or three times before giving up possession—except for your wingers, who dribble with surprising speed down the lines and loft or drive crosses into the penalty box before the goal mouth.

The game is total freedom, and total freedom requires infinite choices. This makes soccer unique: teams have styles, but there are rare moments for set plays. You study the opposing side's system of defense, listen to them talk to one another in hopes of discovering where they feel weakest, who doesn't get the same amount of respect as the others. Next time you receive the ball you head straight for a guy near the sideline—he tends to plant himself, and can't turn or change direction quickly. In that instant, driving toward him, you must have already decided what feint you will use, in which direction will you dip your shoulder, who is the closest man on your side, will you keep the ball or pass it off, has their team pulled over to follow the ball and thus left somebody wide open near the opposite touchline . . . all while keeping the ball under control, and looking at the defender's feet, and allowing quick glances to survey the field while registering the voices of your teammates who bark instructions, possibilities that you have missed.

Air moves easily into your lungs but you have allergies, and you blow snot onto the waist of your jersey, no longer tucked into your shorts because it's more comfortable with the wind rushing up as you run. The beat of your heart presses everywhere: your chest, throat, forehead, eyes, arms and legs. You can smell the heat, and have bruised ribs from a season of thrown elbows, and the soreness stretches across your torso as the breathing comes harder now, through the mouth, after that first forty-yard sprint launched from midfield in a long diagonal run made for nothing—the guy with the ball couldn't get it to you, or he sends it over your head and out of bounds . . . he apologizes, says, *my bad.* The next time the ball comes you charge with it on powering legs, beat one man and prepare for another even as there falls the noise of galloping hooves and a grunt comes from behind and there is a sudden sharp pain in your calf, grass in your teeth, a burning in your palm where you just skinned yourself, falling.

Motherfucker, you mutter under your breath. Who was that? You search him out and stare him down as if to say *I'm memorizing your number* as he makes a calming gesture out of common politeness, but they always do that (you even do it after sliding into a tackle with no other intent than to bring the man down). At least a foul was called and you've got a chance to work up a set play. Now comes another choice: the ball stands thirty yards from the goal, within shooting range, and behind the five-man wall set ten yards before you, their hands cupped protectively over their crotches, three teammates stand ready to make runs toward three separate points and you can choose any of them to hit. Consider: one guy has a great rocket of a shot but can't head the ball with much precision, so his chances are slim; the next is really only there as a distraction as he's too small to pose much of a threat with the ball in the air and with nearly the entire opposing team squeezed into the penalty box; in the third you hold absolute faith that he can nod the ball on the mark if he gets the chance, and he will dart toward the post nearest you. . . .

But maybe free kicks are your particular fetish. The keeper bellows at his defenders to move the wall two steps to the left and to interlace their arms so nothing will get through. He's pulled himself too close to the near post as he aligns them, the ball is already set, and there's no rule saying you have to wait—before the keeper takes position you run three steps and drill that ball with a clean instep, smacking it across that 'sweet spot' with a steady gratifying swing of your leg, and instantly you know Yes you hit it real good because it *feels good* throughout your entire body. By the time your eyes catch up with the ball the shot is already in the upper right corner, bursting into the net.

Triumph pops like fireworks; the aches disappear; you smile as though to crack open your head. Jogging back to midfield you feel light and monstrously confident even if the heat comes back in a wave and your feet can't breathe and they feel like they're roasting in your shoes. New sweat pours over the sticky, dried sweat already caking on your skin; someone nearby has a white streak of salt over his cheek; your tongue is swollen and dry and your eyes hurt from squinting so much against the sunlight. But the match isn't over yet, and the only thing that could make you feel better than scoring that goal would be to score another one.

After the game you lie down in the grass by the sidelines, knees bent, raised, and let water pour from a bottle over your face to cool the sunburned skin. You kick off your shoes and dig into the crusty blades of grass, regard the purple spots popping behind your closed eyes, feel the ache of overexertion in your limbs, regain a temperate rhythm to your breathing. Your scalp and groin itch. Everyone is animated and laughing, telling jokes despite their weariness—it's a gentle weariness, a satisfied one. They each narrate what they were thinking and planning up to the moment of your fine goal, and you feel a hero of sorts, and content. The exhaustion and the headaches that settle in from dehydration are more like forms of a high rather than discomfort. Massaging and stretching your sore muscles in the shower you ask everybody, What are we going to get into tonight? You've never felt as alive as you are right now.

A soccer team in America is a microcosm of the multicultural society. On average each team of eighteen players dressed six or seven home-growns—suburban white boys with names easy to pronounce—and the rest would be immigrants following the money; in this tiny control-group called a professional league, typical economics were reversed: whereas a first-year player like me might make $200 a week, and a veteran like Mies $100 more, a six-foot Nigerian mazy dancer might bring home $500 or $600 which he would send back to his family overseas. Sunday Achebe was the star of the D.C. Ambassadors. A talented goalscorer at twenty-three, he wore the beautiful unblemished ebony skin of central Africans; the darkest man I'd ever seen—and the most gifted, too, with tree-trunk thighs that fell in long gazelle strides across the pitch at unlikely breakaway speed. Broad-shouldered and barrel-chested, he was iron out there and indestructible; defenders slid into vicious tackles which would have left me waiting for the stretcher but which bounced off Sunday. He made waves . . . NFL scouts attended our practices to watch him run, and asked if he'd ever carried an American football. Sunday never wore shin guards and kept his socks rolled down around his ankles—an act of bravado, a way of taunting the other team. Purplish scars skittered over his legs from where any number of cleats had drawn blood.

Then there were the aging English and Scottish players who moonlighted in the American leagues since their European careers were finished. They could do nothing else. —It's *football*, man; soccer sounds like an afternoon diversion for schoolgirls, they'd correct you. Arrogant, hardy, it was usually the Englishmen who started mutinies on the team against the coach, for each of them believed only they understood the true mechanics of the sport and its principals of training. They tended to click only among themselves, sulking and sniggering like huddled groups of unshaved dock-workers, and ignored the rest of us off the field—sometimes on the field.

Blond-haired Dutchmen; mustachioed Cubans with skinny legs; small South Americans quick as dragonflies—they didn't call for the ball but shushed for it, blowing air through pinched cheeks, *shhht, shhht;* stony Germans with penetrating blue eyes and, like Sunday, the air of physical invincibility; stout Eastern Europeans with three or four consonants spluttering their names; each team had its selection from seeds strewn all over the world. But it was Caribbean and African players—from the Antilles, Cameroon, Jamaica—who impressed me most. They tended to be foolhardy and undisciplined and made plenty of silly mistakes from lack of concentration, but their physical gifts were enormous, with speed and strength that never ceased to amaze me, gargantuan thighs and slim calves, squat powerful buttocks that propelled them at a horse's gallop, and ripped torsos of model perfection. Most importantly they seemed to have the most fun; they realized we played a game and nothing more, and that the field made an excellent place for laughter and practical jokes. For them, the sport was only a distraction from the real opportunity they discovered in this country: the pursuit of American women, preferably blonde, with a little money and a girlfriend who might want to join in on the party.

Sunday had two wives and five children in Nigeria, but it did not keep him from tasting the fauna of his adopted nation: —I'm here to learn, man, he said to me with his fringe of English accent, flashing his shockingly white teeth and pink tongue. —Your women here, they are very tight between the legs (he made a fist to demonstrate), I find that profitable. African women, they have big, big, holes. . . . He would cup his hands a foot apart to give me the idea, a fish story, his laugh a spitting one that brought a red rim to his eyes. He saw every moment and encounter as a fleeting one, an adventure, since he knew his body would take him to the real money in Europe some day: he came to America first for a college scholarship as he hadn't had the chance to showcase his skills yet in an international setting. All that would change when he capped for the Nigerians in the next year's World Cup in Italy, after which he signed a $3 million contract with Florence.

After the game, the party always continued into the night. When we were on the road it didn't matter who won or lost once we left the field and came out of the showers, hair still dripping onto the autograph pads held by little kids in T-shirts and indoor soccer shoes, watched by beer-bellied fathers or mothers in sweats; each city housed nightclubs that someone knew well, and our colorful team jackets gave all we needed for an opening line. At the bars I picked up what I could, a young scavenger who nibbled at the flesh remaining on the picked bones that the more-skilled carnivores left behind. In a city like Cleveland, Columbus, Ft. Wayne—Sunday would stand with his back leaned against the bar and have tucked under each arm one shapely bottle-blonde wearing a lot of make up and spilling out of her spandex top—the type of women we called our *Trixies*—and his infectious baritone laugh crowded the smoky room. Mies usually had a conversation going with a woman who looked like she'd left the law office to meet friends at Happy Hour who never turned up; the Anglo faction hunched over huge steins of beer and snickered conspiratorially while stealing glances at the women but saying nothing to them. They regaled themselves and any of us nearby with past tales of their legendary cocksmanship, every woman a beauty of mythic proportions and yet with a taste for the most diabolic sexual games: a career they appeared to no longer practice as they usually left the bar holding up one another and vomiting in the street. —What a night, eh lads? they'd say the next morning on the bus, iced quarts of orange juice battling blistering hangovers, evidence enough that the night had been a worthy addition to the novels they lived in.

I had no discretionary tastes in Trixies. Nearly anything would do— middle-aged divorcees with fat, lonely thighs; young college girls who needed to be put at ease and convinced; the somber army of habitual twenty- and thirty-somethings who were collecting notches on their bedposts just like me. Or they were angry at their boyfriends and the night went farther than they'd originally planned; or they had just broken off a long relationship and needed a break from the new loneliness. On those nights I slept in fitful bursts beside them, afraid of sleeping in, rising early to coax them with a cup of bleary-eyed coffee so that they could speed me back to the waiting bus.

On the long ride home, or to the next dull city on the road, we avoided the coach and trainers because we did not want to be caught nursing hangovers, scratching our crabs, throwing up into the dirty toilet in the back. We settled down low into the narrow seats, pushed our knees up against the back of the seats in front, shaded our eyes with a shaky hand to the forehead and mumbled our night's indiscretion to the next guy, or else gossiped about the sleazy whore we saw somebody else leave the bar with. *Sleaze* was the operative word: it dirtied you, clung to you, soiled your clothes. We didn't pursue nights of love so much as a suitable hole to come in. And getting laid was not enough; the rush lay in a particular depravity or unusual predilection the woman had; the game took life the more sordid it became, so you could describe in detail to your buddies how she looked with her face smeared with semen, or how she scooped your stuff off her breast and stared you down as she licked her finger clean. —Oh man was she an insatiable little minx, we would say, —I won't be able to get up for another week after that. Or, —She was so loose it was like fucking a bucket of water, I had to tell her to squeeze it between her tits or I'd never shoot off. Or, —She wanted me to go down on her and I was like, okay, I'm into it, whatever, but when I got down to her navel there was just this *smell . . .* I tried, I really tried, I got down there and held my breath and while her thighs knock against my head and her roommate's banging on the wall telling us to quiet down because this girl's moaning loud *oh yeah, right there, god that gets me so hot . . .* but I'm thinking you know, when's the last time you took a shower, girl? Or does she always smell that way, and I'm there sticking my tongue up some disease. . . .

—Hey Sunday! Mies called out. —What do you think about the smell of a dirty pussy?

Sunday would get a faraway look in his eyes and his face would break into that regal smile as he said gently, —*Ma-a-a-n, the smellier*

the better . . . I like a girl who sweats and hasn't washed . . . I like to get my
tongue up in their asses sometimes, get my nose up in there. . . . The entire
bus would groan and make sounds of disgust and pummel him with
soda cups and fast-food bags lying about on the floor.

—You're sick, Sunday, you know that?

That smile again. —Yes, yes I do. . . .

Sunday was the team favorite. All of us wanted to hear what he
would say next.

6

Once Ray was released, he met us on the road, at a game in
Columbus. —I wouldn't miss it for the world, boy! Pops said over
the phone. —Your mother can't make it, she's got other plans, but me and
Uncle Crush are driving up together, we'll see you there. Don't get hurt.

During warm-ups, I searched for his crown of shining white hair
in the sparsely-filled stands and paid little attention to what else. I
didn't see him, and coach Ross yelled at me to concentrate on prepara-
tions even though he knew—everybody knew—that today there would
be distractions for me. And then I saw the broad, fubsy and waddling
form of Uncle Crush, tattooed biceps bursting against a taut purple
T-shirt despite the almost-cold air, World Wrestling Federation arched
across the chest, belly overhanging a pair of elastic-waisted training
pants. Behind his crewcut head loomed the halo of white hair, red face
bedecked in mirrored sunglasses, a video camera in one hand, swag-
gering in like he owned the place; Smilin' Ray strolled onto the field.
Nearing our team a security guard motioned him away. Ray laughed as
he waved him off, saying, —I haven't seen my boy outside prison walls
in seven years, pal, and you sure as hell ain't gonna stop me now.

So there the man was: a little fatter since the last time, his shoulders
and neck more muscled from weight-lifting, his face a beaming moon pie

of relaxed delight—looking at him you would have thought life could have never touched this guy. I waited for him to cross the field to me, my feet rooted in place. How to relate the weight of that moment? Within my overwhelming excitement sat an uneasy sadness, a twinge of anger, bulwark nervousness. It had been seven years—almost eight; what would we say to one another? We no longer had the buffer of the telephone; *he was there.* But he was Dad; you don't have to think. I opened my mouth, managed one step forward, reached to shake his hand and he said, —Honey you don't shake hands with your father, and he took me in his arms for a grand embrace. His neck smelled of cologne and cigars.

—How's it feel to be out, Pops?

Ray said nothing; he drew in, then huffed a long sigh of air. He held my shoulders at arm's length away so as to take a long look at his youngest son. With his sunglasses still over his eyes, all I could see was myself: my hair growing long (which I knew he wouldn't like), my round face unusually taut and narrowed. I lay my own hands over the posts of his arms and we held like that for a long time—long enough to be surprised by the sudden whistle signaling time to clear the pitch and field a team. He chuckled and gave my shoulders a last squeeze, my own hands briefly clutching his biceps, and he opened his mouth for a second, but his voice caught. And there's the truth of that moment: two men in a half-embrace, the shouts and cries of an athletic field dying to silence around them, strangers unable to find a word to say; happy and light nevertheless.

—We'll talk after you play, he said. He didn't turn away at first, but rather slowly backed off, shaking his head in good-natured disgust. —That hair. . . .

It made the game a difficult one for me. The place seemed as real as the imagined stadiums roaring around the old YMCA fields, except I was less effective: the ball moved faster, it rolled past without me there to meet it, I didn't understand my teammates or what they were shouting; every touch landed with harsh impact.

The whole team lacked luster. From the sidelines Coach ordered us to calm down and just play, and then at halftime let fall a good tongue-lashing. We had played sluggishly, with reticence—we'd arrived in town only an hour before kickoff after seven hours in the bus—and allowed two goals while scoring none.

—You look like the Optimist leagues out there! I've never seen so many miscues and lost chances! Regroup! Pull it together! You got forty-five minutes to win or it's wait till next year!

As the team filed out of the locker room, goading one another to overcome our reserve and restraint, Coach Ross pulled me aside and said in a voice gone hoarse from yelling: —Tourbie, I know you got a lot on your head right now, but I don't care if your father's here or not, you don't get it together I won't think twice about pulling you. . . .

—I'm in there, coach, I'm fine, don't worry, I said, and I did feel more settled, less concerned about my father. Nobody likes to be shown-up by the other team as if you didn't belong there. This was not the kind of first game Ray needed to see.

We came out hard and aggressive in the second half; our forwards suddenly found their legs and made blistering diagonal runs to confuse the defense and open up wide spaces on the field. Soon we were threatening their goal, getting them set on their heels and missing marks, our shots zipping closer and closer to home. There's nothing worse than a 2–0 lead to lull a team into complacency, and ten minutes into the second half we could feel the menace in our attack as the momentum began to shift our way. We sensed an impending goal; it was now no longer a question of *if* but *when*, and who would be the guy. Jesus, but I pounded that keeper from whatever angle—lofting unlikely shots from thirty yards out which he punched over the crossbar, driving directly at the defender before me then darting aside, drilling the ball from the edge of the penalty area only to see it carom off the post and sail over the heads of our forwards crashing the box. With twenty minutes left, I gathered the ball off my thigh just past midfield, feigned the man on my back and sprinted past him in a bolt toward the touchline, and sent the ball across the goal mouth to Coleman Fines, a six-foot tall hulking Irishman from Londonderry, who headed it home.

—There it is, fellas! there it is, now! we called to one another amid embraces and high-fives. I found Ray and Uncle Crush in the stands and pointed, punched my finger in the air—it wasn't my goal but at least I had a hand in it, there you go, Ray—and he was on his feet with his hands clapping above his head, face red, his sunglasses folded and hanging from the collar of his polo shirt.

We controlled tempo the rest of the game. We attacked incessantly, wildly and without mercy, aggressively chasing down each loose ball; but it wasn't our day. The goalkeeper played above himself; we slammed shots down their throats, our offense streaking bolts through wide open spaces on the field . . . we took something like twenty-six shots in that half alone, but never evened the score. 2–1 to Columbus, booked at the final whistle. Ray's first game was over.

Yet without despair: my father was a free man again, what other consolation could I ask for? We passed the weekend together with Uncle Crush in Washington, eating quietly in restaurants or taking in room service, listening to the races on TV. Ray said he had lost his taste for the track. He didn't appear significantly aged since the day he left; in fact he seemed younger, more jovial, the new fat fading the old worry lines in his face; preserved at the age of forty-eight, rather than his true fifty-five years. Briefly I believed my fantasy had come true and that those years had not counted after all. That illusion flickered in me from beer to beer over the length of the weekend, canceled out by bursts of reality: Olive's alcoholism; Michael's delays in finishing college—he rarely undertook a full course load, and did not come home for Christmas break anymore; the faltering family business that had once seemed on the verge of thriving. —I have my work cut out for me, yes sir. But do I resent it? Hell no! I welcome the challenge. Your mom did a superhuman job keeping it together this long, I tell you.

—Yeah, here's to mother! I made a toast with one bottle of beer.

—She'll be all right. Everything is going to be fine.

And maybe everything would be all right; I wanted to believe him. His face betrayed amusement at the sight of me drinking in front of him for the first time. The three of us sat around a small table by the balcony, getting up only to pull more beers out of the styrofoam cooler, slowly getting drunk, then not so slowly, the TV aclatter with the hype of horse racing. I cussed when he cussed. They asked me about women and I bragged about the Trixies. —Remember this time, son, Ray intoned, —you'll never get more pussy than you get in college.

—I'm not in college, dad.

—Well, whatever. At this time of your life, I mean.

—That true, Crush? Am I missing out on the easy women?

—How would I know? I never made it to no college. Never made it out of high school. Never got much tail either, come to think of it.

Crush's loss only further inspired my own tales. He recounted his memories of my father's career among women—before he married Olive—in a voice low with awe; a voice that only caused my own stories to take on grander dimensions, multiple partners, video cameras, public places. I could see Ray's face begin to pinch, and Crush even muttered, between laughs: *Aw Gaby son I don't need to hear no more of that stuff,* but I kept going, the beer full in my veins and my pride swelling high on the tide of it. Ray's smile slid from his face, and his eyes appeared to slope downward, sadly; he shook his head. He stared at the bottle in his hand, and I understood they were no longer listening to me. I cut my story short and waded into the silence that descended over the table.

—What? I asked, finally.

Crush broke in as a guffaw escaped his lips. He rose from the table and patted my shoulder, then headed toward the bathroom, saying, —That's all too much for me, boy. I guess the women were a little nicer when I was your age.

But I did not pay much attention to Crush; I cared only about my father. Ray looked at me with his face betraying doubt, his bottom lip folded in one corner beneath his teeth. Again, he shook his head in a slow, side-to-side rhythm, staring, until, with a laugh, he said: —It's strange to hear my little boy talking like that. I've been away a long time, haven't I?

—A long time, Dad, I said. And without the slightest understanding to why, I left the table to stand alone for a while on the balcony, looking out over the dirty center of the city; looked away from the monuments to great men of history, my eyes gliding instead over the prefab architecture of the hotel complex, the identical rows of floors and rooms and balconies; and then the hotel next door, and the one next to that, each apparently molded from the same cheap cut, nothing to hold the eye. The lack of any unique detail gave me an odd comfort that I saw no point in trying to analyze.

We had more drinking to do. With a deep breath I went back inside, and the Sunday afternoon descended rapidly over orders of fried buffalo wings and jalapeño peppers, manly belches, piss ringing loudly in the toilet through the open bathroom door. We got loud in our laughter. *Are you guys drunk yet? Who's drunk? I've never been drunk in my life!*

—Well, *I* am drunk, I said as the afternoon began to finish.

—No you're not, come 'ere. . . . No really, come here, stand up and hold on to this table edge. Can you do it? Are you holding on? (I could do it, I held on.) You're only drunk when you can't hold on to anything anymore, Crush said.

Crush's antics made me laugh. At that moment he was the funniest man ever. I began to laugh, began laughing hysterically. I clutched the table, shaking with convulsions, then folded over it, gasping for air, my forehead resting on the pressed-wood surface stinking of ashes. I laughed until a great rush of tears filled me, until I was surprised to find myself caught in sobs.

Neither of them touched me. Crush got up and moved onto the balcony; I could hear his shoes scuffing the astroturf patch out there.

The tears only came more heavily, I had no control over them. My beer bottle felt cool and wet against my forehead, and I seized it desperately. Ray remained in his seat but reached over, across the table, and let lie his hand to my back. His face etched a portrait of stunned disappointment and fatherly concern, but with his hand on my back a comfort started in, and the sobs began to slow. It felt like I was a little kid again, and was disgraced by that. Once the sobs calmed enough that I could speak, I remained there, cheek pressed to table, the wet bottle covering my eyes, sighing. I mumbled a vague apology.

—You need to take better care of yourself, Ray said.

—What? Better care? What do you mean?

—Nothing large, he said, and shrugged. —Just take better care.

I thought over his words, slowly gaining control of myself again. But I did not understand what he meant. It angered me. I shot up from the table and stood before him: —Who are you to tell me that? Who are you?

My father answered only by raising his hands, palms out, a calming gesture. He whispered, *shhhh*. He said nothing more—and I could not respond. Was he angry? Discouraged? What was I doing wrong? I could not figure him; after seven years of phone calls and one-hour visits, I had no idea who my father was, nor did he have any concept of me. And again, like those first moments before the game, we stood close before one another and regarded the stranger before our eyes.

7

Ray said, —You have to put it behind you. I just want to forget and get on with my life. Take care of your mother and my two boys. We can't live in the past son—there's no future in it!

Pleased with his wit, Ray cackled, clapped his thigh. Yet if he expected to dismiss the past for what could only be a brighter future, brushing it away with that practiced golf swing he mimed when he stood and spoke, he could not avoid what the past shouldered into the present. Submissive to her husband before he left, leaving her defiant remarks to herself, Olive was not going to let her independence disappear simply because Ray had returned.

When I returned for a few weeks in the break between the outdoor and indoor season, the house rocked with arguments. Olive remained at the office to help Ray relearn his business and the place was organized by her sensibilities now; she expected him to adapt. Combined with the pressure of two people spending all day together, then all night; the pressure of scarce money, with Ray in bewildered, resentful shock at the new cost of living; and with the strain of readjusting her daily schedule to a man too proud to admit that he understood nothing, Olive and Ray regularly came home from work ready to tear into each other's throats.

—You son of a bitch, I don't care if that is what you think, we do it *my* way around here now!

—Olive, I am not going to argue with you in front of my boy. . . .

—Why not? You think he believes he's from the perfect family? That his parents never argue? I could open your eyes to that "angel boy" of yours, Ray; if you knew half the things he's done while you were locked up—

—What things? What's been going on that I don't know about?

He could not accept that for some time now he had lost his place at the head of the family, that there might have been goings-on of which he knew nothing. Ray would look about himself theatrically, waiting for somebody to answer him. Olive's glance to me would be dismissive and yet sarcastically proud and mocking, her eyes performing a little dance as if to say *well? you see how you let down your father while he was away? who's going to break his bubble—you or me?* But then she would flick her hand and say: —It's nothing, Ray, just a silly old woman raving over what she doesn't know anything about . . . just leave me alone, both of you. . . . She stomped up the stairs to the bedroom from where we could hear the clack of coat hangers shifting in her closet as she changed clothes.

—What's been going on here? Pops asked.

—You were gone a long time, Dad. We had a lot of arguments and fights. It's no big deal.

—I don't understand. That's in the past. Why does she have to hold on to each wrong in her life and parade it for all of us to see? I don't get it. . . .

At last the mood in the house would relax—or at least turn quiet—with the two of them separated by different floors: Olive in the bedroom upstairs paging through glossy fashion magazines and scribbling in crossword puzzles; Ray downstairs snoring on his favorite chair before the TV, the program following some golf tournament or frothing evangelist. I stayed on the mezzanine between them, reading the books I'd skipped during school, when I'd relied on short critical summaries. Later I would wake up Ray to share a bowl of ice cream together; more often than not Olive would eat nothing at all. It felt strange to be there, and I could not wait to leave, to throw myself back into the loose spinning of the world.

8

So Mies and I installed ourselves in Atlanta for the indoor soccer season. We were not far from my brother Michael in Athens, Michael still as skinny and cool as I remembered him, with as little to say as ever; he was excited to show his little brother the scene he moved in. He took me to a house party to celebrate some local band's debut, and it was there, in a dank basement before painfully loud guitars, that I found Emily.

Sashaying sweet Emily of the Georgia Peach cheeks, pale-skinned and perpetually blushed, with a pink rose mouth forever in bloom. She wore cut-off jeans, no shoes, and a man's gabardine sports jacket. She smoked a cigarette held shoulder-height, elbow tucked into her waist and cradled by her free hand—except when talking to a companion, when she held the cigarette at arm's length away. You had to lean your mouth against an ear to be heard. Her strawberry-blonde hair came down in a bob that curved toward her chin; her teeth flashed white in the black light; her nails shone lacquered pearl, a look nobody was doing then. I wandered in and out of the octopus arms of the ancient basement boiler, trying to look inconspicuous. Every time she climbed the stairs to grab another drink or to take some air, I watched after her nervously, ready for disappointment, certain she was about to leave, forever. I had always despised the feeling of helplessness, and yet there I was: smacked, crushed, *smitten.* And helpless.

Then, after the music ended a few hours before dawn, Michael spied her talking to a guy he knew, and the introductions got made.

We stood in the cool of the backyard. Emily spoke with an assured but quiet voice, quiet enough that you had to lean close to hear her clearly. She smiled as she spoke, in a faint southern accent with round vowels and drawled *r's*, and her teeth were small, straight, and marvelously white, despite the fact that she seemed to be a chain-smoker. She knew nothing about soccer; did not even know Atlanta had an indoor team.

Still: —That must be neat, she said. —Can you get us free tickets?

If she said it to mock me I didn't realize it, and answered her seriously. Her continued smile appeared genuine enough, though it seemed to reach beyond the moment's necessity. Her way of speaking, her attitude, made me wonder if I really understood what was being said; made me suspect she was guiding another conversation on a parallel plane, beyond us. She had the habitual gesture of clearing her hair from her eyes by her thumb, hooking it under her bangs at the eyebrow and smoothing it back in a delicate line. The hair, folded behind one ear, kept falling loose as she talked.

And Emily liked to talk; she became more engaged as I listened. She was a literature major at Emory, where her father sat as the Dean of Sciences. Now, I had studied literature—kind-of—at George Mason and had read many of the same books, which she spoke of with an intimidating clarity; I could say only whether I liked them or not. —Dostoevsky was awesome, I said. —We read *Crime & Punishment,* which seemed to me just as suspenseful as any thriller you can find today (a comment stolen from a bright classmate); somebody should make a movie of it. And we read, uhm, *The Possessed.* . . .

—*The Possessed?* Oh, you mean *Demons.* I like Dostoevsky too, but it depends on the translation. Which did you read?

Conversational dead space descended. I shrugged and felt as though she'd pointed out I'd shaved only half my face. She said she preferred the lightness of Chekhov to Dostoevsky's tirades. —But you know, there are so *many* great Russians. Have you read Gorky? Bely? Gogol or Babel?

All of them strangers to the young jock before her, but I saw it as opportunity: —Maybe you could lend me a copy of one you like, we have plenty of time to read after practice.

—I always sell my books back at the end of the semester, she said.

I stared at her feet, browned and dirty between her toes and around her heel, damp from morning dew, the nails flaking creamy silver polish. Her legs were slim and looked soft and already I longed for her in a peculiar, hopeful way. But it was getting late and the word *practice* reminded me that mine would start five hours later. She didn't seem very interested, either; difficult to admit, but there it was. Certainly she thought me dumb. Hell, even *I* thought I was dumb—but stubborn and willful, too, and as Emily was so intelligent and naturally charming, and pretty on top of that, and apparently not a snob (though she had every right to be), I liked her all the more, and would not give up easily. Already I'd begun to bargain and barter with myself, thinking that if I couldn't have her as a lover at least she could be an interesting friend. I would be leaving in a few months anyway.

Since Michael had brought me to the party and planned to stay there for the night, there was the question of a ride home, and Emily offered. Along the drive she asked polite questions about soccer and then pointed questions about health and the nature of injuries, following this line of inquiry with a curious tenacity. When I asked why she was so interested in torn ligaments and separated condyle heads and perpetually

sore backs, she answered, —I think it's foolish the way men batter themselves for the so-called glory of sport. It's another form of unbridled
aggression and you'll spend the rest of your life dealing with the consequences. I bet you have arthritic knees before you're thirty—my father did
a study on it. Do you drink much alcohol? Most athletes do and it'll
make your life painful later, you'll see. It breaks down your body.

She wanted to be a novelist someday and was looking for a theme.
She disliked autobiographical writing and found it narcissistic, —All
those books about what-all someone has *survived*, as though personal
trials are all that's worth exploring, me me me, yes History and society
happen, but what matters is what happened to *me*. Emily laughed, tossed
open her hand, carelessly, and went on to say how she thought perhaps
this, men disparaging their bodies for minor glory, might make an interesting story someday. —Did you know most pro athletes have a shorter
life-span than the rest of the population? It's true. Marathon runners and
cyclists, especially. They tend to die around sixty. Soccer players, too.

—I see, I said, and changed the subject. The rest of the drive
passed over a shared enthusiasm for the short stories of Edgar Allan
Poe. Nearing my neighborhood, I snuck one hand into my jeans and
pulled out my house keys, placing them silently on the floorboard. I
did this without any true forethought. After she dropped me off, I
watched her drive away with the sinking sadness that I had not had
the nerve to ask for her phone number, and felt certain I'd never see
her again whether she found the keys or not. I had to wake up Mies
in order to get to bed. But it was impossible to sleep; I kept him awake
nearly to dawn describing the evening: how aimless I felt before her,
how my self-consciousness had been overwhelming. —I'm not *like*
that, I groaned. Bruck said nothing. To prod him into a response I
asked, —Did you know athletes die younger than normal people?

—From lack of sleep, apparently, he said. —Look, you left her
your keys, surely she'll find them and bring them back. If not, you've
got an excuse to call her.

Dusty sunlight eased into the room, and I tried to trick my body into some semblance of rest before practice, but my mind persisted in the thought that I'd given up a solid education for a soccer ball, and if Emily were right about drinking athletes, then I had a short painful adulthood ahead of me; what a tragedy it would be to find someone . . . someone like her, for instance, to sit and talk to and be fascinated by, only to die soon. Where's the fairness in that? How is it that you could meet a person worth clinging to and not have them? Yes, already I was thinking like that; it was like watching your foot slot a perfect shot home: *the ball slips in like it belongs there.*

9

A day passed without word. I don't know what she thought of me, have no idea what she may have said to her friends about the night. They all studied the arts and had something to say, her friends. When no news came after three days—three days of urgent expectancy and maddening anxiety—it was time to do detective work. Michael said: —She's an English major at Emory, her father's the Dean of Sciences; go look her up.

I did as my brother said. Maybe she hadn't found the keys after all. Judging by the state of her Volkswagen, she didn't spend much time caring for it. I went to Emory in search of the name of the Dean of Sciences, half-concerned with being taken for an obsessed stalker. Apparently they were the family Hague. Another important discovery at the student center was a directory, thirty or so photocopied pages in smeary print, complete with phone numbers. I shouted in triumph and called immediately, only to find Emily was not there. Her roommate answered, an uneasy voice on the other end of the line. —So who are you? Billie asked after ostensibly taking down my name and number. —My name's Gabriel. Like I said.

—Never heard of you, she answered. —What do you want with Emily?

I hung up and, with practice finished for the day and nothing else planned, drove for hours, aimlessly about an Atlanta dreary with clouds and saturating rain, telling myself it would be worthwhile to learn the city.

—You missed a phone call, Mies said upon my return. —Here's her phone number. Nice voice.

Emily answered on the first ring. It took several minutes to clear the confusion: I thought she had merely returned my call, and she believed I was only returning hers; but soon we realized her roommate Billie had not passed on my earlier message. —*Honestly,* Emily said. —Well, she tries to coach me on who I see.

The fact remained that we had both tried to contact one another, at nearly the exact same time. Adding to my happiness—and happiness this surely was, as the somber mood instantly dissolved into the bright, teeming voice at the other end of the line—I learned she had not discovered any keys in her car.

—I've only driven it once since the other night, she said. —I'll look to see if they're there.

—So then why did you call?

—Oh, I called because . . . I don't know. Your name came up on the phone directory. Did you call just to find out if I had your keys?

—No, I admitted. —No, not really. . . .

A pause fell then, as we both mused quietly over the conspicuous admission that we must like each other. Or at least were interested.

Emily and I pursued an old-fashioned courtship, one of manners and mutual kindnesses, one that built momentum slowly, in increments—with me for fear of exposing myself as a mind unequal to her own and so not worth her trouble; with her, perhaps, as she did not quite know what she wanted with a man so atypical to her usual attentions. It was the opposite of my experience with Trixies, and I felt naked in such a situation, cautious. We went to movies that required discussions afterward, a favorite intimacy where in the dark, cool, almost cold theater, she would slip her arm through mine and allow our shoulders to touch, a lambent sensation igniting my arm with pleasant radiance. In the after-noons we window-shopped together after her classes, and I carried her sacks of purchases, oblivious to this tiresome rite which usually made me impatient. I was curious to see what she would buy; she avoided depart-ment stores for consignment shops, having a particular taste for fashions of the Twenties: flapper dresses and floral swimming caps that she sometimes wore as hats, and long bead necklaces she wrapped over and over around her neck and which still spilled over her breasts and small belly. Betty Boop memorabilia gave her a significant thrill, and after buying a poster or comic book or kitschy nightlight, she would parade down the street before me, punching out one hip with each step as she sang *Betty Boop-boop; boop; dee-boop*, flashing her over-mascaraed eyes over a haltered shoulder. We laughed often, in waves; we conversed in whipsaw bursts. We shared mocha milkshakes in a basement cafe, one that she said used to be a speakeasy during Prohibition, and ate guava jelly and cheese sandwiches on loaves of baguettes.

—You should cut your hair, she said, already striving to manipu-late my appearance before we had even kissed for the first time.

—You want me to look like your intellectual friends, I teased. —I'll confess right now, I own only one tie and nothing with elbow patches, and I don't need glasses.

—No, it's not an intellectual look you need, but one that makes you look less like a barbarian, she clarified. —With your locks and burly shoulders and that three-day beard you'd fit happily into the hordes of Genghis Khan. Or the Manson family or something.

—What are you, my mother?

—I could cut it myself, you know. I know how to do it right. And stop wearing your team jacket everywhere, it's cheesy.

I liked her so much, just to be around her, and still felt eager to please her, that I allowed Emily to cut my hair—a critical event as it meant losing the definitive look of the American Soccer Player. Her roommate Billie sat nearby in a wooden chair, sourly drawing on hand-rolled cigarettes and giving Emily needless instructions, confiding to

me in an aside, —I'm a good friend of her ex, you know. Let me say I
don't understand what the interest is here, so don't seek me for help.

We listened to the Glen Miller Orchestra, Marvin Gaye and Al
Green, and a small party started. There was impromptu dancing and
incessant phone calls, the music swirled down at the first ring, then
rushed back up once the receiver fell home; various friends stopped by
with curious, bemused smiles as they watched Emily at work on this
young man whom nobody knew.

—Look at that face! they laughed. —He looks like a little boy
listening to his mother tell the barber what she wants.

—You should be surfing, Mies said, inciting the rest of the team
into merciless taunts. My hair was now parted on one side with long
bangs draping the left eye, streaked with blonde highlights that looked
bronze under the magnesium lights in the practice arena.

—You join some New Wave band? somebody asked.

—Where's the beach, buff boy? the coach called out.

—He hasn't even kissed her yet, Mies confided to everyone in the
locker room, sending a wave of *oohhhs* in a cascade onto my head, and in
the time it took to shower and shave and dress I listened to a procession
of advice on what sort of fool's trouble I'd led myself to.

But I did not care. I looked in the mirror and frowned at the
hair—I hated what she had done—but rather than feeling anger, I
started to laugh to myself anytime I saw my reflection. It was Emily's
work; I sported her mark, now. I did not know what it meant, or if it
meant anything at all.

10

E mily chose books for me to read; she nurtured a special attach-
ment for the sweetness of Proust. She instructed me to read
him, and I tried, I bit my lip and gathered all will to push through, but
simply could not. It was too silvery and lyrical, all those flowers and

hawthorns. I could not read past the coy poise of that voice, its babied affectations: —For example, I argued, —when he starts in about how forlorn and lost he became if his mother didn't stop in for a kiss before he went to bed? *What a pansy,* I thought. All that weeping and swooning. . . . I tried Emily, but I had to close the book. He writes like a fairy.

—He *is* a fairy, she smiled. —The celebrated Proustian women were all based on men he loved . . . philistine.

—See? *See?* I've no doubt that if I'd met Proust as a kid, I would have brained him senseless.

The thought came without consideration, and I looked up as though caught in an awful act. But Emily only giggled; she laughed shamelessly—a laugh to adore, gushing and guileless, face reddening as we both imagined the delicate, pasty-skinned writer as a child, silk kerchief held over a mouth whistling with asthmatic breath, his two huge limpid almond-eyes blackened by the punchy little fists of a ferociously macho Kentucky boy on a city playground.

—Come on, find me somebody else to read, I begged, —a book with teeth and heat. Gimme a writer with muscles.

Emily would not give up on her darling author so easily, however. Her idea of "a writer with teeth" meant Camus, and as I enjoyed the proliferation of bodies piling up within the city walls that composed *The Plague,* she insisted we take time for her to read long passages from her beloved Proust. One in particular attached itself to mind: the scene where Swann finally chooses to seduce Odette, leaning over in his carriage to kiss her by saying he needed to "fix her Cattleyas," the flowers on her dress, and how that phrase—*Fixing the Cattleyas*—became synonymous for making love.

Now, I didn't know what a cattleya looked like, and didn't have to; the phrase stuck as though pinned to my chest like a brooch, aggravating emotion and feeling, and I drifted back to that phrase and its allusions with increasing frequency in the most unlikely places: during drills at practice, waiting in line at the supermarket, on the tour bus. I connected the words to Emily and my deepening sensitivity for her, and when the surge of longing it carried rose to such an alarming degree (my own form of the swoon), I felt forced to kiss her the very next moment I laid eyes on her.

She came by the apartment for coffee. I opened the door; she stood in the hallway wearing a man's suit with the tie loose about the collar and her palms turned out as though to say, *voilà, here I am;* I took two steps and placed my hands at her waist, and kissed her.

—Oh, she said; she stepped back as though I'd mentioned a fact she did not know. Her pale cheeks blushed in blotches. —So you know how to kiss after all. I was beginning to wonder.

We kissed a lot after that. She now came to the apartment in order to study, saying the house she rented with Billie had too many distractions, especially with the phone (*she has any number of male fans,* Billie informed me). Emily would cast herself upon the bed and work steadily at her classes, allowing periodic interruptions for sudden kisses, and I would read whatever she told me I should. We ate Thanksgiving dinner at her family's home. During games I would sometimes lose all focus and gaze at the crowds of four and five thousand, guessing that somewhere in the midst of that whirlwind of faces there was one that was mine, one attached to me. Out of all humanity, a pair. The thought was shocking.

Five weeks after the party Emily said, —I'm in the mood for murder. Let's go to a Hitchcock movie, there's a revival festival at the Savoy.

We took her car, which I preferred as it had no radio and we would be forced to talk; I still could not accept any lapses into silence without fearing such pauses indicated that we might be hopelessly unsuited for one another. She asked me to drive, and on the return to my place she shifted the gears while I worked the clutch.

It was late, the night flat and dark with a moon shining uselessly over a city illuminated by its own means. Crossing one neighborhood we were forced to stop, captured by the pulsing tableau of flashing red lights, two fire engines, and a handful of firemen scurrying over the roof of a burning house. The house looked austere and oddly white within the aimed searchlights, accentuating the black burns smoking in the siding, the black overcoats of the firefighters, the billowing smoke dilating in the light wind. Flashlights crossed and recrossed on the lawn as a crackle of radio voices scratched the air. Firefighters crouched and shimmied over the shingles, their bootfalls pushing tufts of ash as they hacked the walls.

—Don't move, Emily said, —I've never seen a fire before.

—I wonder why they're not spraying anything, I wondered aloud.

We listened to the whipsnap flames. Firefighters were still setting up the hoses; the street hydrants stood far away and were blocked by parked cars, and it took some time to find them. We watched quietly, enchanted by the wicked glow now rising from the roof and licking through the panes, marveling at the boom and furl and the incandescent sparks waving then fading into the night. A crowd of spectators gathered in a lonely huddle, gauzy and gray within the haze silting on the dully-lamped avenue. Emily leaned across me to get a closer look; she placed her hand on my thigh as she craned closer, scrutinizing the scene, perhaps memorizing it as she wondered how this might fit into a future novel about aging, self-crippled athletes. I put my arm around her to make room, hand grazing the back pockets of her jeans, a taste of an intimacy we did not yet share. My nostrils filled with the smell of her perfume, and my eyes closed as I inhaled the scent, mixed with the sting of soot; I pushed back her hair with a gentle prod from my nose so that I could smell the space behind her ear, near her neck. The scent of roses . . . or maybe cattleyas.

Then a man in uniform approached, his face stern, blackened, waving us away. I nodded and obeyed immediately, a primitive shudder shocking me, which I didn't understand until later, rolling slowly down the street. The fireman who'd yelled at me to go home, that afternoon

long ago when I rode my bike through the destroyed neighborhood.
—That was so cool, Emily murmured. —It's beautiful. . . . I've never
seen a fire before, Gabe. Hey, are you all right?

—I'm fine, I insisted.

—You got all strange on me. . . . They're scary, aren't they? It's my
worst fear, dying in a fire. When I was little my parents took me to an
exhibition organized by the local department, you know, to teach the
kids about fire safety? and they showed us all these photos of people
mutilated by house fires, it was sickening, I didn't learn a thing and had
nightmares about it for ages. These *faces*. . . . She shuddered. —I still
have nightmares every now and then.

—Shift, I said, and she did. We drove the rest of the way without
speaking, the first silence to fall without awkwardness, with a sense of
mutual comfort.

That night, Emily followed me into my room without invitation;
it seemed expected now. She said she wanted to hear music, but before
I could turn on the stereo she was kissing me with an open mouth,
lowering us both to bed.

There, we entered into hours of shy, excited searches, unveiled
expectancies, caressive assurances. We fumbled with the invisible
buttons and snaps of clothes, trading garment for garment in a mutual
shell game of guess-where-I-want-to-be-touched-now, breaking our
embrace to pause and admire the texture of a certain thigh, the knots
in my abdomen, the hives in her skin that shivered and puckered when
my mouth grazed her in a certain, light way. We wanted to impress one
another, to show what we knew about loving. Once she was topless she
stood again—she had the studious intellectual's body, not fat, but soft
and in need of exercise; her breasts hung heavily and swayed when she
moved, and just over the white lace rim of her panties graced a slight
dappling of the skin of her belly. —Come here, I said, and raised one
hand to her. —What are you doing over there?

—Looking at you, she whispered. —You have a wonderful body.

—So come here . . . it's yours. . . . And she did come, she lay over me and kissed me deeply, her tongue moist and small as my hands ran the length of her, taking in each soft curve, wandering hesitantly until the moist pulp of her sex.

Once inside her I murmured Emily *I love you, I love you so much*, and it was true. She answered with a careful *shhhh* as though it were a lament. She rocked deeply on top of me, anchoring her weight by pushing down on my shoulders. I sat up and she cradled my head into her breasts, she breathed into my hair, panted into it as the rhythm increased, licked delightfully over my face as I raised it to her.

Afterward, stretched side by side on top of the covers, blue in the room's darkness, we inspected each other's bodies for distinguishing characteristics. Were you born with this blemish, is it a birthmark? Is that your booster shot? How did you get this scar, how old were you when it happened? Emily had an angry red welt on the back of her neck, hidden by her hair, where a doctor once removed a sebaceous cyst when she was twelve—the only scar on her body, so that it seemed to gather an extra force about it, a fascinating gravity. This opened an entire line of inquiry for her, as my body was covered in welts and wounds from tip to foot, from a gash in the crown inflicted by a childhood biking accident to blackened blisters where my toenails used to be. Proudly, I detailed the story behind each one.

—How can you be so careless with your body? she asked. —Don't you realize you get only one? She lit a cigarette and shook her head, not recognizing the irony of the moment which screamed out at me.

—Does it bother you?

—No . . . it's your body, after all. Eventually she allowed that in fact the scars, some hidden by a sketch of body hair, others flaring and swollen, turned her on in a guilty sort of way. —My little warrior-man. . . . It's a primal thing, I guess. To me, the woman can't help but be accepting in sex, it's an act the man does to her—not to say it isn't enjoyable like that. I can enjoy being submissive. But men have to be so violent; guys don't want to simply enter you, they want to thrust and pump. . . .

—Did I hurt you?

Emily smiled. —No, baby. I had a great time. When do you think you'll be ready again?

11

Over that entire season in Atlanta we drew only closer. —Hey, we're a couple now! I exclaimed often, either alone or with her, surprised and grateful for this new turn of events. We ate dinner with her parents once a week. Her family came to games; a Betty Boop dress slinked up the aisles, and suddenly, in that vast landscape of invisible faces, a whole row somewhere mattered.

My ascension to the seat of *companion* caused a rupture between Emily and Billie; an acrimonious parting. —It's not that she hates you, Emily explained, —but she likes Gerald, my old boyfriend, a lot.

—Gerald? You used to date a guy named *Gerald?*

Emily laughed and shrugged. —Oh, stop. . . . He was sweet.

—What happened?

Emily wouldn't tell; she refused to talk about past relationships. I wondered if this was because there had been so many or if it meant they did not matter as much as what she had going with me. It felt important to know—how many men have you slept with? what sort of things did you do together?—but Emily would not budge on this point and I learned to let it slide. Mies explained: —The strange thing about love, which we like to think is all about unspoken understandings, is in that specific amount of our lives that we hold back from our lovers. It's necessary.

Except I loved her, and longed for her to know each detail of me— except for those experiences that seemed unimportant, like thrashing gays in Bluegrass Park, or the event with Catherine Rapagna that shot me from home, or the arrest. She would never learn of the Trixies, the numbers before her. These things were not important. They were embarrassing.

We became what neither had expected: a regular suburban couple, with Gaby taking to the "manly" duties with gusto, washing and polishing her car, changing the oil, repairing the many wounds erupting like a disease as the old clap-trap—she called it the Jayne Mansfield Death Mobile—decomposed before our eyes. I bought a radio for her car and installed it myself. We shaped budgets from minuscule finances. I stopped going home with women while on the road, choosing instead to curl up in my hotel room with a book Emily had assigned.

The changes in behavior were no less shocking for her. Finished or tired by studying, she would search the apartment for chores to do, not willing to leave unless she had to; she began to repair training outfits, sewing buttons on shirts, doing laundry or else cooking dinner for me—and Mies, too. Working over a battered jersey or pair of shorts, she would have to stop in wonder, unbelieving at the work of her hands and the commitment she had to it, announcing, —I am only sewing right now because I *want* to, not because it's my place and expected of me.

—Whatever, Mies would say. —Iron these shirts for me? I got to look nice tonight.

—*Fuck. Off.*

—What, it's like we have a regular family here! I'd enthuse, and the three of us referred to that small two-bedroom apartment as the Family Home for the rest of the season.

As the rigors of indoor soccer bruised and pounded my body, Emily nursed me with almost motherly devotion, bathing me in hot, salted baths; she confessed she enjoyed washing my hair, and I sat patiently as she scoured my scalp with scented, environmentally-approved and non-animal-tested shampoos. She massaged heated creams into my legs, and especially the lower back, which came to be a constant irritant. We thought it must be from the astroturf field and the cement underneath.

—You told me I wouldn't start feeling this way until I was thirty or so, I joked. Over time the pain became so chronic that it forced me to take special care to warm up for nearly an hour before practice or games, stretching through a regimen designed by the trainer to loosen the back and hamstrings. Regardless of such precautions, the muscles would sometimes clutch and bunch after a few sprints, often so badly that I had to sit out games and lie alone on the floor of the dressing room with feet propped on a bench. My joints started to grate and pop worse than the old guys'. Despite a battery of tests, we couldn't find the root of the problem. A fact to live with, the doctors said. *You've got a bum back, Toure,* they reiterated. *Bad genes.* Yeah, well, what about the legs? the pain there?

Warm up properly . . . take time to cool down and stretch . . . here are some anti-inflammatories . . . visit the masseuse daily . . . here are some muscle relaxers . . . stretch morning and evening even on off days. . . . The litany went on forever, and only served to alleviate, never erase, the discomfort.

I did not want to risk missing the outdoor season—my favorite game—by being marked so young as an injured, risky prospect, so I played through the pain, sometimes in agony, finally convincing the trainer to give Novocain shots to numb my back before games. I swore the man to secrecy and did not ever tell Emily, who wouldn't approve. I thought there was something honorable in keeping mute about suffering, and did not consider the ramifications of what might be happening to my body regardless of the constant comments listed by my girlfriend. I had her to take care of me, after all.

Besides, by this time—February—there were more troubling issues. We never talked about what would happen when the inevitable occurred and I would leave. Instead, early Spring brought meaningless arguments.

Once, waiting at home after practice, she told me I stank, blanching visibly at my approach. —My god, take a shower before you kiss me.

—No, come on, girl, let's get it *on*.

—Don't you come near me smelling like that! Get in the shower!

—You'd do it if you loved me.

—Damn it, I would not! and who do you think you are to tell me what I should or shouldn't do! she shouted, and stormed out of the apartment. I waited in a few moments of indifference, casually changing to another T-shirt—a clean one she had laid out on the bed—and with a sudden, inexplicable surge of fear (*you've lost her!*)— sprinted down the stairwell of the building, to find her pacing the yard, fuming, an unlit cigarette shaking in her hand.

—Emily, I'm sorry, I'm sorry. . . .

—I love you, she said.

—I love you, I answered. We embraced for a long time, swaying.

—I was being stupid and selfish.

—No, I was being demanding.

—You're not being demanding to ask me to shower after practice, I said.

We let the matter drop and walked up the street holding hands, and never discussed it again. We didn't have to; there were other things to get angry over: unwashed dishes, empty refrigerators, unavailability because of studies or training. Possible contracts in distant cities hovered about us.

But so much of Emily kept me devoted to her: her unique, adventurous spirit, and culture; her characteristic way of approaching anything new with the idea *why not?* rather than *why?*; her intense, anthropological curiosity toward the aggression of men. —Tell me what turns a man on, she would ask. —Do you like a woman to talk dirty during sex? Don't make a face; I'm serious. Do you like to hear a woman say a word like *fuck*, or *cunt?* Like, don't men want a woman to come up to them, grab the hair on the back of his head and say, *fuck me?* . . .

—Sure. . . . A guy can appreciate that.

She smiled and clutched the back of my head. —I want you to fuck me. . . .

She described her orgasms as more of an emotional experience than a physical one; never has a woman come so fast; she swore it was the first time she had ever managed it with a man. —It's like as soon as you enter me, and I have you in my arms and I'm thinking it's you, Gaby. . . . You only have to move a few times and then it rushes all over me. . . . She was unusually quiet during sex, except for that moment, when she began to sigh and heave and I would open my eyes to watch her face. Sometimes she would have tears on her cheeks after an orgasm, a fact that only led me to think I could not do without her.

12

And then . . . *gone.* This story has no denouement; it breaks. We believed in our love; therefore, we should be willing to give up much to keep it. When the contract came through for another outdoor season, this time in faraway Albany, New York, the question came: who was it going to be? Does Gabriel give up his career in sports? Does Emily transfer schools? She had a free deal at Emory as the daughter of a school dean. She was a year from graduation and a transfer would set her back another year due to lost credits. And she wanted that Ph.D. I wanted her to have it, too.

—I'll move to Albany when I graduate, Emily promised.

—I may be somewhere else by then.

—So I'll move where your next contract goes.

—But what do we do the season after that? You can't keep moving from school to school each year. You'll be forty before you can teach.

—But, she said. —But. . . .

13

Knowing I would crumble before her, I tried to steal off at dawn while Emily slept, dressing at the sight of her sleeping face framed by a warming light from the window; from her chest of drawers I took a purple bandanna that she often used to keep her hair from her eyes. As I stuffed it into my back pocket, I saw her looking at me. *Come here*, she said. I did not move. She raised herself into a sitting position, the sheet falling off her shoulder and baring her, naked, soft with sleep.

She wanted to make love again. Her arms reached toward me. I could not; I could not. I held her hands in both of mine: me standing, her sitting almost side-saddle on the bed, and we stared a long time. I moved to the door and heard her, seconds after, following. Her last word to me, as she gave me a final hug and kiss before I got into my car for the long trek north:

—Gosh. . . . And it perfectly summarized the lightning-strike speed of those five months, a speed that only gathered force as the time wound down to my departure. She did not cry at all, not once in front of me, but as I drove along the lonely highways, missing exit ramps and connections and having to circle back endlessly, I was a mess of sobs and curses.

Wasn't this love? Could it have been anything less? How could two people become so molded to one another in such short time if it wasn't the most necessary of moments? She was my first glimmer of light. What was the point of having it for an instant—just so you could know what you were waving at as it passed? just so you can be able to say, *I've been there?*

Fuck those who say it's better to have loved and lost than never to have loved at all. I don't know what that means. Emily and I did not lose one another; *I left her. She stayed.*

The stadium crowd filled with invisible faces again, one which, unseen as yet, would go home with me that night. One which could be borrowed.

Never since have I seen a strawberry-blonde slinking up the aisles in a Betty Boop dress; no, she's not on the streets, either—nor in bars or parks or gyms or at anybody else's party. She's a figment now. She's a history all to herself, a thought at night when I lie awake in bed; a photo in a drawer. She's a sentence I repeat on evenings when I'm alone and sad and caught up in my life, those evenings when I stretch along my bed and listen to my empty apartment: *Emily I had you, I had you, I had you.*

14

In the disappointing city of Albany, I was coming to the end of a road, though I did not know it then. I knew only that I did not want to be there. I attended every practice and trained as hard as ever, but once off the field, thought little of the game. Instead I would drive to the river wharf and sit in silent rumination—or else shout out over the water, shouting words that signified nothing. Still, they gave me a temporary relief. There was much on my mind, all of it weighted with a general melancholy. Although I trained hard, my back and legs worked as well as a cramped fist. I lived on handfuls of muscle relaxers and anti-inflammatories that brought out small white sores beneath my tongue. I knew no one and missed Emily; the city was a bust and the team a mess—in an effort to save money, many players lived and trained alone in their home cities. They showed up on game days.

Arguments erupted on the field, inevitably between the eight who trained together daily and the other moonlighters: —Who the fuck are you to tell me he was my mark? a defender would rant after the other team scored. —I don't even know your fucking name, get out of my face! It rained continuously over the city, and then with the sun came steam and stilled, sullen ozone. A postcard from Mies underscored his luck and the failure of mine: having accepted a contract in Jacksonville, Florida, he complained of sunburn and the rabid temptation wrought by women in thong bikinis. Also, he'd agreed to a recent appointment to the National Team.

For the first time, I found myself wondering what I might do outside of soccer—and managed only to sit with lips pursed, mind blank, my vague thoughts skittering into darkness like fishfins shooting off into watery shadows. Then Viktor Savic arrived, and presented my life to me in shocking, naked relief.

Savic hailed from Yugoslavia; more exactly, *Serbia*. Nineteen years old and blessed with the gifts of a Sunday Achebe (without the irrepressible joy; Savic played in grim scowl), he fled the Balkans as soon as Croatia and Slovenia declared their unrecognized independence.

—Where is Yugoslavia? I asked, innocent.

—*Serbia*, he corrected me, punching his chest. —I am Serb! Yugoslavia never exists, that was only Tito.

Viktor came from Banja Luka, a town which, at the time, was busy expelling and exterminating Croats and Muslims to purify their soil for Serbians only, a miserable exodus we saw nightly on the news. He told me not to believe the reports of genocide; said he did not care even if they were true, for if the Serbs *were* killing civilians it was only to make up for the years of murder and suffering his ethnicity had endured. I asked, —If you hate Croats and Muslims so much, why didn't you stay and fight?

—And get killed? To waste these skills, this body? You *listen* to me: Viktor Savic was born from a bolt of lightning, raised by lions. . . . He said he didn't hate the other Yugoslavs because you couldn't hate those who were hardly human, and he made a chopping motion with his hand while he shook his head with certainty, professing that this was a question of justice a naive American would never understand.

But it would be misleading to insinuate that we discussed politics often. Before Viktor was a Serb, he was VICTOR SAVIC (born from a bolt of lightning, raised by lions, etc), and his allegiances and concerns evolved from this fine point. Never have I seen a man pass as much time before a mirror, grooming: changing and modeling his many outfits, working with his violent, brilliant, treated hair of tightly undulating waves. He talked to himself constantly, reciting trivial hymns to Savic glory; he spent all of his money on shoes, clothes, and hard liquor, with a particular taste for rum, which led to a constant need for small loans from the rest of the team—loans we learned he would never repay, and so at practice he suffered ferocious tackles during scrimmages. Despite his whining, his 'lightning body' weathered the attacks, so I'll have to recognize the gods had at least built him tough.

If he scored a goal he celebrated a lonely ecstasy, shouting *Yes! Now I am the best!* and ran back to midfield alone, for no one on the team had the heart to congratulate him. We rolled our eyes as he chanted *the best the best the best!* In the locker room after the game he described to us in stilted tongue how he managed such a magnificent performance, and castigated the rest of the team for not giving him more support on the field, for if we just gave him the ball he could do the rest on his own. Despite his detailed descriptions of how to score a beautiful goal, nobody cheered him on; he had a knack for scoring on days the team lost. Eventually he would take his place near me and sulk. —What is every person's problem? he would ask, to which there would be no answer.

Viktor endured an untold number of practical jokes: he filled his water bottle with iced cola rather than water, and sometimes gulped it down before realizing the soda had been replaced with coffee or sugared tea, which he would spew out in a combined spray and curse; he received dubious instructions in English: —Listen Viktor, the ladies love for you to tell them they wear a lot of makeup, it shows you're paying close attention. Here's a good opening line, you say, 'I saw your painted face from across the room.' . . . Works every time.

Or, —Remember to always ask if she showered today. Smell her, show her you're smelling her, they dig that.

—Yes, yes, I will remember. . . . We could see his sallow eyes strain with concentration, the red pimples on his neck flaring as he repeated the words under his breath, but luckily for him he had a poor memory.

The coaching staff assigned him to live with me. —Time for the ladies! he shouted once his bags were unpacked. He divided his clothes with surprising neatness, stacking them on the floor in appropriate little piles grouped by shirts, socks, pants. We did not have a chest of drawers then, and without Emily around to keep me straight, I'd relapsed into a young jock's typically slovenly ways. Viktor perused the apartment with apparent distaste. —The spirits, Gabe? You don't have no rum? And me with no money . . . I pay you later.

Viktor Savic, tornado of pride and conceit, the disaster companion. He moved the portable stereo from my room and cranked heavy metal music, a genre I had lost my taste for, influenced by Emily toward the fineries of fifties' jazz; he was compulsively neat and would wake me in the middle of the night if I left dishes in the sink—*disease there, man!*— or if I shaved and did not clean the water basin after. He borrowed my car when I napped after practice even though he had no driver's license, and brought it back with an empty gas tank and dented fenders, raging over the idiocy of the driving public; he pawned CD's of mine which he didn't like and used the money to buy music more to his taste. Otherwise, in spite of his rampant egotism, if he liked you, he treated you with the respect of a brother. With his accent and athletic body, and his wide local publicity as the first refugee from the Balkans to come to Albany (where he '*anchored* the Capital attack,' a clouded truth that gave another reason for teamwide resentment), the women came home with him in droves, in groups of two or three. Miniature orgies reigned in that apartment, although with questionable bodies, which led me to chauffeuring the man to the doctor a few times; the type of ladies who say please with two syllables, who rasp when they laugh, who ask what your problem is and tell you to loosen up, who shout when they make love and walk around the apartment meaty-naked and jiggling, all cottage-cheese and hirsute flesh, and start the day with a rum and coke then call for weeks afterward asking why they never heard from Viktor.

—Ah, she is in love with me, Viktor would sniff distastefully.
—These American women, always in love. I tell them ridiculous, I leave
soon. (He smiled with his proper elocution of English.) —I play in
France next year, it is certain. My friend Serge helps me find a team.

He spoke of it often, his future in Europe; I chalked it up to empty
bragging, even after he said: —Maybe you come with me, Gabe! You
can play there, I have no respect for the French. You want to play in
France?

—Sure, Viktor, why not.

—I ask my friend Serge to help you. I tell you, I am connected.

We should have both concentrated more on the season at hand
than dreams of European leagues. Albany was a troubled team, with
one win after five games, and attendance in the low hundreds despite
that the regional recreational leagues had rosters in the thousands, with
immigrants from all over. None of us had our heart on the field—me
most of all, with the stiffness of my body and the soreness that came
afterward resigning me to the role of a hearty cheerleader who did
little else than throw a wrench into the other team's attack. But Viktor
wasn't very interested in Albany except for what he could take from
it personally.

15

I awoke one night to Viktor crawling onto my bed with a trixie, whis-
pering into my ear drafts of cigarette smoke and rum, —Gabe . . .
leettle leettle *Gabriel*. . . . He shook me. —Wake up, my dear friend, I
have a surprise for you. Meet Lynette, she wants to say hello.

A drunken giggle came from behind me in the darkness, female
and crafty, a languorous weight at the foot of my bed. I shaded my eyes
from a light that was not there.

—You mad we woke you up?

—No, I mumbled. —What's going on?

—She wants us both, Viktor said, close. I flinched at the stench of the bar they'd left. —She like the soccer players.

—I've seen you Gabriel Toure, you have really nice legs, the woman's voice, gravelly and tired, said to me from the vague end of the bed. She broke off the sentence with a yawn. She began to tug the sheets which covered me, sheets I held lightly and then let go. —Oh look, he sleeps naked, I just *knew* that, she said. To Viktor she asked, — You sure he don't mind?

—Gabriel? Oh, he *loves* this, he answered. —Go on with him, go ... yes yes, go, go! Look, is he stopping you? Listen, Lynette, listen to me, I like the way you smell. Do you shower today?

Lynette answered with a murmured *What?* and snorted swallowed laughter, stopping as she massaged my sex before putting it in her mouth; and me, barely awake, pushed my hand through tough curly hair as I tried to blink dust from my eyes. Viktor announced that he would undress her now, and the stupor of sleep soon left me as things got more active, Emily's phrase of *why not?* rather than *why?* echoing in my head. Viktor whispered, —Ah, look at that, she like that, she like that. ... He entered her from behind, grabbing her whimpled waist and pushing into her with a loud cry of *Hah! Hai! Hah!* Lynette grunted into my stomach and I watched her fleshy body shimmy and shake. —She like that? Tell me, woman, you like that?

She murmured in answer.

—No, you tell me! You say you love the Viktor fuck!

—Yes, baby, I like that. ... Give me some of that cock ... gimme some. ... And then she hushed, and groaned as she swallowed my sex again. I could not help laughing out loud, at the bad porno dialogue, at the ridiculous unreality in the air, the adolescent fantasy which had become my life; and then there was the sight of Viktor with such livid determination on his face, a face fisted with anger and contempt as he drove it home with shouts and curses that would need translation. He slapped her face a few times, playfully at first, then with brutality as

he said he wanted to hear her cry out. Lynette did her best in trying
to please us both, raising herself from me briefly so Viktor could hear
what he wanted, then plunging back down. I got up to my knees so I
could see better, with Lynette down on all fours between us, a soft
white blob capped by wiry brown bush ending below my waist. Viktor
slapped me once and I told him to cut it out, and then we started
laughing again, throwing high-fives to one another as he chanted *I got
the bitch home, I brought her to you, I am your best friend.* —I am Viktor
Savic!

He pulled out and bent over her, biting her hard on the thigh, on
her back, on the cheeks until she complained —Cut that shit out, man,
I fucking don't go in for that! Viktor responded with a sinister *heh heh
heh,* and bit her again, on the neck this time.

—Stop it, dammit!

—Viktor! Relax, man. . . .

He didn't listen. He flipped her over with cruel dexterity, a carnal
anger, and pulled her to him so he could twine his arms about her legs,
holding her ankles against his shoulders. —She don't fool me, she like it!
Do she know who she is fucking? *Huh?* She loves Viktor Savic!

My whore, he shouted. *My cunt.* It was brutal. The show turned
me off and I laid back against the wall, astounded, disturbed.

—Say it, woman! You say my name!

—Viktor Savic. . . . Lynette pressed her hands above her head,
reached for my thighs.

—You like the stick of Viktor Savic! Say it!

—Give me that stick, that Savic stick, she grunted, and it was
then that I realized how drunk she must have been, as her words
slurred so in her mouth that I couldn't tell if she was saying *Savic* or
Savage. He smacked her legs ferociously, the contact flying flat and
sharp in the humid air, in the darkness through which I could still make
out pink handprints glowing on her pale, plump thighs. Her cries
mixed pain and pleasure; she tossed her head from side-to-side saying

stop, and *no*, and *cut out that shit*, but also *give me that stick, baby, that savage stick*. . . . Viktor rode victorious above her.

It drew on forever. I searched the room for something else to look at, but there they were, life-size and unavoidable. The happiest of the bunch was me when finally he pulled out to jerk off onto her belly, sporting a stubby cock barely a fist long that coughed out no more than a tiny gob of white spit, and that, tiredly. I would have expected more from Viktor's much-proclaimed virility. But at least it was over.

Viktor wiped the back of his hand against her thigh. He told her to rub it in with her fingers, which she did with an absent smile and looking around. She seemed satisfied with an air of contentment that I would return to again and again in my mind, once the events of this night came back to haunt me. When he tried to leave her, she caught him for a moment with her legs, locking on to him, giggling as he struggled angrily, her slack breasts shaking. Finally he broke free and stormed from the room as if there had been a vicious argument that had left him offended. He slammed the door behind him, and soon we heard the falling shower in the bathroom, a screech of air through the pipes above my ceiling.

Lynette sighed. I could see her well now with my eyes adjusted to the absence of light—the pockmarked skin, the light mustache, the bulbous belly, an ugly ass that made me think of flatulence. At the time I held rather idealistic, fascist beliefs toward the proper erotic form of the human body. I wanted her to leave. The mood in the room felt prohibitive and sulky. —Are you all right? I asked.

—Is he coming back?

—I don't think so. I don't know. Why don't you go find him.

—You want to give me a go? she asked, looking up at me, her hands kneading her breasts. I turned my head away.

—No . . . no, thank you. You should just go on home, I guess.

—But you didn't even come! she said with a swipe between my legs.

—That's all right . . . thank you. I'm not much in the mood anyway.

She asked if she could crash with me overnight and I told her no. She shrugged again, sighed again, said, *well then . . .* and raised herself from the bed. She dressed slowly, slow enough to suggest she was waiting in case I changed my mind as she searched for her clothes, willing to forgive me. But no more words were coming from my mouth, glad as I was to see her go, and my eyes slipped shut as she shut the door behind her. With the sound of the outside hallway door clicking closed, I went into Viktor's room to check on him, to ask what had gone on that night and where did he find her, only to see him already facedown on his bed—nothing more than a neat cushion of folded blankets on the floor—and snoring.

An awful sense remained. . . . I couldn't go back to sleep for a long time. A corrupt spirit hung in the air, a foreboding ire, a malice that stood me on guard as though I felt watched and judged, as though perturbed ghosts sailed about the room. A certain sickness, an obscenity. . . . Me? I went around the apartment to check the locks, inspected the power fixtures to make sure nothing smoldered there, waiting to erupt; I stared out the window to our street for anything amiss. But there was nothing. My body stood on alert, warning me of an unidentified presence, a bad feeling like a black cloud lingering, pungent, in my room. But there was nothing there. Eventually the only word available for it was Viktor's name. Savic disturbed me. And there we were, not yet halfway through the season.

16

Viktor's infamous friend Serge Criquillion turned out to be as surprisingly real as the Serbian claimed him to be. There was something to this French Connection after all. The man's visit made good timing, too, as my physical problems had started to wane; perhaps it was the stagnant humidity which kept my muscles loose. Somehow the team had managed an unanticipated five-game winning streak and we held outside hopes for a spot in the playoffs; and Gaby Toure, released from the constraints of tight muscles and sore backdom, had recently shown both "flair and ingenuity with long threatening runs from the backfield" (I quote local articles pasted into my tattered scrapbook). As my body improved so did my confidence, and my enjoyment of the game. I was eager to play again.

Criquillion was a sports agent in France who had European rights to Viktor. He planned to sign him to a team in the premier league for the following season. Yugoslavians, famous for their ball control and flashy, Brazilian style of play, had become a hot item in Europe with a diaspora of players fleeing the consequences of the war there. Criquillion arrived in Albany in high July to inspect the condition of his investment, and to film Viktor as a way of presenting him to a host of general managers overseas. But I recruited myself to do everything possible to make the true highlight of that tape. This was my chance.

It made for a big weekend: we played Jacksonville that Saturday, meaning I would see Mies for the first time since Atlanta; there was the hectic hubbub of Serge in Albany, and Viktor's promises that he had wetted the agent's appetite for me, exciting him with the idea that an American had never played professionally in France and would make good publicity; and to top it all, only hours before the game, I drove to the airport to receive Ray, who had announced his visit just two days before. —I get a hankering to see my boy, he barked into the phone. —Show me how you play that game!

But to start with Serge—a short man who looked up to me from my chest, with a tanned skull fanned by feathery silver strands and an eagle's nose that sprouted tufts of gray hair from tightly flared nostrils, and a bony, elegant chin which gave his profile the look of a caricatured crescent moon. He had an icy, canny air, rarefied and fine; he gave the sense that he could listen to what you had to say but felt no need to declare himself. He closed his eyes to speak, or looked at the ground while he gesticulated with one hand holding a thin brown cigarette, the other tucked deep into a stylish trouser pocket. Criquillion came by the apartment as we packed our athletic bags with gear, shaking my hand once upon introduction and nodding to my father on one side of the room, and then casually dismissed us both to concentrate on Viktor: —How are the pains in the ankle now, good, yes? I have two teams interested in you, two teams in south. You play well today to give me a good show for them.

Viktor motioned toward me and Serge craned over his shoulder, cast a glimpse my way: —You think you can play in Europe, no?

—Well Mr. Criquillion, I sure would like the chance.

Serge shrugged in that definitive Gallic way that assures you it means nothing to him. —*Every*one would like the chance. The question, however, is *can* you play. I wish you luck.

—Hey, you'll see, Ray called from across the room, his face red but jovial. —He can play with the best of them, my boy!

—I have no doubts, *monsieur.* He turned away from us again and pulled his trousers up a notch and squatted before Lord Viktor spread-eagled in shorts on the couch, inspecting his legs with the scrutiny of a doctor, turning Viktor's foot one way then the other, asking how many injuries had he sustained this season, what did he think of the American leagues (Viktor: *they are children to me!*), and why weren't his statistics better than average in the nine games played so far. Viktor balked. —It's the team, Serge! You will see! They make me do it all myself, they have no respect for Serbians . . . long ball, long ball, you pass the long ball and only lose it. Gabriel, he is only player on the team I respect—and he is American! But he is not me, of course.

Serge smiled and said Of course, Viktor, of course. He glanced at his watch and said they should go to the stadium, he wanted to see it before the crowds came in. He shouldered Viktor's bag himself and they left together, driving Viktor to the game in the air-conditioned style of a rented Mercedes. A feeling of tension and politeness withdrew along with their exit, and my father and I looked upon one another in smiling relief, happy to have a few moments together.

—They set you up in a nice apartment at least, Pops said as he began to poke his head around. He wiped dust off of a counter, swept his hand over a cobweb on the wall. —You need some furniture. After the game why don't we stop somewhere and I'll buy you a table and some chairs.

There was no reason to have more than what I could fit into my car, I said.

—Well, I sure wish you were playing for that team back in Montreux, but word is they're going to fold . . . bad management or something. They got the attendance they need; 4,000 a game, I hear. It would be nice to have you home again. Good for your mom. Maybe if you were there we could convince Michael to come back, too. Do you talk to your brother? Do you know what he's doing these days? Manages a record store. The boy has a Master's degree in something-biology and the best he can do is sell records for some other guy.

—Last I heard he had himself a good band, he told me they were playing out in Atlanta, had a small following and everything. He was supposed to send me a tape but I don't think I ever gave him this address.

—When's the last time you spoke to your brother?

—I don't know . . . May?

And here it was, late July. We were leaning in close from opposite sides of the kitchen counter, speaking in hushed, knowing familial tones. He helped rub mink oil into my cleats, the leather hardened by our last game played in the rain. —Nah, no more band, he said. —*The Star-Strangled Bastards* are finished, they played their last show back in June. *The Star-Strangled Bastards*—where do you guys find this stuff?

He held up one shoe and inspected his work, then, with a glance to me, advised, —Don't have to use such a big gob of oil there, honey, a little dab will do ya; rub that in, do the rest of the shoe, wait a while, then add another coat. Otherwise you clog up the pores in the leather and it'll crack sooner. See how I get that sheen? Hey look,—(and when

I did he was tapping his finger against his forehead)—*College.* You didn't
know your Dad knew how to shine shoes, did you?

—Right, right, I said.

Ray smiled and stepped back into the kitchen and set his feet
shoulder-width apart, positioned his weight just so as he eyed the wall to
his left, looked down again at his feet, and mimed a picture-perfect golf
swing. He sighed as he shaded his eyes and watched the imaginary ball
sail off toward the green. —It would be good for your mother to have you
two in Montreux again. She misses her boys a lot.

—Olive? She told you this?

—*Olive?* Where do you get off calling your mother *Olive?* She's
your *mother.* (He gave up the golf swing.) —She's not so good, son, not
so good. Still drinks. Smokes as the day is long, I don't know how many
packs. I fixed her a space down in the basement so she could get back
to her needlepoint—you remember all those shirts and pillows she used
to make?—but man, I don't think she's doing anything down there but
drinking. She's hiding the bottles from me now, they turn up from time
to time. We don't even talk anymore.

—You didn't talk that much before, Pop. . . . He looked at me as
though I were a complete stranger who had suddenly arrived to hit him
on the side of his head for no reason at all; he stared at me, his face in
complete, quizzical consternation. I said, —Why don't you take her to
detox? and his face opened again.

—See? That's what I think. But she doesn't want to quit, says she
doesn't need to; she's got this psychiatrist now—and boy that costs me
an arm and a leg, dog-gonnit!—and he tells her she's the greatest thing
ever, no problems at all, just a jewel and what inhibits her is her overpow-
ering desire to please everybody. That's what *she* says, at least. But you
know you can't tell your mother anything she doesn't want to hear.

—You can't tell anybody anything they don't want to hear, I said,
and he answered with Ain't that the truth. He said, —I pray but the
problem just stays there. You learn to focus on other things. The business

is doing great . . . I was in Atlanta a few weeks ago for a conference, saw your brother there. He's got nothing in his apartment but cats, musician stuff, the most insane computer technology you ever saw, and antique furniture. Damnedest thing, your brother. I'll never figure him out.

17

Every so often there happens that most rare of occurrences when you awake refreshed and inexplicably content; the body poses no outrage at your rising; the sun shines not into your eyes but showers gold over the entire day, a day when mistakes and self-doubt and bad luck flee at the mere sight of you, recognizing that, for this hour at least, you are not to be touched. The kind of day when you automatically catch what you drop before it hits the ground; you swerve masterfully without hitting the car that cut you off; favorite songs play unimpeded on the radio. Days of extraordinary hours. . . .

For ninety minutes of play, I could do no wrong. Sweat never fell in my eyes, my head never bowed to fatigue, my legs moved with powered assurance and slashing speed. Every move, every choice, came without forethought, and each was the right one. The goals fell like rain, like stars. We scored two, then three, then the next time I glanced at the scoreboard, we were five goals ahead with none against. The spirit on the field felt like a wild party, a raucous whirling storm, and for the entire ninety minutes our pinwheeling play did not stop. We allowed one goal in the last six minutes, on a penalty, and that was all.

The game ended. I lingered on the field, not wanting to leave. I can do more! I thought. Give me the ball! I had to check the team's statistics to be convinced it had actually happened. Five goals, and I had a hand in four of them: scoring twice and assisting two. For two hours, it was like another soul had taken control of my body.

Ray—jocose, infectious, unstoppable—could not cease talking the rest of the afternoon and into the night; in the car he repeated to me what he had seen in case I had missed what I had done myself. He basked in the congratulations of those around him, repeating over and over *yes, that one is my son, that one there, the kid scoring all the goals,* and confessed in a dominant baritone that none of it surprised him. Afterward at the bar his festive glee continued: —You've got to give me a copy of that tape, Criquillion! Told you he was good, I told you, what didn't I say, hah!

—Yes, yes, *of course* you can have a copy of the tape, Mr. Toure, Serge said. —May I call you Ray?

Pops would not veil his worldliness. —It's not me you need to coax down, pal, but Gaby there. . . .

The restaurant boomed with our boisterous laughter; we annoyed the other patrons, eventually cleared the room. Even Mies was pleased, looking at me with his wry smile, giving me tough-guy punches to the shoulder, mussing my hair, saying he knew I had it in me but why did I have to pull it out today? *You were in a zone,* he said. *We couldn't touch you. You were a freight train.* Sometimes that happens; every athlete prays for that seamless hour when the world becomes mere sense and color. Our coach asked my father if he could make it to every one of our games—*we'd bring a trophy to Albany if I could count on Gabe to always play like that,* he laughed.

Viktor appeared content, too, having scored two goals himself—two powerful and unlikely missiles—although he could not grant full compliments to me, only backhanded ones, teasing that yes mine were nice goals, but could have been knocked in by anyone; it was a question of being the player in the right place at the right time.

—But being in the right place is the whole object of the game, Mies said to take my side. —I wish I'd been rightly placed five times today.

—For that you must rely on your teammates and today your side had nothing, said Viktor.

—What happened to Jacksonville? Ray asked. —Gaby said you boys were tops in the league.

—What happened to us? You should ask what happened to

them! Albany was unstoppable today. If you guys played like that every game. . . .

—Unless the other side had Gaby playing for them! Ray gushed, clapping his hands to point his enthusiasm. —I can't wait to show that tape to your mother. When are you going to leave, Criquillion? You think I could get a tape to take back with me?

—Yes, Viktor continued on his own, unperturbed by our voices clamoring at once, —yes, Mies, but I prefer the goals that go boom! in the back of the net. My shot is a rocket, like lightning. Your keeper does not know I shoot until we are already running back to midfield to celebrate my fine goal. Gabriel, he is precise; I admire that; he passes the ball into the net, we stand and watch it go in, waiting with hope. But the crowd loves a rocket.

Serge began to speak to me in reserved, quiet tones, asking if I had signed with any European agents as yet; when I told him no, he explained how his contract worked, speaking as though we had already committed. Did I really want to play in Europe? he asked. Because if I did, the time to go was now, while I still had some years of strong play ahead of me; he felt sure he could land me a place on a team next year. —It is doubtful for the premier league, of course; not yet. They will want proof that you can play. We will find you someone in the second division. I am sure you can have a future there if you like. At this moment I have no contract with me, but if you have a fax I can send one when I return to Paris. Let me tell you how I work for my clients. . . .

He sat forward with eyes narrowing in an unsettling ferocity as he described the world of sports as similar to Hollywood, how the teams don't matter anymore, it's all about the star, and he would rather work for the star than the movie house. *The star is always the one being pursued.* —At salary time I confront the football team as an enemy to be overwhelmed. I promise you that.

Criquillion left us with a blue burst of silky smoke from his dun-shade cigarette, we continued to drink late into the night, icy drinks roiling, teeth gnawing at our lips, yawns of fatigue stifled and far away. Ray took over with tales of his army days, dissected his jumps for us, his war experiences, the details of battle in the air. His success in racing cars. All of which I could recite by heart already—aside from the new embellishments—but sat forward and listened to anyway, as captivated as the first time. Mies sat enthralled; he'd only heard about Ray from me and now here the man was: flesh, god-like. Well, demigodlike, anyway. The noise of the restaurant whirled about our table but never interfered. —You've had quite some life, Mies said. —Lived it all myself, Pops answered. Viktor belched and looked about the room for available waitresses, thumping his chest with the flat of his palm.

In my excitement and desire to hold this feeling as long as possible I hit up Ray for his calling card and left to make a long-distance connection to Atlanta; though it was Saturday evening, Emily answered.

—I had to tell you, Em, you won't believe the day I've had.

—It sounds fantastic, she answered. —I wish I could've been there to see it.

And there the charm withered into reality returned. Reality with all of its disagreeable facts and unavoidable truths: the cruelty of high-tech communication, the clarity of contact masking the strident distance of place. Her voice so close in my ear we could have been speaking from two sides of a fine drapery, or (more likely) between the flimsy film of a soiled bed sheet. I wanted to roll over on my side and touch her. . . . Two months since we last spoke—not such a long time—but the fact of our story's impermanence, the loss of what we had shared together, fell now as a heavy, sullen weight fallen on the thin copper wire tenuously stretched, carefully buried, for hundreds of miles between us. *Gaby I still think of you often,* she whispered in a hoarse voice. *I miss you all the time,* I answered, my throat low with awful seriousness.

—I'm sure you have lots of girlfriends to help take your mind off of me by now.

—No it's not like that; I don't really have the time, Emily.

The lie brought a disbelieving but playful chuckle from the earpiece of the telephone and she said, —You have more free time than anybody I know.

A long pause, then, rounded and thickened by the twenty-four pinholes in the receiver meeting my ear, the other ear closed from the surrounding noise by my finger. I had to keep moving to avoid the barback hauling crates of bottled beer up the steps of the cellar. —And you? Are you getting help to take your mind off me?

Bottles clinked and tapped against one another, the lowly server mumbling *sorry pal*, and *excuse me, there*, and *it'll only take another minute . . . look out . . . sorry. . . .*

Emily said she had been spending time with somebody nice. —You would like him, Gaby, he used to be an amateur boxer. A guy in the English program, the same age as you but two years behind me. She promised there was nothing big yet.

—But possible?

—Isn't everything possible?

Again the heavy silence, the events of the day fading to the past where they belonged; the triumph and glory of a dream come true set into its proper context of momentary bedding: there, then gone. —Gaby I'm sorry but I don't mean to upset you—this is nothing, he's just a friend I spend time with, I don't even know why I mentioned him. Or why I'm feeling defensive about it, *listen*. . . . I still think of you, every day, awfully, I keep asking myself should I have just chucked it all and come to Albany? You know you can take Literature courses anywhere . . . are you listening to what I'm saying? I keep thinking what we had was so perfect, baby, so right, and therefore shouldn't I have been willing to change my life just a bit to accommodate it? Or even change a whole lot? It was so much fun when you were here and now Atlanta is a terrible bore, it makes *me* boring, life has been just one big yawn since you left. I've been trying to write this down to send you, to make it clear to you how it is. Then I don't. But it's there every day.

—Emily. . . .

—I'm sorry, I'm ruining your perfect day. I never did get to see you play outdoors. And now you're going off to France.

—Jeez, let's hope so.

—Oh yes, *let's,* her voice emphasizing sarcasm. Then: —Gabe, don't listen to me, I do hope it works out for you. You've wanted this so long. Maybe I can come for a visit when you're there, I haven't been to France since I was fifteen. You'll need me to translate for you! To think I've always wanted somebody to speak French to and then I had you, and now you're going to learn it but you'll be so far away. Gosh the more I think about it the more I believe it's all going to happen. There's a lucky star over you, Gaby; you're supposed to have a happy life, I'm sure of it.

Emily had said such things before. When I described the past before we met—accentuating the darker pratfalls and calamities as they seemed the most true (censoring the more violent episodes)—she would answer that hearing of those times surprised her. —It doesn't fit my conception of you. It all seems like a big mistake, she said. She summed up my past and its parade of accidents and false-starts as one big metaphysical misunderstanding. —You have a guardian angel but maybe he's just an apprentice or is absentminded or else he just makes mistakes, she would say.

—Or else I'm too much a handful.

—There could have been a personnel change! They couldn't fill the position for years—

—Yes, because nobody wanted it!

We had this same conversation or a variation upon it several times over those too-few months together, and each time it did not fail to bring us to falling-down laughter. —But it's all behind you now . . .

your Dad is free again and you're doing what you want to do . . . smooth sailing ahead for Gaby Toure.

In the end the gist from her was always the same: for all my mishaps and near-disasters, I was lucky; for every broken bone (having suffered seven by the time I turned twenty-two) there easily could have been a broken neck, paraplegia; for each car wreck (three as a teenager) there was the debris I might not have walked away from. Emily insisted I was meant to lead a fulfilling life, so much so that when around her I believed that I had, as it was now fulfilling with her; she did not think that I could be denied my hopes and expectations.

But standing there in the cranny between the bar and basement, all that seemed very, very long ago, and over. My hopes and expectations did not include Emily anymore.

18

I signed with Criquillion, accepting his fax in the Albany offices—the manager as excited as me at the prospect, for if Serge found a team in France, there would be the question of a transfer fee between clubs—and I signed with barely a glance over the poorly-translated document. The agent worked fast; within another week he called to say he was discussing my transfer with the second-division team in Nice, on the Côte d'Azur, and my imagination swelled with images of green sea and endless sun, topless sunbathers clad only in sandals and thongs. Criquillion faxed a map so I could see where the city was (such was my knowledge of geography) and attached a note to explain within a thirty-minute drive of Nice awaited the town of St. Tropez, glamorous and seductive: *In France we call it St. Trop—trop meaning 'too much,'* he wrote. *You will have to be careful so you do not lose your legs to too often pleasure. Football players are treated well in my country.*

With the team playing with renewed confidence, we flew through a month of summer Sundays, aligning ourselves as wild cards in the playoffs. But summers wane. Near the end of a regular morning practice, the coach called out to me: —Tourbie I need to speak with you and Savic after training.

His tone suggested seriousness but preoccupation, and therefore nothing to get too concerned about; he was a serious man after all; I assumed he needed us for some publicity work, an interview, or a clinic for children. Wealthy parents were always asking if private tutorials could be arranged for their sons. But the coach's grave and saddened face, his fatherlike clasp to my shoulder at the end of practice as he directed me toward his office, the silent walk we covered in meditative and fitful steps, made me feel like a kid caught in the midst of shameful acts. An array of awful possibilities sprang to mind: Olive was gone? Another calamity for Ray? What had my brother been up to all this time?

The problem was composed of none of these things. He told Viktor to wait outside his office while he spoke with me. I sat alone, sweating still from training and with a new bitter sweat sprung in my anxiousness, my thighs sticking to the faux-leather material of an old love seat opposite his desk. The problem had nothing to do with me; it had everything to do with me. Coach handed over an official-looking letter with a return-address of gold-embossed print, a header listing the names of three lawyers. In his heavy Irish brogue he growled, —Okay boy, you tell me who in Christ is Lynette Stern?

I echoed the name without recognizing it, "Stern" falling on a descending query-note.

—Read the friggin' letter, man, coach ordered. He was nervous by temperament and suffered an odd tic: the loose folds beneath his alcoholic eyes wriggled like a pool surface disturbed by water jets, a curious trait that always stole my attention when he lectured the team, so that I rarely understood what he had said; the kind of tic that made conversations maddening internal battles about where to look.

I read over the letter quickly, disbelief gradually heating my face. A lawsuit was being prepared against the management, Viktor Savic, and me. Lynette Stern stated that she had been raped by Viktor one night in my apartment and that I had been an accomplice in the matter; that I had held her down on my bed while Savic raped and sodomized her. I read over the letter again, the dire reality of it sinking in, denial awash throughout me. I dropped it back on the desk. —Coach, this is not true, this never happened.

—I want to believe you, lad, sitting down in a large armchair and lighting a cigarette. —You tell me what happened, then. Who is this woman and what in Christ is going on?

I did my best to remember. In my nervousness and shock it was not so easy, but I knew only one Lynette in my lifetime, a figure by now mostly forgotten. —She's the one who crawled onto my bed and woke me up, my tone raising as the details came, —she got mad when I lost interest and stopped messing with her . . . coach this isn't true, you have to believe me . . . dammit I knew there was something that didn't feel right. Suddenly my pride swelled with self-righteousness: —She was trash, coach, a groupie, a barfly, she complained when she didn't get more of what she wanted!

—How many times have I lectured you boys to be careful? Whether you're in jerseys or not, you are always a representative of this team and its management and owners. You are representing my name! Now I get to be dragged through this tripe! This same letter was sent to the papers, to the TV news. . . .

It got worse. The mayor of the city had a share in the team and sat on the Board of Advisors. The Cuomo family were members—in name only, really—of the booster club. —And here we are starting the playoffs! Coach raged. —Advisors telling me to suspend you both until an investigation is made and me arguing that you don't fuck with a line-up on playoff eve! Don't go anywhere. Get showered and come back. Our lawyers need a deposition from you. Not today, but soon. The police, needless to say, want a word, though the-fuck-don't-you-know they haven't got dick-one from this Stern tramp. We haven't heard from the media yet, but I'm sure they're on their way. Get yourself cleaned up, shave for chrissake, and send Savic in on your way out. I'm tired of looking at you.

I waved in Viktor and headed for the locker room. My mind spun the situation from embryonic seed to gargantuan proportions, the sting of ice water prickling me in the leftover after-steam of the other guys' showers . . . did I deserve this? Did Viktor? How could this woman. . . . Maybe she truly believed she had been raped. Maybe she *had* been and it was only my own insensitivity that prevented me from realizing the fact. Over and over, my head pressed against humid tile, cold water shucking off the tacky morning sweat, eyes closed, I searched for images from nearly-erased memory: the buck of the window unit kicking in lukewarm air; her husky rummy breath—*you don't want to give me a go?* Savic's slaps to her body; the way she said *no,* and *stop*—then *yes* and *more.* I had sat curled in one corner of my bed and watched the entire fiasco.

Fiasco: that was the word. Maybe I didn't realize what had really transpired in my own bed. My initial impulse was to avoid the news; to escape it; to hide from the possibility that anyone could know I was somehow involved in this. Hiding: from Ray and Olive, from Mies, from Serge . . . that seemed paramount. It would be impossible.

The coach's office was used for a series of interviews that week, none of which had the slightest connection to soccer. Viktor wanted to deny the entire incident ever occurred. Lynette's lawyer announced that they possessed photographs taken by her roommate showing red bite marks on the woman's buttocks, back, and thighs. Nevertheless our lawyers felt confident and optimistic: there were unanswered questions posed to the opposing side: why had she not submitted to a medical exam until after the lawsuit was announced (a full month after the alleged rape)? Why did she contact a lawyer first and not the police?

Farce was made of the situation in full-blown, uniquely American style. Being jocks and therefore supposedly insanely virile, and somehow assumed to have enjoyed charmed lives where our society had given us so much so that our personalities must have been warped by lives absent of reality, our guilt was a given. The first step the team took was to abandon us, allowing us use of their lawyers but publicly pronouncing that the event in question had occurred outside the scope of our employment and so they could not be held liable. We became subjects for the local radio call-in shows, where the names Savic and Toure became examples of a society steeped in moral decline; an embodiment of the arrogance sustained by the deep sickness of our sports-mad culture. Feminist activists took to picketing the team office and the sidewalk before our apartment, toting posters announcing *Woman is not an object for sporting appetites* and *Athletes are not above the law* (although no formal charges had been—or ever would be—brought against us; the police decided the case should remain a civil suit for lack of evidence) and then, on the stoop before my home, somebody had posted: *Did you know rapists live here?*

We disconnected the phone to stop the ceaseless ringing, slept on the couches in the apartments of sympathetic teammates. In the midst of all this our training continued, the playoffs neared, and my body remounted its rebellion against me. No length of warm-ups and stretching could alleviate the stress in my muscles. My vertebrae felt as though bone ground against bone; my belly downward hardened to concrete; it took a full hour of light exercise before my feet could flex to a full ninety degree angle.

But, as Olive or Sarah would have said, I tried to pull myself up by my boot straps; I worked to grin and bear it. I endured our casual calisthenics, the drills, the wind sprints, with grinding teeth. Two days before our big playoff opener, however, my body begged, *no more.* During an easy jog to the sideline my left hamstring tightened, pulled, then tore, shouting a searing pain through my leg.

Strange and fascinating, the colors created by the body in pain. Sport can make for a cruel study. The florals of a hard bruise, the snotty yellow which ripens as the tissue heals; the purple and black oily swirl of flesh exposed by a torn-away toenail; the emotive mauve of scars. My torn hamstring swelled with an infant anaconda twining beneath my skin, the burst and flooded tissue mimicking the tropical serpent's patterned pelt: greens and yellows and the deepest of blues, spattered with a crimson that snaked its way among my pores.

They wrapped the leg in ice—there's nothing else for it, save swallow handfuls of the painkillers and more anti-inflammatories and wait for the muscle to heal (and the ulcers to begin), hoping the scar tissue won't inhibit movement enough to require surgery. This is all simple medical information. The fact remained that I could not walk without cane or a crutch's aid, much less jog or run, even less perform. The season was over.

Out of pity the management allowed me to take the bus to Ohio to witness our loss. Not simply a loss, either, but another fiasco: 4–0 by the whistle, with Savic red-carded in the fiftieth minute for fighting. I hate Ohio. In its useless landscape of infinite fields, I found only losses and definitive endings. The entire state has victimized me with the same indifference of a totalitarian bureaucracy. In Ohio it rains perpetually, even when the weather seems fine.

19

Our bus grumbled over miles of dusty pavement. The air seethed with resentment, anger, disappointment. Losses and lawsuits, that's what we'd accomplished in our inaugural season. . . . We left the tension unspoken; allowed it to teem. Our wheels thrummed loudly in the body, in the heart and belly, reminding you of where your flesh sits loose, the places you need to work on, for all of us must be hard. A dull rattle flexed in the Plexiglas windows, and each player sat with a stern regard of bitter self-reflection. All except Savic, our irrepressibly incapable self-reflector, who pressed a set of headphones to his ear, the music ringing a tinny din nearby. His eyes were closed and he sang.

Savic's indifference upset the goalkeeper. He glared at his large hands resting empty and ineffectual in his lap. His name was Terence but he was still six-foot four and weighed well over 200 pounds, bald and bulge-eyed, bloodshot. He said in a sneer: —Somebody shut that frigging thing off before I do it meself. His hands worked over one another, and his tone left no doubts to his seriousness. I tapped Viktor on the shoulder.

—What? What is it you say? Viktor pulled one speaker from his ear and leaned toward me, showering our space with harsh rock.

—I said turn off your headphones.

—Move somewhere else. . . . Savic shrugged and let the headphone snap back into place. The bus windows rattled over a dip in the road. Terence now glared at me.

—Gabe. Listen mate. Tell the punk to turn off those headphones.

—He says he's not bothering anybody.

—The hell! He's bothering *me*. I can't friggin' hear myself think.

—Then you tell him. What am I, the message boy?

Terence snorted. He rubbed his awesome hands in an undulating row over his thighs. Air pumped out of his nostrils, which flared and whitened in the passing street lights. He wadded a cheeseburger wrapper and threw it at Savic, hitting him square in the forehead. Savic picked it up and flicked the wad at me, saying —Don't be foolish, Gabe, why do a thing like that? even though he knew the missile originated elsewhere.

Terence spoke loudly: —Turn off the fucking music, man. You should be thinking about this afternoon, this is no time for a celebration.

—What do I have to think about? Savic asked. —I played today. It was not me who watched four goals pass.

No one had to direct this boy on what to do—I moved from my seat to another across the aisle, to keep my bad leg protected. Terence was already rising; he approached Viktor slowly, his full bearing swollen with menace, his posture one of fatigued patience lost. He was not a bully of a man but rather a failed thinker in an angry bull's body, his face pinched with dull consideration rather than sweltering rage, as though he wanted to approach the problem philosophically but was led to the physicality of it without choice. He stood at the booth, where Savic was curled against the window. —'Ay, he retched hoarsely. —'Ay, Viktor. He poked Viktor's arm with one meaty finger, inclined his bound-ham-sized head at him. —What's with the rumpus? Turn off the fucking noise, man.

Viktor said nothing; he stared back. Everyone in the bus was watching them now.

Terence's philosophical thread must have met an irreconcilable knot, the kind that can only be torn through rather than slipped out of. He struck with a casual swipe of a bear's paw, tearing the headphones from Savic's head. —I said turn it off.

A moment of regard, then. Rock music splashed up from the floor of the bus, *three, four!* Savic sprang at our goalkeeper with nary a word of warning. Not a peep or grunt from him and the fight was on, with everyone suddenly yelling and shouting, a holler alive in the bus, our hostilities happily sparked into the open.

Savic benefitted from the unexpected quickness of his attack and the cramped space. They slammed against bus seats and the bathroom door, grunts hurled and hustled above the encouragements and exclamations from the rest of us—stilled as we were by the certainty that something should be done yet glad to see our bitterness erupt . . . arms flailed, punches were thrown. Grunt-grunt, punch-punch, huff-huff, *Fuck* flitted about the metal walls and ceiling. For an instant it looked as though Savic would get the better of him, but Terence rallied. By the time our coach had stormed shouting into the roar, Viktor was bloodied and mussed, his tight wavy hair sprung in spliffs of brush-wire, and still he parried and struck, screeching in a tongue none of us knew.

—All right that's enough! Bastards, enough! the coach shouted, before he himself became entangled in the muck of it. He tried to push them apart, needle between them, and ended by simply becoming an old man lodged there. Then it was three wills at odds: Frozen like that, tensely coiled, three bodies of muscle in one intense flex and huffing breath, until the old man finally won through and the two flew apart—Savic to the floor and Terence's 200-plus pounds onto me, where the thick of my leg broke the weight of his fall.

The pain sent me under for a few seconds. My cry silenced all. Hostilities seeped out the windows and were swept off by the cooling autumn air, and I awoke to tones of concern and helpful touches, a tenderizing. Gaby the martyr! *Fuck off and leave me alone,* is what I said. Somebody finally turned off the noise of Viktor's radio, still thinly rampaging from beneath a seat somewhere, and the coach took his place in the back with the rest of us, beside Savic, with Terence sentenced to the seat up front. Like a bunch of third-graders.

Well, we were all through with one another. Sick of it, of the whole thing. That bus ride lasted as long as the entire season. By the time we pulled into our training facility to regain our cars and to leave without speaking, the only pleasure came in knowing that both, night journey and season, were over. Finally.

20

Savic flew off to Auxerre before the weekend was out. Another week passed with me alone in the apartment waiting to hear from the courts. There was no melodramatic scene between Lynette Stern and me before a grand jury. She had tried to claim *respondiat superior,* that the master was responsible for the acts of the slave, but once it became apparent that there would be no exaggerated prize money—the court ruled out the team management's accountability— her lawyers must have lost interest. A summary judgment came down in that the court accepted all of Stern's accusations as true, but still could not see that a reasonable jury could find us liable. Hardly a complete vindication; one could argue that I might be a rapist, still (the radio stations did). Yet the threat of punishment was over.

The last I heard from Savic was when he called to introduce me to an associate of Criquillon's. —Gabriel hello, I am giving you Iohannis Vassilis, Viktor said, —I am sorry my good friend but there is bad news. . . . Perfect that the phrase *bad news* would be the last I ever heard from his voice. Criquillon had suffered a stroke and was now incapacitated, and all deals were currently off. Vassilis promised to do what he could, he said; evidently this meant nothing. Nobody wanted an American who could not prove himself in a try-out. Again, there would be none of Europe for me.

The Greeks had it right: they constructed statues to their victorious athletes, and the defeated were held in shame—sometimes exiled. The victor did not shake hands with the loser after a contest; the loser hid himself; there was no such thing as an honorable loss. An honorable loss is democracy at its worst. All or nothing: this was the philosophy I had banked myself on, committed to, and I had failed. The cat I'd been trying to fuck turned and slashed me, the tough mouse. Maybe one could say my body had failed me. A sympathetic soul might argue that my luck simply ran out—that I'd never been quite good enough, that for three years I had played above myself, riding the hem of Myer Bruck's jersey, and luck decided it had seen enough. Regardless, with Albany's contract finished, I had nowhere to go. Nowhere to go but home—to Montreux, and Ray. To Olive.

Cripplefears and Everything After

1

Parade's End. If my ambition had been to bolt from here to make my mark, to ram myself into the world on my own, to be the mouse that fucked the cat, then this was failure. The torn hamstring in my left leg was merely a symptom of an unknown malady, as my musculature had completely mutinied—the athletic bull's body had come home a stiff, a stone, a statue. In three years this body seemed to have aged thirty.

How to truly relate subjective pain to anyone else? At this time there was no word for what wronged me: The pain and stiffness and cackling joints felt like the day after a hard workout when trying to regain game-fitness, nothing more, but intermittently there shot sharp searing streaks of agony, like glass shards caught within the folds of muscle, pinpoint screwdrivers spiked deep into the tissue, a seizing. Eyes closed, I pictured muscles torqued and twisted like the satellite photograph of a hurricane, the eye my center of pain. My thighs, hamstrings, glutes, and lower back jumped and jerked at random while I lay on the nylon bed of the living room floor before the TV, pillows behind my knees and head, zoning on morphine derivatives appropriated by

Ray, my hopeful and helpful pusher. The aches grounded by a constant and unyielding fatigue, a rich soil readying flowers of agony.

All this, and no name to attribute to it. To multiply insecurities exponentially, place yourself in chronic distress and watch the doctors shake their heads in wonder. —There's nothing viral here, they pronounce before large white printouts of numbered paper. —I see no skeletal damage aside from the disc degeneration, and that doesn't account for the rest of your son's symptoms.

—All this is in my son's head? Ray asked. —Is that what you're saying?

No; they were all very careful not to assert as much—but how can one feel confident before the baffled eyes of onetwothree doctors in a matter of weeks? Blood tests, X rays, MRIs and CAT-scans yielded nothing. Ray's face blanched before the bills, since with the end of my contract came the end of health insurance, and even though he struck deals with most of these physicians—having known them through business of the last twenty years—the numbers still added up. Besides the painkillers and muscle relaxers (which Ray could yank for free as if they grew on a local vine), and bed rest, the single treatment we found came from a theory of pain management involving spinal-tap needles, location of painful pressure points, and steeping four inches deep to saturate the area with loving lidocaine. We visited this doctor three times a week, an aging physician with rumpled hair and sleepy eyes who made 7:00 A. M. appointments and showed up at eight-thirty or later. 400 ccs, 600 ccs, my body sponged it all up, there could never be enough. The rest of my time passed on that downstairs floor before a wide-screen TV. For the last three months of that dark year, this was my life, a floating bloated body on a sea of synthetic fiber, surrounded by Olive's stale tobacco smoke and murmuring curses.

Once, Ray caught me staring out the living room window that gave to the great maple in our front yard.

—You and Godfrey never did post a flag up there, did you? he asked, looking past my shoulder to the tree outside.

At first I did not even grasp what he meant. I didn't remember ever telling him about our legendary Eagle Point. He seemed to know what I was thinking, though, and his smile to me at that moment was warm as with understanding, his hand atop my head.

—The things kids consider important, he said, and we both laughed at that, although my heart seemed to rise into my throat and float there, choking me, and it was difficult not to show tears. I was not quite sure where Eagle Point was anymore; the tree had grown so much larger by then, engulfing the place that had once seemed as high as heaven to me.

Two levels above, silently reading what she called her 'soft-porn' novels, Olive sat in bed, cigarette smoldering within reach, the radio or TV turned low. She set her alarm so as not to miss particular programs— talk shows, talk radio, all the talk of strangers which she longed to hear and which comprised her social life. She had retired from the office, announcing that the demands there were too destructive, an antagonist to her Serenity. This in response to Ray's confrontation that her drinking affected her health, her business performance, their marriage, him.

Olive was alcoholic and saw no shame in it. She was wasting away; her eyes slightly jaundiced, the flesh on her face pruned; her lips now formed a cruel sneer when she smiled. She rarely ate more than candy bars and maybe an egg or two. The most dramatic change was in her belly, where the liver had swollen so much she looked like a starved African. Within weeks of my arrival, the lifetime of cigarettes had her dragging oxygen on metal casters behind her, a yellowed feeding line attached at the nose.

She made stabs at Recovery. Still, we suspected—no, we knew but ignored—her clear plastic glass of ginger ale, with the felt-patch putting green and little flag inscribed *The 19th Hole* on the side, con- cealing a taste of bourbon inside it. My father and I made for excellent enablers. This, despite the shock of what she'd become, physically.

A part of her did want health. In the years since her two boys had been gone—Michael still in Athens, me all over the place—Olive had detoxed twice, gone a few months clean, then fell back. Maybe it was the boredom and the isolation; she now left the house for two reasons only: her AA meetings and twice-a-week sessions with a psychiatrist. Everything now revolved around her goal to reach the oasis of Serenity; a number of reminders and items of support littered the house for this purpose to keep her focused and us aware: framed needlepoint mats with the "God grant me the serenity to accept what I cannot change" prayer/poem throughout the house; a scattering of positive visualization and self-hypnosis tapes discarded at random; tiny chapbooks stuffed with daily affirmations composed of all the depth of a Hallmark card. *Tell yourself how wonderful you are . . . Each day that passes with you in the world is a marvelous day . . . What do you want?—Lord knows you're worth it!*

She started at any sudden entry to her bedroom, so that Ray had to begin talking as he mounted the stairs to bring her food. She leapt upon any perceived remark which questioned her sincerity—a statement as simple as congratulating her on continuing with her AA meetings, her recovery, provoked the venomous reply of —What? do you think I can clean up on my own? It's a *disease* and I'm not going to find any help from you or Ray . . . surrounded by nothing but selfish bastards! Then she fell to murmuring, —Think little Olive will just stay put with her pretty face, well those days are over, lemme tell you. . . . I take care of myself now! All my life's been given over to you men. I'm through with that 360-degree son of a bitch.

—360-degree son of a bitch?

—He's a son of a bitch no matter how you look at him.

Ray was at a loss to understand them: his wife or the disease. —Because they *are* two different things. She doesn't know what she's saying half of the time anyway, he said.

—Maybe it would help if you went to some of the meetings with her, showed her your support.

—Why all this anger, all the time? She blames me for the train wreck and the hospital stays, for the time in prison, as if it'd been a vacation. And you go to these meetings, it's a bunch of drunks talking about how they've ruined their lives, you'd be amazed to hear how low a person can go. I just find the whole thing too depressing. Life is not as debilitating as these people insist. And your mother goes on to criticize me afterward anyway.

Ray feared that Olive had missed the entire point of Recovery—he suspected nearly everyone at those meetings had misplaced their goal. Most fundamentally because he believed that they (and Olive in particular) denied responsibility for their pasts, and he despised turning over one's fears and "disease" to faith in a Higher Power—a power that had nothing to do with the God of either the Old or New Testaments.

—This whole idea of calling alcoholism a disease, he complained.
—There's nothing proving that. This is *behavior*. Your mother . . . she always had the urge for tragedy.

For Olive, the meetings were a social function, and on those mornings, she took the time to shower and perfume, dress to the nines and adorn herself in jewelry. Ready to leave, she would waddle down the steps, cradling her growing belly before her, and say, —This lady is off to her confession. . . . When she returned two hours later, sometimes having taken lunch at a cafeteria with AA acquaintances afterward, she scowled and grumbled over my inert body on the floor as she moved upstairs, casting off clothes along the way, to collapse into a faded blue nightgown with a sigh: —What a day. . . . The house would fill with her snores, for hours.

2

They shared the same house now and little else. They kept different rooms, with Ray having moved into Michael's old bedroom and Olive now bearing full reign of the master bedroom. They slept with doors closed.

I can walk through Olive's room in my mind as easily as when emptying the place those first few days after she was gone. Alive, she clutched that shelter close to her soul, and rarely were any of us allowed inside; dead, her presence still pervaded the space so thoroughly that Ray never moved to reclaim it. The door, painted a gray mustard, scooted in jags over a high-pile carpet so that a scraping *shhroom* skidded to the ears as you entered. On the back hung white-wire racks crammed with tattered mass market paperbacks. The bed swallowed most of the square footage; on either side stood two stained-oak night-stands capped by matching blue-shaded lamps. To accommodate this cramped feeling, mirrors were placed on each wall. The closets on one side were mirror-doored, and two large mirrors hung on the wall above the dresser—which you had to be careful not to catch your hip on the corner of as you entered—so that when the closets were folded open upon her racks of burgeoning dresses, some never worn and still bearing tags, you walked in to find your image endlessly replicated.

The sheets and bedcovers are disheveled and wadded to one side. Weeks of daily newspapers stack precariously along the edge of the bed, crossword puzzles completed and checked off, sections of paper strewn and crumpled to the floor. The papers, yellowed and grayed by sunlight, enhance the sting of tobacco and dust in the nostrils, drawing the eye to the three or four ashtrays overflowing with cinders and crushed butts. Candy wrappers lie scattered and torn over the bed, the night-stands, the floor, particularly in the small niche between the bed and wall on the side she claimed as her own (although she had the entire bed she remained to the one side that had been hers before). And there you find the piles of empty bourbon bottles, our harsh Kentucky bracer, spilling from inside the nightstand and from underneath the bed because there is no more room to hide them; in the end she stopped caring that we knew. The TV murmurs on, tunelessly, and the room eases out its emptiness and sadness so that you have no choice but to accept this place as the hovel of a madness, a beaten psyche; the headboard and wall above it scorched black, emphasizing the sense that here came an end, the chromium blue wallpaper peeled back to frayed splinters singed brown and white, heat still emanating from this spot as if the nebulous mind itself had exploded.

Ray's room sits adjacent to Olive's. It has a monastic austerity to it. The space is much smaller, with room only for two twin beds separated by a narrow aisle, and there's only one small nightstand of glass framed in bronzed steel. Stacked there are a few small books of biblical study—Billy Graham titles, Arthur Bloomfield—beside the large book itself, Old and New testaments with Apocrypha in a single volume. A single book of low-risk investment strategies. The only novel in the room is a western: —A real novel has someone die on every page, he liked to tell me.

The room is immaculately clean. On the nightstand there is the stained ring of either a coffee cup or a glass of water, a scattering of castaway change, and the folded bifocals which he needed to read lying next to an imitation-leather case. The bed in use is made up perfectly so that it appears that nobody has slept there for some time, even though it is his place every night.

Within that house exists a story from which I feel excluded. The story of Olive, the woman whom you may have noticed I've never been able to address or refer to here as Mom. Ray and Olive—what brought them to who they'd become? Adjacent to their story, my own can be summed up in the back of a closet, where three team jackets hang, ignored, hidden. Ray and Olive—who will remember them, mourn them, once Michael and I are gone? Who remembers those who never enter History but lived domestic, small, private lives? No one. It is for this reason that we have invented Heaven.

But these people were real, and it was obvious to anybody who cared to look that Olive was slowly, incrementally, *maddeningly* dying. A liver transplant was out of the question for an alcoholic who insisted on her continuing to drink, although Ray queried every doctor he could find. Olive wanted to die.

—Have you ever given thought to suicide? her psychiatrist once told me he had asked her, once she was gone.

—Often. All the time. But I'm not strong enough.

This, from a woman of such often, fierce rage. Olive insisted she was weak and frightened and that's why she drank. Or she'd had no say in it because it was a disease and there you go, that's why she drank. Or her life had been nothing but perpetual disappointment and suffering and she deserved whatever escape she could find, or it was her mother's fault and the difficult relationship between them, the fact it could never be reconciled since Sarah had died while I was in Atlanta, a stroke; that's why she drank. Or it was the cause of Ray, the three hundred sixty degree son of a bitch.

—Every family gets a grog blossom, she insisted.

But Olive was still a mother who wanted good lives for her children, even if they had "abandoned her"; she often mentioned that her life could never be regarded as a complete failure since she had placed two healthy boys in the world. She enjoyed the idea of doing things with them, if not actually doing them. Or, better yet, have them perform some task for her—preferably before the witness of a house-guest. When I think of my mother I remember most clearly the words *Gaby get up and come here there's something I want you to do for me. . . . Gaby while you're here why don't you. Gaby move this. Gaby I need, I want.* Still, her anger allowed infrequent breaks. We tried to approach, console, understand one another at times; glimpses of her goodness could yet be stolen.

In early December Ray left for a sales conference in Tennessee and I was still scheduled for my trigger-point/lidocaine therapy. Olive had no choice but to drive me to the doctor. Anxiety-prone and ago-raphobic, this was no small task for her. She talked as a way to keep herself calm, her small red oxygen tank resting between us.

—We might get snow this week, she said, motioning to me to switch off the tank so she could light a cigarette. She cracked open her window. —Maybe we'll have a white Christmas this year, I love snow on Christmas, don't you? I want snow on Christmas and then I want it to go away the next day because other than on Christmas I hate snow . . . those awful long gray winter days . . . it would be nice for your brother, you know he says he hasn't seen snow in eight years, they never get it down there in Georgia, did you know that? I've never been to Georgia. Been all the way across the Atlantic to Spain, but you know I've never made it two states away to Georgia. Hey look out you!

A driver coming our way moved into the center turning lane, a fraction too close to the lane in which we were driving, his headlights set on high beam in the after-dawn murk. —Well what else did you get for Christmas! she yelled as we swerved and passed. —People here think they're the only ones on the road. Oh look, there's a squirrel, I bet *he's* cold; get out of the road Mr. Squirrel or else you're going to get squashed, go on, get out . . . go on go on go on GET OUT OF THE ROAD YOU DUMB ANIMAL! and she fisted the horn, car screeching to a halt as the squirrel scampered in one direction, then the other, panicked, more car horns wailing behind us in a trail of suddenly-braked autos, until finally the squirrel dashed to the curb and the safety of one tree.

—Damn! she shouted, glancing past her shoulder at the clamor behind us, —You'd think people would just run over whatever wanders into the road, that could have been a little child there and you think they'd have horned then? Bunch of complainers YES I SEE YOU BACK THERE SIR THANK YOU VERY MUCH now look out I'm going to turn . . . ugh all those trees over there, look Gaby, naked and spiny all of them . . . what a gray morning. You just want to stay in bed. God I hate winter.

At the sight of the huge syringe Olive fanned herself quietly with one hand, then announced she would wait in the outside room until the procedure had finished. The needle hurts at first and you have to lie very still or else risk snapping it. The doctor asks where the pain is localized, and you run your hand down the back until you find a minuscule knot and point, *Directly below my finger,* and he replaces yours with his, tells you to relax, and you try and then there's the pressure of the needle against your skin then the tissue giving then ripping as he steeps it deeply until BANG it hits the center like a hammer on a raw nerve and you cry out, *Oh!* His gloved palm comes down on your spine. He tells you don't jerk or move. Sudden sweat opens out over your entire body, muscles twitching, and breaths come quick and pulsing until the relief, *mmmm it's all good,* you feel the flood of chemical warmth. You don't feel the needle come out, yet you know when it's gone—it leaves the body like a sigh. Then you start over, —Show me where it hurts. . . . A nurse towels off the sweat with a quick swipe. —Stuff really brings the heat out quick, huh? the doctor says with a laugh.

Afterward, I tottered out of the office in shaking drunken baby steps, my body lidocained, quivering. It took us a good fifteen minutes to shuffle to the car, saying nothing, our short steps counted out by a squeak in one of her casters that called once on each turn. Inside the car she asked, —Do you have the strength to do anything else before going home?

—What do you want to do?

—We're not far from The Pug Mill. I want to stop by for a quick look-see. For Christmas you might want to have a few pieces to round out Sarah's collection.

Mama Sarah had not been a wealthy woman by any standards, and she did not leave much behind. But, like Olive, she cultivated a small ceramic collection from The Pug Mill, a celebrated factory of folk-art wares crafted by hand. This she left to me, so that whenever her namesake settled into a place secure enough to call home he would have a reminder of her any time he sat to eat, or drink a cup of coffee.

Olive stopped at the crumbling curb before the warehouse and stared a moment at the entrance. A dramatic, nervous pause, then:

—Oh, Mom, she groaned, lending the morning a gravity that always struck the rest of the family as pretense. As though she felt, because of her mother's death, the visit was now laden with a weight and emotion inexpressible. I waited patiently for the tears to come to mother's eyes—which they did, dutifully, in time. She wiped them away with a quiet display of pink tissues pulled from her glove compartment. Cars on their morning commute rolled dully by. Trucks headed toward the interstate lolled the car lightly.

—Well, shouldn't we go in? Olive asked, smiling with reddened eyes designed to exhibit her fortitude despite a life of unresolved pain.

We entered the small warehouse cramped with rows of fifteen-foot shelves of unstained wood, arranged by stoneware and ironstone, crackleware, and the cheaper castoffs where you could find good pottery with perhaps a blister in the glaze, an uneven balance to a plate. Olive knew her ceramics. She inspected the various washes with utmost care, identified which pieces were made of argil and which of kaolin; —And see, look at the smalt on everything in this section—what a rich blue! Don't you think these would go with your set, Gaby? Everything Sarah left you has a blue theme.

She moved quickly despite the oxygen tank. It was as though Olive had decided, once surrounded by stacks of possible purchases, to live. As though she *could* decide. Each plate, serving bowl, salad bowl, ladle, coffee cup, teapot, became an invitation to be. —You'll need one of these for your set once you get an apartment of your own, fingering a large bowl with a ram across the body of it, —for when you have people over, you can serve a salad or something. I'm not saying let's buy it now.

Soon she was spouting ideas of interior decor for an apartment that did not yet exist and was not even planned: mounted tiles of the same blue smalt and ash glaze as my dinette set would warm a kitchen into more of a homelike atmosphere. Set the table with fictile candlesticks. Olive made the choices, and with animated insouciance presented them to me, her casters squeaking on the warped wood ancient floor: *and this? see the ram? It goes with yours, right?* I had to smile at her childlike enthusiasm, mixed with a dash of haughty *nouveau riche* (which we weren't, though Olive had faith in Ray's ability to keep cash in hand) indifference. She was a small jaundiced woman whose hands shook so that holding a pen was a conscious, infuriating effort, yet there in that dusty warehouse of a cold late morning she appeared to be fifteen years younger, nearly-not-wrecked, almost confident. She reveled in stacking plates and cups on one corner of the front desk without glancing at the price, as my future kitchen gathered its abstract shape.

—I like those coffee bowls there, I said, entering into the spirit, pointing to bowled mugs with an ash glaze, ones that reminded me of a French movie I'd once seen with Emily. Olive hawed and exclaimed Of Course! and brought four over to the desk. —And what about you, mother? Don't you need anything? but she shook her head while inspecting a set of ladles and serving forks touted by ceramic handles, exquisitely made and sporting her farmer pattern.

—I'd like to have some of these, she said, —Come here, Gaby, look at the work they've done here.

So I go to the pewter ladles to fawn and coo over excellent craftsmanship, our rare camaraderie making this no effort at all. —But I don't want to buy them now, she said. —This is a Christmas Day afternoon and I'll tell you these ladles would make a perfect birthday gift for your mother . . . you tell Ray I told you that, you all never know what to buy me anyway and he just goes off for a lot of junk at the last minute. Not that I'm hard to shop for—(here she rolled her eyes coquettishly at the young clerk who idled nearby)—but any gift does require a bit of forethought and my men have never been particularly talented in that department! They can't think unless the pressure's on.

A beam of understanding from the young clerk; a knowing smile. Olive began to discuss with her what she would like to do with some tiles for her kitchen and how she could put them over the stove or set them above the counter. . . .

—Your mother has a wonderful sense for decor, the clerk said to me in a voice tinied by awe, reacting to what Olive had imagined for her kitchen. The three of us sidled up to the warehouse register and mother asked for the damage. It cost hundreds of dollars, but she did not react with the least surprise. —Get my checkbook out of my purse, will you hon? I did as told while watching her trembling fist clutch the Pug Mill's gnawed ballpoint pen. —Your daddy would have a fit if he knew how much I am spending on you today, Gaby. He thinks taking away the credit cards can stop me, but I still hold the coffers here.

She scribbled her illegible signature—a powerful enough symbol of decay to make me glance aside, for she had always prided herself on her excellent penmanship (chiding the rest of the family for our sloppy, manly ways). The clerk wrapped our purchases in yellowed newspaper and stacked them carefully in a limp cardboard shipping box with tattered packing tape frayed off the corners.

Olive smiled the genuine smile of years and years ago, the one which had long since gone foreign to her face. She said, That was fun, wasn't it. I nodded. We moved to the car but halted, lingered a moment on the sidewalk holding hands, me pulling her oxygen behind her, briefly mother and doting son on the day together.

3

The most anticipated gift of that season, however, was Michael's arrival for the holidays—his first visit home in some five years. And when he appeared the afternoon of Christmas Eve, he brought his own Noël surprise: an unannounced guest. I opened the door upon my brother and a tall, solid man with blond-flecked eyebrows, startling blue eyes, and short hair that lent him a rakish, boyish charm. Alan said he'd never been to Kentucky before and that he'd heard so much of Olive and Ray that he was pleased to have the chance to meet them.

—And you, too, he said, giving over an outstretched hand as he added, —I hear you're down for the count.

A long count, I said. He smiled and introduced himself: —Alan Oakley from Athens, Georgia. His voice was pitched higher than I'd expected from somebody his size. Not feminine, exactly, but like the voice of a sixteen-year-old in the body of a man. His teeth were wide-set, broad, and looked made for champing. —A companion from school, Michael said. —He doesn't have family for the holidays so I figured why not put him through this. He asked for the punishment.

A sheepish grin from Alan. His hands were plunged deeply into the back hip pockets of faded jeans. —I hope I'm not causing any problems for you all by showing up unannounced.

—Not at all! Not at all, no sir, Ray said hurriedly as he scooped the man within his arm and pulled him out of the doorway and into the house. —Welcome to the house of Toure. We've got plenty of everything here. You'll find this family likes to eat, so we tend to overbuy anyway–

—Do you care if we take my old room? Michael asked. —You still got the two beds up there?

—That's what I was about to say, you boys go on and I'll just sleep in Gaby's bedroom.

—I sleep on the floor downstairs, I answered. —It's better on my back. I'd offer to take your bags up, but you see, I've got this *malady*— (the catch-word we'd invented for my condition). Everyone laughed briefly, eager to invite a holiday spirit.

—My youngest son's got a body older than all of us put together, Ray said.

—Michael told me. Let's talk about it, Gabe. You know we're hearing about this kind of condition more and more–

—Alan's getting his Ph.D., Michael called from the stairs as he grunted from beneath the two bags shouldered at once. Alan nodded to us and followed him up to his room while Ray, Olive and I watched them until they shut the bedroom door behind with a carpet-shush. They said they were wasted by the drive and they wanted to rest a while.

We stood in a line staring at the closed door. Ray tapped his belly and glanced somewhere near my feet. —Well. Looks like we got company. Gaby you set another place at the table.

—Ray don't you say a word, Olive rushed in a dominating whisper.

—What, I'm not saying anything! The more the merrier. Shoot, I'm just sorry we don't have a gift for him to open tomorrow.

Olive looked to me and spoke loud enough for the entire house to hear. —Oh, the mama hen's happy to have her nest full again!

We started about our business. Ray checked on the turkey basting in the oven, filling the rooms with its flavor. It was a buttered, marinated heap that filled the entire oven. As I opened a drawer to pull out another place setting from mother's fine set of silver, she interrupted me with a hand closing over mine and said, —Gaby you come downstairs with me a minute, I need help wrapping. Already she was taking the first step at the top of the stairs and spoke loud enough as though she'd had to call for me from somewhere deep in the house. Her other hand graced her swollen abdomen with affected tenderness, and I grabbed her dolly to carry it down the stairs to the basement where she'd cleared her sewing table for the ribbons and wrap and tape.

—If that doesn't just change the color of your whole holiday, Olive said. A crackle of gift wrap wrenched from her hands.

—What? I asked, and without speaking she motioned with her head toward the ceiling with a wry and worldly smirk. She paused from her tasks to start a cigarette; I leapt to turn off her oxygen.

—I keep forgetting to do that.

—Some Christmas it would make if you blew us all up for a cigarette.

—Oh, get off my back. Nobody's going to blow anybody up. She waved the match in the air before her and smiled as the smoke's blue chalk wandered and wafted and then fell to rest in a slowly spreading haze. My nostrils tingled, adjusted. With a dismissive gesture she turned back to the small pile of gifts to be wrapped and said, —Well I don't care really. As long as he's happy and they're playing it safe. I just hope your father doesn't go off and ruin the holidays by embarrassing the both of them. I've always suspected it. Dreaded the day I'd know for sure.

—Know what for sure.

—Oh come on, Gaby. Surely you're not so naive after all the living *you've* done. Look at your brother. He's what, twenty-nine? And never had himself a girl? He's not an ugly man, I don't think he is.

—So you think Alan? . . .

—Don't you breathe a word. I just hope your father doesn't figure it out. Has Michael said anything to you?

—Michael and I don't even talk.

—I hate that, shaking her head slowly, cigarette smoldering in the corner of her mouth, her eyes squinched to slits. —Brothers like you all were when your dad was gone. You two were so close as kids. Two darlings is what you were. Well, so what. It's his choice and I don't profess to understand it. As long as they watch out for one another, I guess. Looks like I don't get to have any grandchildren.

—Maybe they're just friends.

—And that would be fine, it's true, I don't know anything! I'm speculating is all. Now don't you say a word, you keep this between us. Mother'll shoulder the burden as always, so your dad can think he's got real stars for boys.

Christmas dinner had always been a large affair at our house. Festive and slightly formal in the requirements of good silver and china and candlelight. Ties were not mandatory, but jeans and sneakers were forbidden. For the sake of photographs. The dog had been perfumed and groomed down to red-painted nails and green ribbons flopping off her ears. Olive spent hours on her own hair and make-up, and appeared smelling of age and that heavy perfume old women drench themselves in, as though to hide the stench of decay. Coffee waited in a glass decanter heated by votive candle. The chandelier above the dining table was set to an intimate glow.

—You boys go on and sit down while I get these rolls in the microwave. No first, Michael? why don't you see who wants what to drink? Alan would you like some wine? The wine is for you all because I don't drink anymore, hon. And I think Gaby will want water, his medications dry him out.

—Water and a glass of wine for me, I said, taking my seat and stripping off the porcelain ring around my napkin.

—What? You're not even old enough to drink! barked Ray.

The room shrank for a brief instant with everyone staring at another, a mood of musing disbelief. Michael spoke quietly. —Pops, Gabe is twenty-three years old?

—Oh. He is, isn't he?

—Just remember those pills double the effect of alcohol, Olive said, adding to Alan, —Lord knows we need only one drunk in the family! Now you sit tight and let Ray do everything, that's what he's here for.

—Ain't that the truth, Ray mumbled, slouching into the chair at the head of the table.

—Ray! Olive snapped from the kitchen. —Don't you sit down until everybody else is ready, come here and give me a hand. Where're your manners, boy?

He rolled his eyes and with theatrical weariness stood from the table again, smiling at me. —I thought the cook got to take a break from serving the food once everything is ready. I been on my feet all day just so we could all have enough to eat! Now you tell me I got to serve, too? He winked at me, and started toward the kitchen.

—Watch these rolls, Olive answered, —I forgot something upstairs.

She returned several moments later to find the rest of us sitting at the table staring at empty plates. Her perfume wafted into the room and settled around us, and her voice leapt loudly over the table, taking an exaggerated, homespun tone that the entire family mimicked around this time of year, God knows why; Ray's voice would slow and deepen its drawl, and Olive would begin to speak in casual country contractions: —What are y'all sitting there like that for? Git yerselves somethin to eat, it won't stay hot forever.

—We thought this being Christmas, you'd want us to wait for you, Ray said.

—Please don't be stupid, Ray. Boys, I hope you don't mind serving yourselves? Olive reached for her chair and stumbled into it, grabbing the chair-back just at the instant she should have fallen. She made a point not to look up again.

We lined up at the long credenza opposite the table, laden with the candled dishes, spooning ourselves mashed potatoes, three-bean casserole, and broccoli and stuffing while Ray sliced the turkey, setting aside the legs for Michael. —Alan I hope you're not a leg man; tradition in our family's that they go to the number one son, it's the only part he likes.

Alan smiled, said no sir, he preferred the white meat to everything else.

—Why don't you boys spoon up some of that oyster casserole? What, nobody likes oysters? Took me two days to get that dish done! You all don't know what you're missing.

—Oh dammit Ray everybody hates oysters but you, Olive said from her chair. She insisted on being served last. —Ugh those things are so slimy and salty.

—Not in a casserole they're not! Well I don't care. That much more left to me.

—Like you need it as fat as you're getting!

—Who's fat? Ray asked. He tapped his sloped belly and smoothed his white bangs to one side. —Besides, I've worked hard all my life, I can eat what I want now.

—Oh Ray, you've never worked a hard day in your whole life, Olive said quietly, disdainfully. Nobody responded. I asked what she would like on her plate and followed her instructions then set the plate before her and finally took my seat alongside the others. Michael cut the meat from his drumstick and already had some wadded on his fork headed toward his open mouth when Ray interrupted: —Michael! Can't you wait until we say grace first?

He set the fork down, and after some time remembered to close his mouth. He bowed his head and the entire table held hands. A sudden solemnity descended. —Gaby? You want to lead us in prayer tonight?

—No Pops, you do it.

—Okay, *I'll* say it then. . . . Lord, we want to thank you for bringing us here together to enjoy this meal which we hope will nourish our bodies, and for allowing us to be here as a family again. We thank you Lord for bringing Alan here to be with us tonight, and we hope you will continue to watch over him, and both of my sons Michael and Gabriel–

—*My* sons too, Olive interrupted, her eyes still closed and head bowed.

—Excuse me, I made a mistake there Lord as my wife was all too alert to point out. They're Olive's sons too. Couldn't of done it without her. . . . Okay. We ask that you watch over Michael and give him the direction and fortitude he needs to finish his Ph.D. program, and we ask especially for you to see fit to rid Gaby of his health problems cause Lord, he's still such a young boy and everybody needs their health.

Olive squeezed my hand to let me know she was thinking of me too. Her hand was cold and I could feel the slight tremors that started deep in her arm. Ray allowed a minute of pause while he thought. His head still bowed, he looked to Alan and asked, —Hey Alan do you have any special requests?

—Uh, no, thank you, Mr. Toure, I'm just happy to be with your family tonight.

—We're happy to have you here too. Okay then. Please bless this food and this family and all of our loved ones who are not here with us tonight. Amen.

Everyone chimed in with the amens and again there was a short quiet pause as we stirred ourselves and Ray announced, —Okay! let's eat.

—You boys go on and get started, don't mind me I'll be right back.

—Olive where are you going? We just sat down!

—I said I'll be right back! Go on and eat, don't mind me. As she shuffled through the kitchen toward her room, she continued: —Not like you mind me anyhow, why start tonight just because it's Christmas and we have company?

—What is it, dear? What are you saying? I can't *hear* you all over the house!

—I'm not saying anything Ray, I just think it's bad manners that you take time to pray for everybody else at the table but not your loving wife.

By now she was up the stairs and though we could still hear her voice, she spoke too low to be understood.

Ray's hands raised helplessly from the table and then dropped in defeat. —I guess I'm just the bad guy, he said. —Guess it doesn't matter that I pray about those problems every day, right? Oh well boys, looks like you get to eat dinner tonight with the bad guy.

—What is she doing up there anyway? asked Michael.

—Come on, let's eat this before it gets cold. This is good nourishing food.

We started the meal in earnest, Michael and Alan providing conversation where there was none. They described their Athens lives and studies—Michael in neurobiology and Alan in physiology. Michael was playing guitar now in a band that practiced several times a week, yet at this point they had not played out anywhere. I detailed my condition and symptoms and the lidocaine treatments while Alan nodded his head and agreed with my prescriptions.

—Is the treatment helping?

—Better than anything else I've tried. But I don't feel up to exercising or anything like that. I miss running.

—Your doctor sounds with it. That's not a real widespread treatment yet, you know. It's kind of new wave.

—I hope he's going to get him better. I want to see a full recuperation, Ray said.

—Yeah, me too, Alan agreed.

He had grown up on a thoroughbred horse farm outside of Athens. He said he'd never played any team sports but had lettered in cross country running three years in a row in high school. In fact he did not like the horses all that much and had sold the family farm once his parents died in an air accident, flying to Baltimore on a chartered jet for the Preakness Stakes two years before, in May.

—My God Alan, that must have been awful, Olive said as she returned through the kitchen. The bounty of her perfume raked our nostrils.

—Your food's got to be cold by now, hon, Ray said.

—I'll eat it anyway, Ray, don't you let it bother you.

—I like to think they didn't know what was happening to them but for a few seconds and by then it was all over, Alan continued. —We were not especially close, as you can imagine. Since I wasn't into the horses. A horse family like us.

—What is it you don't like about horses? Ray asked. —You don't like racing?

—Racing's great and I still go sometimes. I still have friends there who get me in for free. I try to get Michael to go but you know, he never wants to. Rather read a book.

—I don't want to waste my money betting.

—He doesn't know anything about wagers anyway, Olive said.

—I tell him he can go without placing a bet–

—But I always tell him what's the point of watching horses run if you don't place a bet? It makes as much sense as watching golf on TV, Michael said.

—Hey I *like* to watch golf on TV, Ray answered, almost ruefully.

—He watches golf as an excuse to nap, Olive added.

—Oh I do not!

—Gaby isn't that right? Have you ever seen your father sit awake through an afternoon of golf without disturbing the dog with his snores?

—I can't say I have, Pops, I answered as an apology, shrugging.

—Well what the hell, an old man needs his rest. I work for a living.

Olive clucked in victory. She took on a peculiar shine when she spoke, aware of the attention centered upon her, straightening herself in her chair, almost girlishly. —The dog'll be down there sleeping all peaceful and not bothering a soul by Ray's chair, all content and Ray goes down and flips on the TV and it's not ten minutes before the house starts rocking with the man's snores. . . . She made a low guttural neighing noise and laughed. —So she can't stand it like anybody else and she'll come upstairs to me and look at me from the end of the bed with these poor tired eyes and I ask 'Honey? You want to get in bed with your Mama?' and so I pick her up and she gets comfortable and it isn't long before *she* starts snoring and huffing while she dreams. I tell you it gets so loud in the house I have to turn the TV way up, you can forget about trying to concentrate on a crossword puzzle and believe me I've tried.

—All of this is true, I said, and the room jellied with laughter.

Alan continued, —What it comes down to is I'm not real keen on hard physical labor the day long. Working on a farm—I did it for eighteen years and I guess it burned me out.

—Well . . . that's natural, Ray agreed. To me he added, —Boy go fix your father a piece of pecan pie. And give me a scoop of ice cream on top. He winked at Alan, —See? Being the cook has its perks.

—I'll be right back, Olive announced.

—Olive! You've barely touched your food!

—I'm going to eat, can I help it if I have to go the bathroom?

—Can't taste anything anyway, the way she smokes.

The four of us sat for a long time enclosed in an enervated silence. The votive candles warming the food kept an erratic pulse in the room, the light dappling the walls and ceiling. We listened to the noises from the floor above: the toilet flushed, but she did not come back down; she crossed the floor and must have sat for a minute or two; her footsteps recrossed the floor and then there came the flush of the toilet again. The clink of silver against china as Ray pushed around his pecan pie and ice cream on the dish without eating it. His mouth worked from side to side although it was empty—no one was eating any longer. Ray sighed and pushed away his plate. —I apologize, Alan, but you can see my wife is very ill.

—It's all right, I understand. It's a horrible disease.

Ray's face pinched. —Well, I hope it hasn't ruined your dinner.

—Not at all, Alan mumbled. Michael stared at his plate, his face gone hangdog and heavy, irritated. He glanced at me but I turned away to the sound of Olive's approaching steps returning through the kitchen. Her casters whistled across the linoleum then fell quiet on the dining room carpet.

—Ohhh, that's much better now, as she eased herself down onto the seat, palms flat on the table. —Now where were we? (Or at least that's what she meant to say; it came to us as *now weahwuhwee.*)

—Your food must be frigid by now Olive, give it to me and I'll throw it in the microwave, Ray said.

—That's okay, I'm not very hungry anyway, she said in a voice gone tired and heavy, soft enough that it seemed as though she were having trouble staying awake, —I get too emotional with the family together again I can't eat a thing. Gaby you clear the table for us. Do it now.

Another cigarette was soon alight and Ray barked *Is your oxygen still on?* and there, with a question posed more as accusation, the evening finally fell into full argument. Dammit no I'm not going to blow up the whole house and Why do you keep smoking anyway it's what got you on oxygen in the first place and It's my life, fuck-all and You don't see how the way you hurt yourself affects those of us who love you and Love me? I didn't know anybody loved me in this empty household when was the last time you touched your wife Ray? and the crescendo mounted until Ray clapped his hands over his ears with eyes blinded shut and shouting *aye aye aye aye aye, enough!*

—Olive, it's obvious you're drunk and I'm not about to get into an argument here before a guest and the boys when you can't even be reasonable.

—You stupid bastard you're already IN an argument, you're so stupid you don't even know when you're yelling at somebody. What's there to hide, Ray? You think the boys don't know what a disaster this house is? Why you think Michael stays away so much? Gaby's only here cause he's got nowhere else to go, and I didn't invite the guest—no offense Alan I'm just stating the facts, I'm glad to have you here (she reached over to pat his hand)—so what is it, you don't want them to know we don't even touch much less sleep together? Is that bad for the big man's image? Look at him boys, this is what you get to look forward to.

Ray's voice tumbled from his angry, tirade level (since the wreck he had constant tinnitus and often spoke loudly without realizing it), down into a register more like forced calm, a fatigue. —That's really wonderful, he mumbled at his hands, appearing to measure the lengths of the fingers of one hand against the other. —When's the last time you looked at yourself, Olive? You want to complain about not touching, why not start with yourself?

Olive's trips to the bathroom and the bottle there had armored her too completely to be fazed. A laugh and a shrug and her attitude of the worldly woman whom nobody could put anything over that she hadn't seen before, the woman she liked to imagine herself to be, she'd seen it *all*, rose, and she shared a conspiratorial look with Alan and Michael as though she knew—it must have been obvious to her—that they were on her side against Ray, the Bastard, the Lord in his decline, Her Persecutor (no, the persecutor of us all), the 360-sixty degree son of a bitch. She inclined her head toward my brother with the same camaraderie of two drunks sitting side-by-side in their favorite bar exchanging dirty jokes: —You know your father hasn't been able to get it up for years. . . .

—Olive! This is our Christmas Dinner!

—And Ray if you want to try and belittle me in front of everyone here don't you know I'm going to hit back, you better know that I look like this because of you. You did this to me.

—No. . . . Ray shook his head sadly. How he managed to remain in his seat without leaving, how I, or my brother or even Alan managed to remain silent through the length of this, continues to amaze me. We were frozen in embarrassment, too shocked by the explosion to react to it. —No, Ray began again, absently folding the corners of his crocheted place mat, —No Olive, what you've done to yourself you've managed on your own.

She sneered even as she sucked so hard on her cigarette that it popped. Michael exhaled in an infinite exhaustive sigh. —Okay, Alan added, —Let's all just calm down.

Ray was apologizing to him again and making light of the moment by mentioning that he'd never been able to master the more rudimentary elements of social graces, but I was watching Olive. Her face seemed to be noticing our guest for the first time tonight, giving me over to a shrinking, haunted worry. My back hurt; my thighs winched in small spasms. I asked Michael to pass the coffee. The decanter was set beside him and he nodded while pouring a cup for everybody but Olive, who insisted she could only drink decaf as she was not allowed to have any sort of addictive chemicals in her body as part of her effort to detox. No one made comment. The room bristled again with the clink of saucers and the slurp of coffee poured and the dog whimpered under the table from leg to leg finally settling on Ray as she begged for the last leftover scraps of food. —Get down, honey, Ray remarked offhand, lovingly.

—So Alan, Olive began, —do you and Michael share the same apartment?

—As a matter of fact we do, I just moved in a couple months ago.

—But I've always understood that place to be a studio. Isn't that right Michael? Your apartment's a studio? or did you move without telling us? Where on earth do you sleep, Alan?

—Mother, Michael and I warned in unison.

—Leave the boy alone, Olive, said Ray.

—Oh, you. Shut up. I'm just curious as to how they manage in such a small apartment, that's all. You must have to live all over one another!

—What? What is going on here? Ray demanded, mystified. —What is with you tonight?

—We share the same bed, Mother, Michael said firmly. —There. You want to know and there it is. Alan's not just a friend, we're *together*. Okay?

He pushed his chair back and stood from the table and told Alan to come with him, who obeyed, silently following, his face reddening— even his hands were red—and they went to the hallway closet and pulled on their jackets and said they would go for a walk to get out into the cold clear air. Ray's stunned eyes followed after them, his face the ideal of astonishment. —The hell? . . . he whispered.

—You see, Ray? See what a great father you've been? How proud you must be, you got one boy a fag and the other a physical wreck. Bravo, baby!

—Gaby did you know this? Is this true?

I didn't answer, what could I say? The swirls of milk mixing into my coffee had become unnaturally compelling. The corner of my eye gave onto Olive's face in contractions of terrible joy, her eyes crimped and lacerating with triumph.

—Olive . . . , Ray started, then stopped. He hesitated in his voice and in his body as if his entire being had become deadlocked in the desire to make some decision, to perform some act. He managed to stand from the table. —Olive, he started again, stammering briefly, —I don't think . . . I don't believe I can speak to you . . . anymore. Not tonight.

—Go on! You get out of this house right now! I don't want to speak to you anymore than you do me! You get out of my house . . . and it is *mine*, Ray, I've gone over the papers and everything and you signed this house over to me and it's in my name and nobody else's! I want you out of it now!

He nodded, slowly, as though in agreement, waved his hand as he turned away from us, a defeated gesture that seemed to signify an absence of concern. To the hallway as Michael and Alan had gone, opening the four-panel closet there and rummaging through the coats and sweats and the hangers sliding metallically along the post until he stopped at his old leather flight jacket from his years in the 101st, the brown hide cracked and veined, the lambswool collar no longer white but yellow as old lard. —I think I'll go for a walk myself, he said, and quietly, almost silently, shut the door behind him. Then he opened the front door and called for the dog to join him, and she sprinted out through his legs and into the yard.

The door clicked shut. The overhead chandelier hummed lightly. I finished my coffee with deliberate slowness as Olive lit another cigarette, crumpling the old pack and opening a new one. Her labored breathing wheezed over the table and collapsed there, a dead weight. I searched by glances, surreptitiously inspecting her face for some modicum of sadness, some hint that she realized the damage she had just caused to a number of people in such a small stitch of time; I looked for one sharp clue of the woman who had taken me to The Pug Mill just five days before, but she only smiled confidently, regally, at me; the single gesture toward her humanity came in the spastic shaking of her hands.

—Your mother will never be too ill to defend herself, Gaby, and you better not let your illness get the better of you either. People will try to take advantage. She studied her cigarette and we both watched the ash lengthen and smolder. Her eyes glazed in either enhanced drunkenness or perhaps the effort to stifle tears. —Look I'm gonna ask you to do the dishes, frankly I'm too tired. I'm going upstairs, going to watch TV.

—Finish your cigarette first, Mother. You sound awful, you need some oxygen.

Rather than finishing it she crushed the cigarette quickly in the nearby ashtray saying, —Little ram, you wouldn't want to see anything happen to your dear old mother, would you? You'll always look after me.

I nodded, hesitantly. Sure. With her cigarette now extinguished I reached over and switched the oxygen valve and told her to go on upstairs, that I'd clear the kitchen. She left, leaving me with the thump and clunk of her dolly following her up to her room. Each step was accented by a sigh or grunt. Her body eased onto the bed, and eventually there came the dancing tumble of a TV commercial, louder than necessary.

The dishes mounted in the sink as I waited for it to fill with hot water and soap. The window there gave out to the backyard upon the new in-ground pool closed for the season, covered by a nylon tarpaulin; the dead thistles of what was a pleasure garden in summer, something she claimed she needed as a project to keep her busy but which was only another expense for Ray, as rather than working the garden herself she hired tenders to come and plant the flowers she envisioned for it over winter, from her bed. It was snowing. I turned off the fluorescent light in order to erase my prednisone-bloated reflection from the paned glass, allowing the cold moonlight to wash into the room, the light reflecting off the snow bed and into the kitchen, the moon a limp saucer in the sinkwater surface. My hands turned ghostly, trembled slightly, and I pictured them opening the latch on my mother's oxygen tank and the oxygen flowing into her haggard, self-battered body, seeping into the rags of her lungs, those lungs working overtime to fulfill their purpose and distribute that blue-tinged element into a bloodstream polluted with alcohol and Librium and Wellbutrin and nicotine and whatever-all other chemicals. I rinsed and dried and set the next clean dish aside and the snow kept falling in heavy and larger amounts, a cold shiver upon the world, and then I shivered too, thinking that's what she was to us now, she was like a stew of foreign chemicals and that's why we didn't know her anymore. Where had she gone? The *real* Olive. Or was this the actual, and the woman she had been while I was a child just a mask, a wall of civilized conscience that had eventually stripped away? I didn't know. I had no answer for this; not even a theory.

I continued to consider the world outside the window. Somewhere out there my brother was walking with Alan, his lover, a man; Ray was with his dog; I wondered if the four of them had met and if they did what were they saying and was Ray recriminating them and prophesying doom as is his wont for lying down together to form an abomination on the earth as his good book contended, or was he too tired of the anger in this house and after all Michael was his own son and he was professing not to understand them but loving them anyway. As I was. I hardly knew my brother but I loved him anyway simply because he was my brother. I thought of those hustlers and my violence upon them as a teenager inflamed by Cody's *burn* and I said it was okay now, I regretted these things and wouldn't do them today and would never do it to my brother or to Alan and what was the difference between that life and mine, where the trixies were nothing more than a hustle of my own; I was tricking before and would be tricking now if my body had not collapsed on me. I thought of the boys I'd beaten and hoped they were doing okay now, that I was the worst to be visited upon them. A tremor came to my eyes, an unfortunate side effect of the prescriptions mixed with coffee. I set aside another clean dish and watched the snow fall and wished it could just erase this house and this neighborhood and let us all start over again.

Looking at the moon I remembered that the harsh light there was only a reflection from the sun on the other side of the world and no matter how bright the moon appeared to the eye, the light came from somewhere else, and this thought held me with a certain gravity. As though it meant something, signified something important. Well, my body was going to heal, I could feel it. I may never play my game again but I could feel the muscles someday loosening, feel that they would come to relax. The question of the day, of the new year to come, was how to heal; how to wipe out the coward from my heart; how to continue.

At last the final dishes were dried and set on the matted rack beside the sink.

The explosion came from upstairs, a hard sucking *whooosh* and then crackle and not a word of exclamation from Olive. A cracking, a clatter, and I was up running the stairs unaware of any pain to find her flailing, writhing within a tight rope of flames about her head and neck and already creeping up the blue wallpaper behind her, and I stood there, stilled for one brief instant only, before yanking at the comforter and leaping upon her with it, burying her beneath my body and smacking at her, practically beating her until the flames were gone and all that was left was the smell, the strongest odor imaginable, fried flesh and hair. A lapping flame continued on the wall and in thoughtless panic I smacked at it with my bare hand, searing the flesh so that wallpaper attached itself, ash melted into the skin of my palm. Finally the wall smoldered, a wiry glow on the dry edges enough to make me nervous so I went to the bathroom and came back with a wet washcloth and dampened the area. It was then that the throb overtook my hand, quaked in my arm. I wrapped it in the washcloth and beneath it, my palm blistered.

I don't know how much time passed. It seemed like several long minutes before I dared look at her, peeling back the comforter even as the front door downstairs rattled open, a figure entering unaware of the change in this house, the heavy clomp of boots shedding snow in the foyer. Her head was a greasy char, her mouth open and black about her exposed gums, the lips flayed back. Her fingers clutched in a motionless claw at her throat. Michael's voice came up the stairs: —What is that? Do you smell that?

I didn't call out. I sat on the bed, my head in the untouched hand, and waited, staring.

4

Olive did not want a burial; she wanted to be ashes. We did that much for her—a cold and clouded, close and lonesome day, the heat of the crematorium stifling and dry, stinking. Ray wept, his silver-shocked hair closer to a somber, bone yellow beneath those fluorescent lights. Uncle Crush arrived, and he came to sit with us. Aside from Crush there was only Ray, Alan, Michael, and me, sitting in the quiet in snow-wet leather loafers on rickety wooden chairs. The oily mustard brick of the crematorium looked like a kiln. Cards and flowers arrived from Olive's psychiatrist and AA acquaintances; a few from school, friends who read her obituary in the paper. We heard nothing from her sister in Oregon. Most of the condolences came from the multitude of business associates, bookie contacts, and horse people who knew Ray—hundreds of them, easily. We received more fruit in the most ornate baskets than we could ever eat. Ray arranged to have them delivered to charities.

Michael and Alan drove back to Athens on New Years Day. The week between her death and their departure was filled by the business of arrangements and the will, and afterward, the long and final silences of four men lost in a room of awkward contemplation. Conversation started and drifted into drawn spaces.

—We met in the summer of '59, we lived in the same apartment house, Ray would say, —and my roommate—you remember Bobby

Owen? he was around a lot when you all were just little boys—he started dating her friend Doll Demalion. Doll Demalion, that was the woman's given name. . . . His confusion over Alan and Michael was subdued if obvious. He preferred not to think about it. He stared at them both, sitting beside one another on a faux-satin divan that Olive had chosen, and then examined with boyish befuddlement his strong, scarred hands, the heavy yellow, drycracked fingernails. Once, when he hurled into sudden great sobs and awful shudders, weeping into his palms, Alan came up behind him with a blue tissue box and placed his hand on my father's shoulder. Ray patted the proffered hand, nodding a grateful while, until he glanced upward and the look of surprise couldn't be hidden: he started, his lips parted with a dry smack. Then he recovered. He patted the hand again but didn't look at Alan anymore.

—You know the first time we met she was all dolled up, she had her hair done in a beehive like it was popular back then, and her nails were lacquered white, even her toenails, something I'd never seen before then, and she wore these fake diamond earrings that I believed were real and I was thinking, hey, this girl comes from a good family, right? But her mom was poorer than mine. Not that it matters. Still, you hope you'll marry up, you know. And I was kind of looking to get married. Anyway. Your mother had on this sensible—she always dressed 'sensibly,' that was her word for it—this black dress. She was a real looker, too. You wouldn't know it by the way you saw her, Alan, but she was good-looking all the way up to the last ten years or so, then the alcohol. . . . I was half-drunk with Bobby, it was summer I remember and we'd probably spent the day on the river, and I saw Olive putting on the Ritz and said *Darlin', you look like a Playboy bunny all done up like that.* She thought that was the greatest. That was a compliment back in our day.

I would like to say that Ray was full of sweetness and understanding toward Michael and Alan by the time they left, but he had his beliefs, and they were deeply held. What I can say is there was no emotional leave-taking; Ray never came to some Hollywood epiphany where he held Alan by the shoulders at a manly arm's-length distance and said, *Take care of my son*. Nothing so sentimental as that; Ray simply did not have it. But he did follow them out to their car, carrying their bags. He spoke to Michael of auto maintenance, having taken the car the morning before to fill the gas tank and have the oil changed, all fluids topped off, the tires aired. Once they were settled in he set his hands on the open window and said, —Don't you boys remain strangers. Come back whenever you want.

That was the best he could do. Some have the gift of innocence, and Ray could not live with any conscious contradictions. So in his mind the men were simply good friends. I guess it is unfair, a thread-like rent in his character, but Ray held his innocence in all matters except business; in his innocence he resisted hatred and welcomed love (or at least generosity), and this was the only way he had of showing his love to Michael and Alan. For a beginning, it was enough. But it began and ended there. We had no time left for more.

5

With Olive gone, the air in the house cleared. Once the cloud of her death dissipated, the House of Toure lost its tension; it became a place of peace murmuring with the play-by-play of golf games on TV, the fingerpicked trots on the Martin 000-18, the one-sided conversations overheard on the phone. Ray said, Okay enough of all this convalescing, what you need is a job, and took me into work with him, where he set me up as a kind of office manager. I answered the phone and hung around with his secretary and typed out state-ments on late accounts, learned to strong-arm insurance companies who denied payment on services that had been preauthorized. Ray and

I took lunches together, we learned one another again, played gin rummy at night with some of his old friends—Bobby Owens and Uncle Crush among them. He tried to get me to take up golf, and even though my body was slowly coming around and I could move without pain—more like a continual discomfort—I never could get into that game.

Soccer no longer interested me, either. Although it is still the most beautiful game, when played well, I have never been able to sit through an entire match, either live or on TV. I have not touched a soccer ball since the day my hamstring tore. Ray would be flabbergasted whenever we came across a game on a weekend afternoon, from England or Italy by satellite, as he would set down the remote and get relaxed only to have me change the channel again. Yet he never asked me why; he would simply mumble *sorry boy, I thought you'd want to watch.*

At night the house turned into a parlor for crusty old men smoking cigars and playing cards and dismissing/lamenting the rising profile of women in the world—*you got more women in the world than you do pussies,* Uncle Crush often sighed, *how you figure that?*; they laughed over the days of whorehouse carousing, when they had the time and the virility to patronize escort services; they enjoyed relating their unique adventures of sexual youth, of fights won and lost, of lawsuits and divorces, of being alive. They tossed their fuming snipes into an old-time cuspidor. At their age they said it was gravy and they did not have to care anymore. Ray no longer blanched when I was present to hear his friends ribbing him about such-and-such, and how about that one three-day drunk, or that other time, and remember that one lady, did you hear what happened to so-and-so after? He would laugh with them and even more heartily to me, shuffle his cards and shout *You boys are so bad, you're going to corrupt my son, honey it was never like that don't believe a word these guys say.* Which only led to loud reprisals and good-timing of how yes, Gaby, all of it was true.

—Your old man wants you to think he's been godfearing all his life! Uncle Crush said.

—No, no. Nothing to fear in God, Crush. God takes care of his own, Ray would answer, mindfully. And then Crush would ask to see Ray's scar from when a bullet scraped him as he sat in the waiting room of a whorehouse, back before he was married.

On those nights the house enlivened with these old men and the rattleclink of shaken martinis, the shuffle of cards, the light pad of orthopedic shoes. They shouted in hoarse and phlegmy voices. Although she'd lost control of her kingdom, Olive remained, a hidden presence in her cinerarium; the silver urn that initially made its place on our hearth, then a bookshelf, then to her sewing desk in the basement, until finally she settled in to the top shelf of Ray's closet. It may sound disrespectful, her remains being taken from view like that; but in fact it was a constant reminder for Ray and Ray only, as each morning when he dressed for work he would have to open those mirrored doors (although he never moved back in to their bedroom, he did donate all of her clothes to charity and claim the closet) and that urn would be the first thing he would see; Olive in the morning, Olive in the evening, and then, once he changed his clothes for sleep, he would close those doors again and be presented with an image of himself.

Although it wasn't apparent then, it seems to me now that we were governed by a sense of our time winding down. Ray often referred to the end of the twentieth century as the Time of Last Things. He listened to Billy Graham and Chuck Colson. He studied Revelation and tried to come to his own terms with its meaning. He read the paper and watched the evening news and proclaimed he could hear the distant thunder of approaching hoofbeats—the white horse, red horse, black horse; the pale horse and rider. He began to work over his memories and his life; although he should have had plenty of time left, he wanted to take account of what he had known and seen.

Ray was too impatient to put his hand to a work as intensive as a memoir or autobiography. Instead he chose the more precise and spare form of a chronology, and often of an evening, I'd bring him a martini and peer over his shoulder at his neat handwriting on a thick legal pad, his mind lost in remembrance, the dates scrawled in the left margin:

1932 Nov. 18: born in Bowling Green. Daddy said I had a hard forehead and hoped that didn't say anything about the kind of man I'd be.

1948 Fall: fell off roof while watching Anne Hicksie walk by in her famous white dress. broke leg. started drawing while in bed. set state record in long jump earlier, in spring.

Et cetera. He rarely waited for me to ask a question; automatically he would start to address what he assumed was on my mind. —I trust you'll have a child someday, he said, —and I don't know if I'll be here for him. But I want him to know that I was here; that he comes from someplace deeper than just you and his mother. (It was a given to Ray that if I ever had a child it would be a son.)

He finished his project within a week or two, not being given to too many details, and handed it to me to be typed up. I handled it with the same care I gave my portrait he'd drawn in prison—it was lost, eventually. I resisted the work, kept putting it off and saying I'd get to it every time he'd ask if it were finished or not. A proper chronology can be made only once its subject is dead, and I didn't like the idea of my father approaching his life as though it were already finished. It was impossible to imagine my world without Ray. In a few weeks he appeared to have forgotten about it, and the pages were buried beneath more pressing papers on my office desk.

Still, in the age I think of as After Olive, he maintained the notion that the great period of his life was over, finished—his future one long, bucolic pastoral—and he must have felt unsure how to continue; he'd been conditioned for drama and hijinks, by fate and character. He was forever referring to the past and its turmoils and confrontations (all overcome), and/or how the past led to this present moment—rarely did he ever mention the future unless it was to pronounce that one day I might have a son, with allusions that he would not be there to see that happen. Or else he spoke of the future in terms of the Second Coming.

Once, in his office on a weekday morning as he prepared to make his delivery rounds to the city's clinics, he sat on the floor in his suit and tie, polishing his leather shoes. I shuffled papers nearby and noticed the crown of his hair had begun to thin, his pink scalp veiled but visible underneath.

—All my life and it comes down to this, Ray mused to me, his tone hardly somber but closer to his usual lightness, —sixty-two years old and shining my own shoes. Would've thought it'd be more climactic. Some day, the whole 'veil will be removed,' you know, that's what *apocalypse* actually means. Did you know that, Gaby? You might even be here to see it.

And then, suddenly lighter: —Hey, where you want to go to lunch today? You think you can make the time? he asked, and laughed, knowing exactly how much free time I had. He paid for every lunch no matter where we went or how many people came with us. Each time he would slap the money down onto the table so that I could pay, and never would he allow me to return the change. As we left he would say the waitress had been eyeing me the entire hour, why didn't I pay attention to such things? We would leave with his big hand clasping the back of my neck—Ray's version of a hug—and I felt like I'd never grown older than the last time I saw him before prison, his large head silhouetted in the back window of his car, snow falling, the brake lights of his white cadillac rosing pink as he slowed near the intersection at the end of my school's drive, and turned left, past the trees.

6

The last time I saw him was under normal and unsuspecting circumstances: Monday morning, the top of summer. He had a number of deliveries to make and we had finished planning for the day. —I won't be able to make lunch, boy, he said. —There's just too much to do. I'll have to eat in the car. He spotted me a ten so I could eat somewhere on my own.

He took his lunch in a downtown cafe. A receipt from his pocket tells me what he ate: a BLT with a side of baked potatoes, washed down with iced tea (which he would have taken without sugar). He left—clad in beige short-sleeved dress shirt and loosened polyester tie as it was hot and steamy July—and walked toward his car with keys in hand. Another parked car caught his eye and he stopped before his past in a 1958 Corvette convertible, red with the white swoosh on the side, just like the one he used to own, when he raced. It was a beauty; completely restored down to whitewall tires. Still had the single headlights, a 283 engine, the original radio with switches rather than buttons, the enormous steering wheel. A red leather interior—the whole bit. I can imagine how Ray must have stopped to inspect it; I can imagine him actually getting into the car to sit at the steering wheel (he did).

And then a calamity. From the throng of lunch hour traffic, two youths came forward, one holding a sawed-off shotgun. They ordered him to hand over the keys. Ray started to protest—to explain—but the boy with the gun held it straight out and pointed to his chest and shouted, *now!* And Ray handed him the keys to his own car, a small Mercedes parked further up the street. He stepped out of the Corvette, one boy got in on the passenger side, and as Pops stood watching, the other shot him square in the chest before jumping into the driver's seat.

The ridiculousness of it. Ray sprawled in the street, a bowl of a hole just below his sternum, still conscious. The boys thought they'd simply roar off in midday confusion. But the car wouldn't start without the proper keys, and as a crowd began to form and shout and swirl about them they struck out on foot, waving the gun wildly. The police caught them within the hour. They fished the gun from a dumpster before the day was out. And Ray found himself being operated on by one of his closest business associates.

They had him in the operating room twelve hours. He never regained consciousness after entering the hospital. He held on long enough until Michael arrived, and then he went, with the two of us by his side, holding his hands, saying nothing, surrounded by hospital smells and noises, computerized beeps and breathing pumps, the sight of it all white and off-white, sheets and painted walls, sterile air, machinery. Ray went quietly without sound or sigh, without moving; he was there and he was gone. He had apologized for not being able to have lunch with me, said we'd do it tomorrow, and then the next I knew, he was gone. I was typing invoices, stuck in the snare of life's daily littleness.

You want to take so much of it back, that last moment, *hold it,* Ray's face solar-boiled red by spring golf afternoons, the sun making a seraphic-white crown of his hair, the sport jacket that he'd paid low-dollar for on a real bargain tossed over his shoulder, the office door open and summer heat bellowing in, the clank of his loafered feet descending the metal stairs, the heavy door clicking shut again. —See you at home tonight, he called back.

You want to take it back and be there, *embracing it,* and him, again, knowing this was the last time you'd see your man on his feet, the last time you saw him breathing, the last time you'd hear his voice, the last time, the last time for everything. You want to have the forewarning to be prepared: from here on out, you're on your own.

But you never get that. Your father is here, and then he's gone. The final step of coming into one's own occurs at the burial of both parents, when you are left a sudden orphan with no one to answer to, nobody to impress. You lose all borders to who you are. No more mirror to reflect upon.

7

He did not want to be cremated. We buried him in an old cemetery once decimated by the tornadoes of April 3, 1974. He had his entire funeral already planned and paid for, down to a white granite gravestone with the epitaph *Goodbye, World; Hello Jesus.* We cast Olive's ashes over the ground above, and planted a rose bush per his request—an odd request, it seemed to me, as my father had never shown any interest in flowers or even nature of any kind.

The day threatened storms and rain, the clouds curled in dark and blackened fists that spread across the sky, shadowing the city underneath in a crude mustard. As the procession of cars parked and emptied along the gravestones, a wind rose and flung cut grass, harsh like straw, into our faces. People held unopened umbrellas, and the wind was powerful enough for women to keep one hand pressed low on their thighs to keep their skirts from rising. It took time for the entire cortege to arrive. I waited briefly on the paved road, cracked by winter icing, the corrugated trenches filled with cigarette butts and grass, dried crisps of flower petals, then moved among the stones and sepulchers, ankles flexing and easing on the uneven earth, avoiding the fresher barrows, examining the dates framing lives lived, the gifts left behind— silk flowers in green plastic buckets, laminated photographs—and smelled the dust off the stones, fingering the rusted doorway to a small family mausoleum, the stained glass portal broken, in shards.

Despite the wind, I was sweating in my double-breasted linen suit; the air pushed humid and close, the breeze brought tufts of heat. My hands shook with nervous tremors and I kept them in my pockets, feeling the damp in my palms. Thunder rumbled in from the distant west—the sound of approaching hoofbeats—and the sky darkened, tightening the large crowd with the tension and slight fear that comes with being outside during angry weather. The priest held the floral arrangement on Ray's casket with one hand while he read, to prevent it from flying into our faces; the tent in which we sat shook and quaked. We were all ready to bolt to our cars when the impact should hit.

Yet the storm never came. By the time the casket was lowered we were standing beneath a light, spitting rain, more annoying than anything else, and the wind eased, lifted; the trees quieted, presenting us the greener side of their leaves; the sky lost its darkness. The storm moved around the city and left us under a wan blanket of shifting gray.

I watched it go. With the funeral over I wandered after it the way home, following the line of forceful clouds, the shimmers of lightning. As a child I would have taken it as a sign, an invitation, an overture; but now, stopping beneath the reach of branches of that silver maple tree in our front yard, I could see it for what it was: just weather, and that which passes.

The tree towered over the house now. Ivy covered its roots and half of the trunk, and Eagle Point had long ago disappeared into the body of it. I could reach the thick bottom branches by simply lifting my hands. I had the presence of mind to discard my jacket, folding it over my arm and draping it over the passenger seat of my car; then I went back to the maple and hauled myself up. My loafers slipped on the bark, but otherwise the tree accepted my weight easily, and I climbed as far as it was possible to go, leaning into the thick arm of a newer shoot. There, I rested, gazing out over my city, waiting for brightness to fall with the sun's return; waiting for the day to continue, and end, and start over as it does in its soft parade. Eventually those rays of light came, inflaming the late afternoon clouds with pink and gold outline, turning me over to a Kentucky summer evening: open, and fair, hinting toward the promise of destination.

Acknowledgments

Portions of this novel have appeared, in somewhat different form, in *bananafish: short fiction* and *Witness.*

Blessings on the heads of the following: Michael Carroll, Virginie Bonnerot, Kristin Herbert, Patrick Donley, and Curtis Smith, who all read drafts of this novel and gave thoughtful advice and encouragement; thanks also to Neff, who saw me through the final revisions and everything after.

Heartfelt gratitude to Judy Long for her sympathetic reading and editing, and to Colleen Subasic, also.

A Reader's Guide

1. Gabriel refers to his parents as Olive and Ray, not Mom and Dad. How does this relationship with his parents affect his own identity?

2. Gabriel spends more time describing the events of his past than his feelings about those events. The author presents the reader with the events in a straightforward and objective manner. Is the narrator/author inviting the reader to judge the characters with this style of presentation? What are the author's intentions in writing this story as opposed to Gabriel's intentions in telling it? What does Gabriel want you to think about his mother, his father, and his life?

3. "Rather than thank God for saving my father's life, I felt as though He had saved him simply to take him away, and I resented it" [page 37]. What does Gabriel believe are the reasons for his father's survival from the parachute incident and the train

accident? What does the author suggest is Ray's purpose for surviving these accidents? What does the author suggest is Ray's purpose for going to jail? How do these incidents improve Gabriel and Ray's relationship overall?

4. "As he dropped us off . . . I was already subtracting the four days we would be apart. It seemed like trying to imagine four days when I would not exist" [page 38]. Gabriel also states, "what use would anyone have for me, if they did not want Ray?" [page 38]. Why does Gabriel feel that his own existence and identity depend on his father's? Is Ray really the innocent, idealistic father that Gabriel believes him to be?

5. What is Gabriel's exposure and relationship to God before Ray's arrest? How does this change after the arrest? Does Ray comfort his children with the correct approach by using Isaiah 54:13? What does the appearance of this passage predict about the ending of the narrative?

6. Does Gabriel suggest that the events of his childhood led him to have an affair with Catherine? Or would any teenage boy act the same in that situation? Is Olive justified in throwing him out of the house?

7. After reading Parts I and II of *The Barbarian Parade*, how did you predict the relationship between Gabriel and Olive would end? What evidence from the text do you have to support this prediction?

8. What meanings do the title and subtitle bring to Gabriel's story? What do they suggest about Gabriel's coming-of-age process? What is the author trying to convey about a child's classic movement from innocence to experience?

9. "The strange thing about love, which we like to think is all about unspoken understandings, is in that specific amount of our lives that we hold back from our lovers. It's necessary" [page 159]. What exactly does Mies mean when he says this to Gabriel? What does this quote explain about Gabriel's relationships with the ones he loves, (Ray, Olive, Michael, Emily, etc.)?

10. After Ray returns home from jail, he points out Gabriel's failure to post a flag on Eagle Point. Throughout the book, Gabriel never seems to be able to reach his goals due to life's disasters. Is Gabriel actually lucky the way Emily suggests, or is he an unfortunate youth bound by the limits of fate? What is the author finally trying to assert about life's challenges?

11. Gabriel asks the reader, "who remembers those who never enter History but live domestic, small, private lives? No one. It is for this reason that we invented Heaven." Why does Gabriel believe that his life is unimportant? What does the author suggest is important about Gabriel's life?